Berkley Prime Crime titles by Casey Mayes

A DEADLY ROW
A KILLER COLUMN
A GRID FOR MURDER

A GRID
FOR MURDER

Casey Mayes

BERKLEY PRIME CRIME, NEW YORK

THE BERKLEY PUBLISHING GROUP
Published by the Penguin Group
Penguin Group (USA) Inc.
375 Hudson Street, New York, New York 10014, USA

Penguin Group (Canada), 90 Eglinton Avenue East, Suite 700, Toronto, Ontario M4P 2Y3, Canada (a division of Pearson Penguin Canada Inc.) • Penguin Books Ltd., 80 Strand, London WC2R 0RL, England • Penguin Group Ireland, 25 St. Stephen's Green, Dublin 2, Ireland (a division of Penguin Books Ltd.) • Penguin Group (Australia), 250 Camberwell Road, Camberwell, Victoria 3124, Australia (a division of Pearson Australia Group Pty. Ltd.) • Penguin Books India Pvt. Ltd., 11 Community Centre, Panchsheel Park, New Delhi—110 017, India • Penguin Group (NZ), 67 Apollo Drive, Rosedale, Auckland 0632, New Zealand (a division of Pearson New Zealand Ltd.) • Penguin Books (South Africa) (Pty.) Ltd., 24 Sturdee Avenue, Rosebank, Johannesburg 2196, South Africa

Penguin Books Ltd., Registered Offices: 80 Strand, London WC2R 0RL, England

This is a work of fiction. Names, characters, places, and incidents either are the product of the author's imagination or are used fictitiously, and any resemblance to actual persons, living or dead, business establishments, events, or locales is entirely coincidental. The publisher does not have any control over and does not assume any responsibility for author or third-party websites or their content.

A GRID FOR MURDER

A Berkley Prime Crime Book / published by arrangement with the author

PUBLISHING HISTORY
Berkley Prime Crime mass-market edition / October 2012

ISBN: 978-0-425-25164-5

BERKLEY® PRIME CRIME
Berkley Prime Crime Books are published by The Berkley Publishing Group, a division of Penguin Group (USA) Inc., 375 Hudson Street, New York, New York 10014.
BERKLEY® PRIME CRIME and the PRIME CRIME logo are trademarks of Penguin Group (USA) Inc.

PRINTED IN THE UNITED STATES OF AMERICA

10 9 8 7 6 5 4 3 2 1

ALWAYS LEARNING   **PEARSON**

For Emily Myers,
and all of the books we've shared together over the years!

AUTHOR'S NOTE

Asheville, North Carolina, is without a doubt one of my favorite places in the world. It offers beautiful vistas, an eclectic downtown, quirky citizens, and the ambience of what a city should be, at least for me. As always, I've taken liberties with some of the locations, distances, and manner in which the police operate, but many of the places I write about, from the obelisk downtown to the Botanical Gardens, are very real indeed, and well worth the visit.

As always, I hope the people of Asheville forgive me for making murder a resident in their beautiful city.

Chapter 1

...

SHE DESERVED TO DIE.

    If I hadn't done it, someone else would have, so I don't feel like a killer. I just saved someone else the trouble of taking care of her. My conscience is clean enough.

    You can't treat people like that and expect to keep getting away with it.

    I tried telling her that again and again, but she wouldn't listen to me.

    And then all of a sudden, she ran out of chances.

    The world will be a better place without her.

    If I'm being honest about it, I'm not even sorry for what I did.

    And if that snoopy Savannah Stone doesn't stop nosing around business that isn't hers, I'm going to add her to my list.

    It's got to get easier the more times you do it.

Chapter 2

...

"**I**'M GOING INTO ASHEVILLE," I CALLED OUT TO MY HUS-band, Zach, who was currently picking up fallen branches in our cottage's front yard and hauling them into the nearby woods. Zach was the retired chief of police of Charlotte, North Carolina, but now he worked as a consultant for any law enforcement agency that had a tough case, and the budget to pay him. My income writing puzzles was a nice supplement to that, and we were fairly comfortable living on what we had, though we weren't wealthy by any stretch of the imagination.

I loved all of the seasons on our land, but this was my favorite time of year. It was the beginning of the end of autumn, and we'd had a pretty intense storm the night before.

I looked at Zach. He wasn't paying me all that much

attention, because he was focused on getting the grounds cleared. That was his style. Whenever he tackled a problem, no matter how large or small, it tended to occupy the whole of his concentration. "Do you need anything while I'm gone?" I asked again, this time loud enough to make it impossible for him to continue ignoring me.

"Did you say something?" he asked with a grin. It was tough being angry with my husband when he smiled at me like that.

"Do you need anything from Asheville?"

"How about grabbing me a new chain saw while you're there, Savannah?" Zach asked as he wiped the perspiration from his forehead, though there was still the hint of a chill in the air. "I think it would be easier if I just go ahead and cut all of our trees down and be done with it once and for all."

I knew he was kidding. My husband loved the hickory, oak, maple, and pine forest that populated our property as much as I did. We'd wanted to escape the hectic pace and energy of Charlotte, and I'd dreamed of living in the mountains since I'd been a little girl, so when a bullet in the chest had forced my husband to retire, a place near Asheville was the obvious choice for both of us.

Not that it didn't bring its own share of challenges along with it.

I smiled at him and said, "While we're at it, why don't we go ahead and tear up all of the grass and put down artificial turf like they use on football fields? That way there wouldn't be any yard work to do at all."

He took a long drink from the glass of cool water I'd brought him earlier before he spoke again. "You've got the right idea. We could even plant plastic fruit and vegetables. Think about it, Savannah; no weeding, no pests, no work."

I laughed out loud. "Admit it; you'd go crazy in a week if you didn't have anything to do outside, and we both know it."

He grinned. "You're right, but sometimes it's fun to dream about that simpler life we promised ourselves once upon a time."

"I like things just the way they are. Don't work too hard," I added, my smile suddenly fading for an instant. I knew the doctors had cleared Zach for a moderate amount of strenuous activity, but I still worried about him every time he tried to do too much physical labor.

He must have seen the concern in my eyes. "Stop worrying about me, Savannah. I'm as healthy as a horse," he said, and then added, "At least one that's been shot in the chest."

"How healthy would that be, exactly?" I asked.

"I'm strong enough to do what needs to be done," he said as he threw a branch onto the pile. Zach reached for another fallen branch and added, "What are you doing racing off into town? Don't you have a puzzle that's due today?"

I loved my job creating the math puzzles that were found in some of the best secondary newspaper markets in the country, but it wasn't my entire life. There were times when I resented how the puzzle creations could intrude on other things I would rather be doing with my time, but mostly I'd found the ideal occupation for myself. My puzzles offered the perfect opportunity to set order to chaos, and in a way, what Zach and I did wasn't really all that different. "I already finished it. That's why I'm going into Asheville. My fax is on the fritz again."

"I keep telling you that it's time to buy a new one."

"I'm one step ahead of you. After I send this," I said,

waving the folder containing my latest puzzle and its solution in the air, "I'm going shopping for a new one. If you want to get cleaned up and go with me, I'd be more than happy to wait around for you." My husband's consulting business was surprisingly quiet at the moment, and I knew that he was getting restless with the inactivity of his brain, if not his body.

Zach peered around the yard, and then he shook his head. "It's tempting, but I really do need to finish this. You know how I get when I start a project."

"I know, but I thought it wouldn't hurt to ask anyway." I kissed him quickly, and then got into my car and headed for the city. We lived two miles from the center of Parson's Valley, and less than thirty minutes from downtown Asheville, nestled in the western part of North Carolina. We'd both immediately fallen in love with our cottage the moment we'd seen it, and we'd bought it with plans to retire there someday. That day came much sooner than either one of us had expected, but it was our home now, and I loved it.

ONCE I GOT INTO ASHEVILLE, I WENT BY MY FAVORITE OF-fice supply store, faxed my puzzle to my syndicator from there, and then indulged myself and bought a brand-new fax machine. Most of my fellow puzzlemakers had switched to computer-generated puzzles long ago, but I had to have the feel of the pencil in my hand and the note-pad on my lap to be able to create. My boss had to convert the puzzles into an electronic format before they could go out to our newspaper clients, and I had been hearing rumblings for months about updating our system, but so far, I'd resisted it at every turn. It wasn't that I was some kind of Luddite—I enjoyed technology as much as the next woman—but it didn't mesh well with my creativity, at least not my brand of it. In all honesty, my puzzles were only part of the equation of what I gave my readers. Many folks I spoke with told me that it was my accompanying snippet that they enjoyed the most, even surpassing the joy of working a puzzle. A combination of my ruminations, advice, and the occasional diatribe made up the second half of what I loved doing most in the world, and oftentimes I worked as hard on my brief commentaries as I did creating the puzzles they accompanied.

After I was finished with my errands, I knew that if I rushed back home, Zach would just put me to work with him in the yard. There had to be some way to stall my return until those branches had been transported deep into the woods. It wasn't that I didn't enjoy helping my husband; it was just that we both liked to be in charge of most of the things we did together. I knew from experience that my presence would take away some of his laser focus on getting the job done, and besides, we spent plenty of time together every day without going out of our way to add to it. I decided to treat myself to lunch at Café Noir, a place with outdoor tables near the downtown area of Asheville known as Pack Square. I loved sitting at one of the tables outside and staring up at the gray stone obelisk, a Washington Monument–like structure dedicated to our Civil War–era governor Zebulon Vance. As I sat at a table watching the world go by, no matter what time of year, the range of people there always amazed me. The entire city of Asheville was a study in contrasts, from the nearby Asheville Art Museum to the bohemian coffee shops and galleries strewn throughout the streets. Sitting outside in the sunshine, it was not uncommon to see a bank executive on vacation walking in one direction wearing J.Crew and L.L.Bean passing a genuine tie-dyed hippie in flip-flops and blue jeans coming the other way.

In other words, if I was going to be close to a city anywhere in America, this was the one I wanted to be able to visit whenever the mood struck me.

I'd been lucky enough to find a parking spot on Patton Avenue near the café, something not to be taken lightly, and I'd captured a table near the square where I could see just about everything going on around me.

Unfortunately, two tables away, someone I had no interest in spending a second with saw me as I started to sit down.

"Savannah. Savannah Stone," Joanne Clayton called out. Joanne's olive-skinned face was narrow and elongated, her nose constantly threatening to tip over her entire head; every time I saw her, a fresh-faced ferret popped into my mind: an image that wouldn't go away no matter how hard I tried to banish it.

I was trapped. I couldn't ignore her, and it was too late to pretend that I was heading somewhere else. Maybe there was still a way that I could avoid the inevitable.

"Hi, Joanne," I said as I pulled out my chair without making a single move in her direction. "Nice to see you."

I pretended to study the menu on the table as I chanted softly to myself, *Don't come over, don't come over, don't come over.*

Of course, she came over.

"Mind if I join you?" she asked, carrying an oversized coffee cup with her.

"Of course," I said.

There was a sharp look on her face as she asked me

pointedly, "Are you truly saying that you do mind? Surely I'm mistaken."

That was exactly what I was saying, but I knew if I turned her away, I'd be fodder for the gossip mill in Parson's Valley until she found a new victim to focus on, and that could take days, or even weeks. Joanne was an uncomfortable acquaintance, but she was an even worse enemy, and I had no desire to go from the nice list to the naughty one.

"No, I meant that of course you can join me." As Joanne pulled out a chair and put her bags on the table, I pointed to her cup and asked, "What's that you're drinking?"

"They have the most delicious tea here. This is Daybreak Delight. It's almost savory in taste. You must try some."

I didn't feel like some strange type of tea brew at the moment, but before I could protest, she waved to a waitress and placed my order for me. Wonderful. I'd hoped to have a nice lunch and enjoy the brisk autumn weather, but Joanne had managed to suddenly kill my appetite. If I could share a cup of tea with her and be done with it, that was going to be my new goal. I'd grab something else on the way home. It served me right, trying to skip out on my husband when there was work to be done back at the cottage. I was a firm believer in Karma, but this payback was so fast it was enough to snap my neck with its suddenness.

I knew in my heart that I was going to have to endure at least some of her company, so I decided to be as gracious about it as I could be. "What brings you to Asheville this fine autumn day?" I asked as nicely as I could muster.

"A moment like this is meant to be enjoyed out in civilization," she said. "And clearly, I'm not the only resident of Parson's Valley who wanted to get away from our sleepy little town for a few hours."

"I had some business to take care of in town," I said, finding it odd to be justifying my trip into Asheville to this woman. If I had my way, I'd rather be home sitting on the sofa in front of the fireplace writing a new snippet with Zach in the next chair nodding off than where I was at the moment.

"I don't mean you, necessarily. Well, of course I do. Not just you, though. The odd thing is that I spoke with Harry Pike not two minutes ago right here. As a matter of fact, you just missed him." Harry ran a nursery in Parson's Valley, and was known for his dexterity with the ladies. At fifty-seven, his tastes were eclectic, and from what I'd heard, he had only one rule: He would go on no dates with any woman under fifty. Rumors around town said that he stayed busy enough even with that caveat, always indulging whenever time and opportunity allowed it.

"How is Harry?" I asked.

"Disappointing," Joanne said. "I'm afraid we had a bit of a spat. I do so hate to argue in public. He'll regret his words to me today, I can promise you that."

There was no doubt in my mind that was true enough. "Sometimes it can be a small world, can't it?"

"Come now, don't exaggerate. Parson's Valley isn't that far away; it's not such a huge coincidence to find folks we both know here." Joanne looked smug for an instant, and then she added, "Actually, I'm glad I ran into you today. I'd been planning to make a trip to your place as soon as I finished up here."

Wonderful. Now it appeared that she had a reason to see me, and I was pretty sure I wasn't going to like it. Well, I might as well nip it in the bud. If I let Zach anywhere near this woman, he'd say something that I was certain she'd find offensive, but the odd thing was, I knew that I'd be the one in hot water. "Why is that? Is it time for the Moonlight fund-raiser again already? You know you can always count on us for a contribution." The one good thing Joanne did in the world, at least as far as I could tell, was run the Moonlight fund-raiser every year. The manner in which she raised money varied, but the cause was always the same, and the fact that the events always happened after dark never wavered. Joanne felt that there were a disturbing number of children in our part of the state who lived in dire poverty, and while others sent their money abroad to help children in Third World countries, Joanne believed that we should start by helping those closer to home. It was most likely the one thing in the world that justified the otherwise abrasive and mean-spirited woman's existence, and it was that kernel of goodness within her that I tried to focus on whenever I was around her, no matter how hard it usually was for me to keep smiling in her presence.

She bit her lower lip, and the ferret image instantly reappeared in my mind. "No, I'm not ready to announce this year's event yet, but believe me, it is going to be absolutely amazing."

The waitress brought me an identical cup of tea to the one in front of Joanne, and I took a sip of the bitter brew. I couldn't believe that she actually liked this dreck.

"It's wonderful, isn't it?"

"Mmmmm," I replied. "I'm not exactly sure that it's my taste," which was the only safe answer I could muster as the bitter aftertaste assaulted my mouth.

Joanne smiled at me, and it was clear in that instant that she knew exactly what I was experiencing. "Don't worry, dear. Not everyone can appreciate it for its layers of subtlety. It takes a true sophisticated palate to enjoy it."

Or a dead one, I thought to myself. Hang on, Savannah, you can do this. "I believe it," I said as I pushed the cup away. Better to be labeled as a commoner than drink another sip of that muck.

It was time to change the subject away from the devil's brew in front of me. "If you don't want to talk to me about the fund-raiser, then why did you want to see me?"

Instead of answering the question directly, she asked me, "Have you seen today's paper?"

"No, I've been working on my latest puzzle all morning," I said. "Why? Is there a story written in there about you?"

"Of course not," she said. It was obvious that Joanne was going to say something more, when two women from Parson's Valley approached us from the square. Why did I bother living out in the country if I was going to keep running into people I knew in Asheville? This was getting more than a little crazy.

"Sandra, Laura," Joanne said loudly as she beckoned to the women. "You must join us. Come, we'll make it a party."

"Hello," the two women said to us in unison. Laura Moon looked at me and added, "I'm surprised to find you here as well, Savannah. Where's that handsome husband of yours?" Laura was a statuesque brunette who weighed more than I did, though hers was mostly muscle, while my curves tended to be softer.

I shrugged slightly. "He's home doing hard labor. It shouldn't come as a shock to know that I venture into the city alone every now and then."

"Of course not," she said with a slight smile that lacked any real warmth. I didn't know Laura all that well, and if I was being fair about it, I couldn't hold her reaction against her. If our places had been reversed, I'm not entirely certain that I wouldn't have feigned deafness and run for the fountain across the street. To avoid the situation I was in at the moment, a dunk in the icy water wouldn't be all that unwelcome compared to what I was experiencing right now.

In an effort to keep Joanne's focus off me, I asked them, "How about you two? What brings you to Asheville?"

"We were just out shopping. Laura and I decided it was too chilly to take a run in the Botanical Gardens this morning like we'd planned, so after a little browsing, we thought we'd treat ourselves to lunch," Sandra Oliver said. Sandra was blonde, an inch taller than Laura, and there wasn't an unneeded ounce of body fat on her. She looked as though she could have run to Asheville from Parson's Valley without breaking a sweat, and I wondered how Laura ever managed to keep up with her.

"This is so delightfully unexpected. I really must insist that you join us," Joanne said forcefully. It would take someone with an iron will to go against her, and clearly neither of the other women had any more spine than I did. To their credit, the women looked as unhappy about receiving the invitation as I had been.

I didn't know them all that well, but misery loves company. If there were two more people at our table, perhaps some of Joanne's barbed comments would be directed their way instead of mine.

"Don't worry about crowding us. We'll make room," I said, doing my best to paste a smile on my lips.

The two women sat down, and before they could order anything for themselves, Joanne called out to our waitress, "Two more of those special teas, please."

If they wanted to fight her move, they both resisted the impulse. Too soon, we had four mugs of the wretched brew in front of us, though mine had been touched just once.

I watched their faces as they each took a sip, and with great satisfaction, I noted that neither appeared to enjoy it. At least I wasn't the only one there with an unsophisticated palate.

I was about to comment on it when my cell phone suddenly started quacking at me, a sure sign that my husband was calling.

"Excuse me," I said as I stood and stepped away from the group. I moved out onto the sidewalk and watched people walking around the obelisk as I talked to my husband.

"Save me," I said in a near whisper. I didn't think anyone at the table could hear me, but I wasn't about to take any chances.

"What's wrong?"

"I'm at a table at Café Noir in Asheville with Joanne Clayton and two other women from Parson's Valley."

He laughed. "Tough luck. Listen, on your way home, could you stop by the hardware store and get me another pair of work gloves?"

"What happened to the ones I bought you for your last birthday?" Zach was a huge fan of practical gifts, and it drove me crazy every year coming up with something to buy for him that he would actually use.

"They have a brand-new hole in them. You know the ones I like."

"Sure, I'll be glad to. Is that all you need?"

"You bet. Enjoy your lunch."

Raising my voice a little, I asked, "Do you need them as soon as possible? It sounds urgent to me."

My husband laughed. "Sure, why not? Go ahead and use me as an excuse. I don't mind a bit."

I wanted to smile, but I was afraid that I'd blow my cover. "Okay. I'll take care of it immediately."

As soon as I got back to the group, but before I could make my excuses, Laura asked me, "Savannah, do you know if there's a powder room here?"

"There's one inside," I answered as I hovered near the edge of the table. "It's back by the kitchen."

"I'll be right back," she said.

"Wait, I'll go with you," Sandra added quickly. It was clear she had no interest in being left alone with us.

"Listen, I hate to run, but Zach needs me back home."

"Oh, sit down. You have time to finish your tea."

I wasn't about to budge, or let her bully me into backing down. "Sorry. Wish I could."

"Can't you do anything without him? It's not natural to be that dependent on a man, Savannah."

I was about to say something even if it meant putting myself squarely in her sights when Joanne asked, "Is that Johnny Depp over there?"

I turned to look, but it was just another local with straggly hair and a partial beard. Honestly, Joanne's eyesight must be going; this man looked nothing like the movie star.

"No, I don't think so," I said.

"Are you sure?"

I looked again, but the man still bore little resemblance to the actor. "I'm pretty sure."

Joanne shrugged. "I watched him in an old movie last night," she said. "I must have him on my mind."

"I could think of worse things to have on my mind," I said.

I was reaching for my purse when Joanne accidentally knocked it onto the ground as she tried to take a sugar packet from the dispenser.

"Forgive me. I'm so clumsy," she said.

"It's fine," I replied as I bent over and started retrieving the contents, which had managed to spread out all around us upon impact with the ground.

"I think that's it," I said, as I finally collected everything and put it back in haphazardly. It was odd that Joanne hadn't made a single effort to help me, but I was just as glad. It was hard to imagine what she might have made of the contents of my purse, and I'd just as soon skip the analysis.

I looked at my mug of tea, and I had the distinct impression that it had moved since I'd last touched it.

"You should finish that," Joanne said as she followed my gaze.

I was about to say something to Joanne when Sandra and Laura returned.

"Did we miss anything?" they asked.

"Just Johnny Depp," I said, joking.

They didn't think it was all that amusing. "He was here?"

"Someone who looked remarkably like him," Joanne explained.

Laura smiled. "Still, if he was that close, he was probably worth looking at."

I was about to make my excuses when Sandra's cell phone rang. She had a brief conversation, and then said, "Sorry, but I've got to go. My husband is leaving for a business trip this afternoon, and he can't find his overnight bag. I swear, I don't know how that man manages without me. Sorry we couldn't stay," she said to us as she flipped a ten on the table, "but I'm Laura's ride home."

"We're really so sorry," Laura added.

"I'll go with you," I said as they started to leave.

Joanne's ferret fingers struck out and grabbed my arm. "We still need to talk, remember?"

"Can't it wait?"

"If you'd rather I come to your home later, I can do that," she said.

I shrugged and sagged back down into my chair. I'd been so close to escaping, only to have the opportunity snatched away from me at the last second.

After Sandra and Laura left, Joanne said, "It's just as well they're gone. I've been having difficulties with both of them lately, for entirely different reasons." She smiled slightly, and then added, "They didn't like what I had to tell them yesterday, but I couldn't just leave the things I knew alone, could I?"

I didn't even know how to answer that. I glanced at my watch, and decided that I'd had enough of Joanne for one day. If she wanted to hound me at my house later, then so be it. "I'm sorry, but I really must be going as well."

"We're not finished with our conversation," she said sternly. "This won't take more than a moment."

When she saw that I was going to stay, no matter how reluctantly, Joanne grinned and reached into her bag. I wasn't sure what to expect, but I was still surprised when she pulled out a folded newspaper with a logic puzzle displayed prominently on it.

"What's this?" I asked as I barely glanced at it.

"It's my puzzle," Joanne said smugly.

"I can see that," I said. "Would you like me to auto-

graph it for you?" I asked as I took it from her. I got that
request sometimes, and was always glad to oblige, though
I was surprised that Joanne was the one asking.

She looked offended by my comment. "*You* didn't create this. Look at it more carefully, Savannah."

I examined the header and saw that it was from an
Asheville alternative newspaper. I'd been trying to get into
that paper for years, but they'd steadfastly refused me.

That's when I saw the byline.

It was created by Joanne Clayton.

MY FIRST REACTION WAS TO THROW THE NEWSPAPER IN
her face, but I managed to hold my temper. It
wouldn't do to melt down until I got more information.

"How nice for you," I said. "I didn't know you were
interested in puzzles, Joanne."

"I have been for years. What amazes me is how easy
these are to create. I'm thinking about branching out to
other newspapers. Who is your contact, and how do I go
about getting my puzzles syndicated?"

Had she lost her mind? I wasn't about to offer her the
slightest bit of help in putting me out of business. Intro-
ducing her to any of my connections would be cutting my
own throat. "I can't make any promises, but I'll speak with
my syndicator and see if there's room on the roster." *When
the moon turns bright green and cows give chocolate milk*,
I added to myself. "Don't get your hopes up, though. It's
a tough market to break into."

"I'm sure once they see what I have to offer, there
won't be any problems." Joanne looked lovingly at the
newspaper still in my hand, and then said, "I'd be happy
to sign this for you, if you'd like."

"That would be nice," I said, still managing to keep my cool. I'd put it in my recycling bin at the first opportunity, but for now, I decided to let her have her moment.

It was clear that Joanne was finished with me after she signed the puzzle with a flourish, and I added a five to the table just so I could finally escape. There was a smug expression on her face as I left, but I didn't care; not as long as I could get away from her. I considered calling Zach to tell him what had happened, but then I decided that I was in no mood to talk to him just yet. That confrontation with Joanne had rattled me, and I needed some time to put it behind me. I turned onto the Blue Ridge Parkway on a whim when I saw an entrance ramp, and drove steadily for an hour in one direction, enjoying the spectacular mountain views and trying to get that vile woman out of my head. By the time I turned around and headed back toward home, I was in a much better place.

When I pulled the car into our drive, Zach was on the telephone. I waved to him as I got out, but he held up one hand for me to wait. The call didn't last very long, and when he got off, he had a somber expression on his face.

At that moment, I realized that I'd forgotten to go by the hardware store for his gloves. "I forgot the gloves. I'm so sorry. I'll go back right now."

"It's not important."

"It is so. You asked me for one thing, and I let you down."

"Savannah, take a breath and let me talk, will you? You're not going to believe this," Zach said.

"Why? What's going on?"

"Someone poisoned Joanne Clayton."

Chapter 3

∎∎∎

"**P**OISONED? YOU CAN'T BE SERIOUS."

He nodded. "I just found out. I'm still on hold trying to dig up more information about what happened."

"Is she going to be okay?" I asked, the life suddenly going out of me.

He looked so sad as he said, "I'm sorry. She's dead, Savannah."

"But I just saw her," I protested. "We even shared a cup of tea. This can't be happening."

"Believe it. Hang on a second. Are you saying that you actually drank out of the same cup that she did?"

"No, of course not. That would be gross. But we both had the same blend. Why? Is that how it happened?" I couldn't believe how close I'd come to being poisoned. What if whoever had done it had mistaken my mug for hers? It might be my husband in mourning. And then I wondered who would be saddened by Joanne's untimely demise. The fact that I couldn't come up with anyone right away was answer enough.

"It looks like we might have a problem," Zach replied, still holding the telephone to his shoulder. "They want me to investigate."

"You already turned down the Asheville job," I said. They'd asked him to replace the sheriff, who had been caught embezzling from his department, but after careful consideration, Zach had said no.

"This would be on a temporary basis only," he said, "but I can't do it if you're one of the suspects."

I hadn't put that part of it together yet. "Why would I be a suspect?"

"If you're not on the lead detective's list, at the very least you're a witness. Based on that alone, it wouldn't be right for me to investigate the case."

I took a deep breath. "Zach? Maybe I'm a little more than a witness here after all."

"How much more?" he asked as a frown started to appear.

Instead of answering, I handed him the autographed puzzle from my bag.

"It's bad, isn't it?" I asked him as he studied the puzzle's creator and matched it to the signature.

"It isn't good," he said as he kept staring at Joanne's name.

"Should I call Jenny?" Jenny Blake was my former college roommate and now an attorney in Raleigh. She'd helped me out of a sticky situation before, and had promised to come to my rescue if I ever needed her sharp legal mind again. I'd protested that I hadn't paid her for the last services she'd so ably provided, but Jenny had claimed that the money I'd loaned her in college was serving to cover her bill with interest that had accumulated over the years. If I had to, Zach and I could cover the tab, though it would put us in a financial bind, but I might just ask my uncle, who happened to have more than he would ever need, and had offered any and all of it to me if I just asked.

Zach stroked his chin and finally broke his stare from the puzzle printed in the paper. "It's not that bad. At least not yet."

I looked around. There wasn't a stick or a branch out of place. "The yard looks good."

He surveyed the yard, and then nodded absently. "I should have just left it and gone with you to Asheville."

"I don't need a chaperone every time I go to the city," I said.

His only reply was one raised eyebrow.

"Okay," I said, "maybe this time it would have been nice, but we had no way of knowing what was going to happen."

He put his arm around me, and I didn't even mind the fact that he hadn't showered yet. "Let's go inside," Zach said. "I'll get cleaned up, and you can tell me everything that happened today." He must have seen something in my expression, because he quietly added, "Don't worry, Savannah. It's going to be all right."

"I love hearing you say that; I just wish that I could believe you," I said.

"FIRST THINGS FIRST," ZACH SAID AFTER HE'D TAKEN THE time to grab a shower and shave before joining me in the living room by the fire, "I need to hear all of the details about your meeting with Joanne." As he said it, my husband retrieved a little red notepad from his pocket, along with a pen. It was the identical type he used when he was investigating a case, and the notepad's presence somehow eased my troubles a little bit.

"Okay. I went to the office supply store and faxed my puzzle to my editor. After that I shopped for a new fax machine. It's in the car, by the way. Remind me later that I need to get it so I can set it up."

"Savannah, did you run into Joanne at the office supply shop?"

"No, of course not," I said.

"Then why are you telling me about your shopping trip, when the woman's murder is what we're interested in?"

"You said that I should tell you everything, Zach. I was just doing my best to follow your orders."

He bit his lip, and after a few seconds, my husband said, "You're right. That's exactly what I said. Tell you what. Why don't we fast-forward to when you saw Joanne."

I nodded. "I can do that. I decided to have lunch outside, so I went to Café Noir, that cute little café downtown across from the obelisk. Do you know the one I mean?"

"I've been there with you, Savannah."

"Right. I forgot. Well, I didn't even see Joanne until I approached a table outside, and I tried to ignore her when she called out to me."

"Why?"

"Come on, you knew her, too. She could rain on any parade with that sharp tongue of hers, and I didn't want to wreck my good mood."

"But she persisted," Zach prodded gently.

"Oh yes. She joined me at my table."

"But she was alone at that point?"

"As far as I could tell."

Zach frowned. "Were there any plates or cups on the table where she was sitting when you arrived?"

"Just the teacup she was drinking from. There weren't any other plates on the table, but that doesn't really mean anything. Those waitresses there are fast." I thought about the time I'd lost my salad after taking a quick restroom break. Worse yet, someone else was sitting at my table. I could have made a fuss, but I was mostly full anyway, so I paid my bill and left.

My husband nodded as he made another note on his pad. "We'll assume that Joanne was alone at the time, until and unless we hear differently. Then what happened?"

"The second I sat down, she ordered me the most dreadful tea you can imagine. I took a polite sip as soon as the waitress brought it, but I never touched it again after that."

Zach looked concerned. "You drank the same tea she had?"

"Yes, of course, that's what I just said. Why, what's wrong?" That's when it hit me. "That's how Joanne was poisoned, wasn't it?"

He nodded somberly. "Luckily, one of the EMTs is taking a toxicology class at night school. She's trying to get into Pharmacy School, and she spotted it right away."

I felt queasy about the news. "But I'm fine. Mine had to be all right."

"Apparently just one of the mugs at the table contained any poison," Zach said. "But there were four of them on the table. Did you each get two?"

"No, of course not. Listen, you can ask more questions

and make me keep losing my train of thought, or you can save them all until I finish telling you what I know. It's your choice."

"I'm sorry, Savannah. Old habits die hard. Go ahead."

I took a deep breath, and then said, "Joanne was in rare spirits, I must say. She was smug about something the entire time I was there, but I didn't know why until the end."

I saw that Zach wanted to interrupt, but he fought it back, and I continued. "Anyway, I'm getting ahead of myself. When she first sat down with me, I remarked how odd it was to find her in Asheville, and she admitted that she'd just spoken with Harry Pike before I'd come along. Joanne made a remark that implied the two of them were battling over something, but she didn't give me any more details than that."

Zach tried to fight his impulse to ask me something again, and I didn't want him to strain anything. I shook my head and tried to hide my smile. "Go ahead. I know that you're just dying to ask me something."

The words came rushing out in a flood of release. "Do you know if he had any tea himself?"

"Not that I'm aware of," I said. "A minute or two after I sat down, Laura Moon and Sandra Oliver joined us, at Joanne's insistence. They didn't look as though they wanted to be there any more than I did, but we all knew how sharp Joanne's tongue could be. She forced them to get the same dreadful tea blend as well. Theirs had just been delivered when you called about me getting you more gloves."

"Did you stay at the table while we talked?"

I frowned. "No, I didn't want them to hear my side of the conversation. I walked onto the sidewalk and stared at the obelisk while we chatted."

"Then what happened?" he asked as he jotted something else down in his notepad.

"Laura and Sandra went to the ladies' room, and then they excused themselves as soon as they got back. I tried to make my own excuses, but Joanne insisted that I stay. I threatened to leave anyway, but she told me that she was coming by the house if we didn't have that chat immediately, so I decided to save ourselves the grief of having to entertain her here."

He grinned at me, despite the serious nature of our conversation. "Good call."

"I thought you'd feel that way. Anyway, Joanne said something negative about both of the women, too, but you know how she could be. She was always stirring the pot to get people flustered and react to her goading."

"I know," Zach said. "Did you leave then, too?"

"I wanted to, but Joanne wasn't finished with me yet. She wanted to show me her puzzle."

Zach stared at it for a full minute before he said, "I can't believe that she actually got this published."

"It's really not that bad," I said. "Maybe a little rough around the edges, but she had potential."

"I'll bet she loved rubbing your face in this," Zach said.

"She tried, but I wouldn't let her. I decided to take the high road." I tapped the newspaper with one finger. "I don't know who she paid off or slept with to get this in the newspaper, but however she did it, it was more than I would have been willing to do."

Zach frowned as he continued to stare at the puzzle.

"What is it?" I asked. "Why are you scowling?"

"I hate that you're going to be dragged into this. Whoever ends up investigating is just going to see this as a motive for you to have killed her. You realize that, don't you?"

"Are you serious? She couldn't hurt me with one puzzle, especially in this cheap little alternative paper in one city. My markets may all be secondary, but they are spread out all over the country."

"We both know that, but whoever's running the investigation might not realize how insignificant this is."

"Then what should we do?"

Zach thought about it, rubbing his ear as he did so. After a full minute, he said, "We don't have any choice. We need to go to Asheville."

"I just left there," I said. "Do you really need those gloves so badly? The yard looks fine to me."

"This isn't a shopping trip, Savannah. We need to find out who's in charge and tell them everything you know before they find out from someone else."

"Who would tell them?" I asked, and then quickly added, "Strike that. Laura and Sandra are probably already spreading it around town that I was there, too."

"Maybe not. They'd have to admit that they were there as well. Still, it's not a bad idea to get this out in the open as soon as we can."

I grabbed my coat. "Okay, I'm convinced. We need to go to Asheville. Do you want to drive, or should I?"

"You can," he said. "I need to make a few telephone calls while we're on our way."

I led the way back to my car, and then I remembered that I still had that boxed fax machine in the trunk. It looked like it was going to take another ride to Asheville and back before it ever made it into the house.

The second I pulled down our drive, Zach started working the telephone. It took him three tries and nearly twenty minutes, but he finally got through to the mayor of Asheville herself.

"This is Zach Stone . . . No, I haven't changed my mind. Have you found anyone to take the job yet? . . . Really." He pulled out his notepad and started scribbling. "And when will she be taking over? . . . That soon?" He jotted something else down. "I'm on my way into town. Would you call her and give her a heads-up that I'm coming? . . . No, I'm not going to get involved myself, but there's something I need to discuss with her as soon as possible. Thanks. Bye."

I whistled once he was off the telephone. "Wow, mister, you must be important. You know the mayor and everything."

"Don't kid yourself. If I hadn't met her at that fundraiser last month, she wouldn't have had any idea who I was."

"From the sound of your side of the conversation, I'm guessing they've already got someone to take the sheriff's place."

"On a temporary basis only," he said. "The state police are loaning them one of their investigators."

"A woman, if I heard right."

He laughed. "Savannah, I should have just put the call on speakerphone so you could hear both sides of the conversation."

"There wasn't any need to," I said as I drove into downtown Asheville. The autumn colors were just fading away from the mountains, displaying a blanket filled with browns and grays, with spots of green left where the evergreens stood. I loved the changing color of the leaves, but the absence of tourists looking at them was welcome as well. Many of the city's part-time residents were heading back to their winter homes in Florida and Arizona, and Asheville would become a good deal less crowded once that happened. "Do you know this woman in charge?"

"No, I've never heard of her, but I'm willing to bet that she's never heard of me, either."

"It might make things more difficult for you to get information from her," I said as I found a parking place near the sheriff's office.

"We're here to give her some information, not ask about any," he said.

"Sure. Of course. I believe you." I knew my husband better than that. For every item he told her, I was sure he'd glean a few things himself.

The police station looked imposing; there was no doubt about it. I'd been there with Zach a few times since we'd moved to Parson's Valley. No matter where we visited, the first thing my husband did was check in with the local law enforcement and identify himself as the former chief of police for Charlotte.

"Do you really think she'll talk to you?"

He shrugged. "I've got the mayor vouching for me, and that can't hurt. We'll see what happens."

We got out, and I asked, "Do you think she'll let you stay with me when I tell her what happened today?"

"I can't make any promises, but I don't see why not."

Knowing he felt that way helped, at least a little.

After Zach identified himself at the front desk, we were told to wait in some chairs near the door. It was less than five minutes later when a pretty but severe-looking woman in her thirties walked out to greet us. She was tall, at least six inches taller than I was, and her blonde hair was pulled back into a tight bun. She wore a state trooper's uniform, and from the way she moved, I could tell that she was confident in her ability to handle the world. I wouldn't want to cross her, and hoped that I didn't have to.

"Chief Stone?" she asked.

Zach smiled and offered his hand, which she took. "You can call me Zach," he said.

"I'm Captain North," she said, ignoring his offer of pleasantries. "I appreciate you stopping by, but I'm sure you'll understand that I don't have time for social visits. I've been here less than eight hours and I've already got a homicide and a carjacking to deal with."

"I can appreciate that," Zach said. If her brusque tone bothered him, he didn't show it. "My wife is a material witness in the murder case you're working on, so we thought you might like to interview her while the events of today are still fresh in her mind."

That caused a raised eyebrow as she looked at me with those hard eyes. "You're Savannah Stone?"

"I am," I admitted, for some reason feeling guilty about confessing it. There was something about that woman's cold stare that cut right through me.

She nodded once. "Then you've saved me a trip to Parson's Valley. If you'll come this way, we can begin."

Zach started to follow as well, and the captain stopped and said, "Thank you, but we won't need you for this interview."

He touched my arm lightly, and I stopped in my tracks.

Zach took a deep breath, let half of it out, and then said, "I go with her now and my wife makes a statement voluntarily, or we call an attorney and let her handle it. It's your choice."

Captain North shook her head slightly. "We both know that just makes her look guilty, don't we?"

Zach laughed at that comment, though I didn't see any

humor in it. He was actually smiling as he said, "Captain, you don't know me, but you can ask around. I've got a reputation for being stubborn, but the woman beside me makes me look like an amateur. Now, are all three of us going to have a nice polite chat, or is this interview over?"

She shook her head as she nearly spat out her words. "Come on."

"Thanks," Zach answered, as if the police captain had just extended a cordial invitation to him.

Once we were all seated in her new office, she commanded me, "Tell me everything that happened today, and don't leave anything out."

I grinned in immediate reaction, since Zach had asked me the same question earlier, and Captain North caught it. "Is there something you find amusing about murder, Mrs. Stone?"

"Me? No. You just reminded me of my husband with the way you worded your question."

She shook her head slightly, and then clearly decided to let it go, much to my relief. As she took out a notebook and a pen, Captain North said, "Let's get started, then."

AFTER I'D TOLD MY STORY THREE DIFFERENT TIMES, THE state police captain closed her notebook and said, "Thank you for coming forward."

"Is that it?" I asked.

"For now. The investigation is just beginning, so I'm sure I'll need to speak with you again."

We stood, and I started for the door. That's when I realized that Zach wasn't right behind me.

He glanced at me and asked, "Savannah, why don't you wait for me in the car?"

"I don't mind hanging out here," I said.

"Please," he replied, and I knew from his tone of voice that arguing with him would be pointless. We each had a way of speaking that the other respected. It was an "I mean business" tone that brooked no argument. I nodded, and then made my way outside. I wasn't sure what Zach wanted to talk to the acting sheriff about, but I knew it wasn't meant for me to hear. If he'd pulled something like that when we'd first gotten married, I would have howled in protest, but there was an advantage in being married to the same man for so many years. We both knew when to push, and when to back off. This was clearly a time for me to back off.

It was a beautiful day, with a crispness and joy in the air that couldn't be muted by Joanne Clayton's murder. I would never have wished her fate upon her, but I certainly understood how someone might be pushed to the limit by the woman. If I was indeed a suspect in the case, I knew I'd have a place along with a dozen other folks, and that was in Parson's Valley alone.

Zach came out twenty minutes later, and I couldn't miss his smile.

Before he could say a word, I asked, "Is there actually some good news for us today?"

"She's not that bad once you get to know her," Zach said.

"And exactly how long is that going to take?"

"Once you were gone, I gave her a few references of fellow officers around the state, and she called a few she knew while I waited outside. The frost zone retreated quite a bit once she talked to some folks we both know and respect. It should make life at least a little easier for you now."

"Thanks," I said. "I appreciate that."

"Hey, if I can't pull strings for my wife, what good is it having them?" Zach put a hand through his hair, and I knew that was a sign that there was something he needed to speak with me about but was not all that crazy about bringing up.

I saved him the quandary. "Go on; just spit it out. What is it?"

"What are you talking about?"

"You've got something you have to tell me, but you don't want to do it."

He shook his head. "How can you read me like that? Remind me never to play poker with you."

"You're stalling," I said.

"You're right." He shifted a little in his stance, and avoided eye contact with me as he blurted out, "I want to hang around here awhile, if you don't mind."

I nodded. "It's fine with me. Should we go over to Mast General Store, or would you like to go by the Mellow Mushroom and get a bite to eat?"

A frown crossed his face. "You don't understand, Savannah. I'm going to stay. You're the one leaving."

I was puzzled by that. "Are you finally getting tired of me, Zach?"

"No, but I managed to get North to loosen up some, and she's willing to take some outside advice, as long as it's not directly related to you. It's a fine line she's dancing, but she knows that she might be in over her head, so she's willing to cut me a little slack." He smiled at me, and then added, "This is a step forward, Savannah. It keeps me close enough to the investigation so I'll know what's going on."

I couldn't argue with that, even though I knew the

prospect of staying pleased him. Zach made no secret about the fact that he loved being around an active police department, so it wasn't exactly a sacrifice on his part, but he was still doing it for my benefit. "How are you going to get home if I go back to Parson's Valley? I don't mind waiting for you."

He shook his head. "It's not necessary. North's going to drop me off later. She's decided to go talk to Laura, Sandra, and Harry today. By the way, you did a great job in there. You were calm and rational as you pointed out the other prime suspects who had contact with Joanne today. I was really proud of you."

"Thanks. It wasn't pleasant going over it again and again, but having you there beside me really helped."

He hugged me, and then said, "I'll call you later with an update. Are you going to stay in town for a while?"

I thought about doing some browsing in Asheville, but I was suddenly in no mood to shop. "No, I think I'll head back home."

"That sounds like a plan. See you there," he said.

As I left Zach, I glanced back and saw him walking briskly into the police station. It wouldn't have surprised me if he'd started skipping. My husband loved being around an active case, no matter how much he protested to the contrary.

But at least this time he was on my side.

As I drove back to Parson's Valley, I suddenly knew that going straight home wasn't really an option for me, either. Though Zach was watching my back with the police, there was another group of people that might not believe so readily in my innocence. If the folks in our town thought I was a murderer, it could make life miserable for us both. I was the newcomer there, still an outsider in many of their minds. It just made sense that I'd be the first one they suspected, especially after they heard about Joanne's puzzle, and my supposed competition. It didn't take a genius to know that the events today could easily be skewed toward painting me as a murderer. I didn't doubt some people would find it heroic, but they weren't people I cared to associate with. It was likely that either Sandra or Laura had already mentioned my presence at the crime scene, and I was pretty sure the telephone lines were already heating up.

I had to stop the rumors before they had a chance to grow and spread.

If nothing else, I could start getting the word out myself that I'd had nothing to do with Joanne Clayton's murder.

I just hoped the people of Parson's Valley believed me.

Chapter 4

...

ICAN'T BELIEVE JOANNE CLAYTON IS DEAD," BARBARA Brewster said the second I walked into Brewster's Brews, her coffee shop on 2nd Street and Main in downtown Parson's Valley. "Savannah Stone, what have you done?" Her voice was loud and brash, and several heads in the coffee shop turned toward me. Perhaps I would have been better off going straight home after all.

"I didn't kill her," I said, matching Barbara's volume so no one would miss my denial. "Believe me when I tell you that I'm not the only one from town who saw her today."

Barbara, a petite woman in her fifties with brown hair and sharp blue eyes, stared at me a few seconds before she answered. She wasn't about to let go of it just yet. "That's not the way I heard it."

"Who have you been listening to?" I asked. "Whoever it was, believe me, they got it wrong."

"So, you weren't having lunch today with Joanne just before she was murdered?"

"We had tea," I said, and then realized how that must sound, since the herbal nightmare she'd been drinking was probably what had killed her. "But she was fine when I left her."

Barbara and I had always gotten along, but we wouldn't be considered best friends by anyone's standards. She had her finger on the pulse of Parson's Valley, though, and if I was going to have any luck finding out who killed Joanne, I would need Barbara's help.

She stared at me again, and then to her credit, she announced loudly, "You know what? I believe you, Savannah. I have a hard time seeing you poisoning anyone."

"Thanks," I said.

"Now, if she'd been hit over the head with a chair, I might think that was more your style."

I'd had about enough of that. "I didn't do that, either." I lowered my voice as I added, "I just came in for a cup of coffee, and I was hoping for the chance to have a quiet conversation with you."

If there was anything Barbara liked more than playing the role of public accuser, it was being on the inside of anything. "Lucky for you, I can do both today," she said. "What can I get you to drink?"

"Let's start with a cup of plain coffee."

"That's easy enough to do," Barbara said as she drew a coffee and handed it to me.

I slid my money across the counter to her, and said softly, "I really do need to speak with you. I'm not asking for help out of idle curiosity. I don't want folks around here thinking I'm capable of murder."

Barbara frowned, and then said, "I hate to be the one to break it to you, but it might be a little late for that, Savannah."

"You're kidding," I said, not wanting to believe that the rumors had spread already. "Sandra Oliver was there with Joanne and me, and so was Laura Moon. I didn't see Harry Pike, but Joanne herself told me that she just saw him. Why couldn't it have been one of them?"

"It could have been, I'll grant you that, but you've only lived in town for a few years, and they all grew up around here."

"That doesn't make me guilty of murder."

"Of course it doesn't," Barbara said, "but it doesn't make you innocent, either. If you ask me, people want to believe that no one who's lived here all their lives is capable of killing someone. It makes things too uncomfortable, if you know what I mean."

I'd suspected the same thing myself when I'd walked in there, and having my worst fears realized didn't make matters any better. "What am I going to do, Barbara?"

She seemed surprised by the way I asked her for advice, and she didn't know quite how to react at first. "I wish I could tell you," she said after a moment's thought, "but at the moment, I don't have a clue what you can do, and that's the honest truth."

"Thanks for the coffee, anyway," I said as I walked out of the shop. Before I could get three steps beyond the coffeehouse door, I heard someone calling my name.

It was Barbara.

"You forgot your change," she said loudly.

"I did not."

As she approached, Barbara whispered, "Would you hush and listen to me? Do you know where the back entrance to my shop is?"

"No, but I could probably find it," I said. "Why do you ask?"

"Meet me back there in five minutes. We need to talk."

I shrugged, not sure I liked being shuffled off to the back room. "Why can't we speak in front of everyone else?"

Barbara looked me straight in the eye as she said, "It's simple. If it turns out that you did kill Joanne, not everyone in this town is going to want to give you a medal, though I admit you could probably raise enough money from the folks who did want her dead to buy yourself a new automobile. Either way, though, they're all customers of mine, and I can't afford to alienate any of them. Do we understand each other?"

"I've got it," I said. "See you soon." Much louder, I added, "Thanks for my change," though if anyone had been watching us, they would have to be a stone fool not to realize that we'd just been conspiring about something.

I did as Barbara asked, and found the rear entrance easily enough. I knocked once, waited, and then knocked again.

There was no reply.

Had she just been taunting me with her offer to help? What would she gain by making me look like a fool? I glanced around, but no one was watching me, so at least I wasn't performing for an audience.

Maybe she hadn't heard me. I rapped on the door again, this time rattling it in its frame.

"What are you trying to do, wake the dead?" Barbara asked as she opened the door.

"I knocked a few times when I first got here, but I didn't think you could hear me."

"I heard you just fine," she said, "but Ramona Ridge is working here today, and that woman couldn't keep a secret if it would save her life. Go back in my office, and I'll be right there. I need to send her on some kind of fool's errand so we can have some privacy."

I did as I was asked and made my way deeper into the back of the shop. Calling the space I found an office was a gross misrepresentation of the truth. I wasn't even sure it had enough square footage to qualify it as a nook, but somehow Barbara had managed to wedge a small desk and two chairs into the space, though there wasn't a great deal of room left for pesky things like actually being able to use any of the area.

"I know it's tight," she said before I could comment on it, "but I had to make do with what I had. Every square inch I use back here is lost for customers, and that's where I make my money." She managed to wedge herself behind her desk and asked, "What exactly do you think I can do to help you?"

"I figure you know more about what's happening in Parson's Valley than anyone else, and right now, I'm in desperate need of information."

"I'm not sure I agree with that, but I'll help if I can." She looked happy that I'd come to her, and I was going to do my best to foster that joy.

"First off, who would want to see Joanne Clayton dead?"

Barbara laughed, and then caught herself. "I shouldn't

chuckle about it, but it's hard not to, isn't it? The woman had her claws into a dozen people, any of whom might want to wish her ill." She tapped a pencil on her desktop, and then added, "I need to do a little digging. Can you wait here for a few minutes?"

"Hey, you're doing me a favor, remember? I can stay here as long as you'd like," I said.

As I waited in Barbara's cramped office, I wondered if what she'd said was true. I'd been under the impression that the folks in Parson's Valley had accepted Zach and me as one of their own since we'd moved there a few years before, but maybe I'd been mistaken. Was there still a basic mistrust of newcomers in this day and age? I couldn't believe it. I'd made some wonderful friends since we'd arrived, and I couldn't imagine any of them turning their backs on me. Then again, I'd never before been tied to a murder so close to the town where we lived. There was a mob mentality that mistrusted the outsider. The question was how many folks still considered me to be a stranger, and not a friend?

That line of thought would just drive me crazy. To distract myself from my problems, I looked around Barbara's tiny office. It was amazing that the woman could get any work done there at all. Papers were stacked four inches high on her desktop, and the few free spaces there were on the floor were covered with books. Barbara was well-known around town as a big reader, and she had a constant battle going on with Nancy Jenkins, the town's librarian. It seemed that Barbara believed due dates were merely suggestions, and Nancy kept threatening to cut off her supply until she started returning books on a more regular basis. The two had endured a silent feud for a few weeks until they reached a compromise. Barbara could continue to disregard her due dates, but Nancy would keep track of the amounts, billing Barbara every month for her accumulated fines. I was shocked that Barbara had been willing to pay that way, since she was notoriously tight with her money, but she claimed that it didn't bother her at all. She considered the bills as leasing fees, though she could have had the books for free if she'd just been a little more diligent about returning them. I started going through the titles, curious about what would attract her fancy, and maybe I'd even find something to read while I waited. If I was going to be there awhile, I didn't plan to be idle, and creating a new puzzle with all that was on my mind was out of the question.

I scanned through the titles, hoping to find anything that was interesting to me. I hadn't realized just how eclectic Barbara's reading tastes were until I started reading through her stacks. Titles like *The Great Gatsby*, *War and Peace*, *Modern Jazz Composition*, *Advanced Loom Weaving*, *Native North Carolina Plants*, *Mythical Creatures of Ireland*, and *The Dead Sea Scrolls* were mixed in with *Where the Wild Things Are*, *The Mysterious Affair at Styles*, and *'Salem's Lot*.

I still hadn't picked one to read when Barbara abruptly came back in. "What on earth are you doing, Savannah?"

I got up from my crouching position. "I was looking for something to read," I admitted.

"Well, you're not going to find anything there. Those are books that I've checked out. The library has plenty more, believe me."

I glanced at the piles. "I doubt they have many more than you do."

Barbara grinned. "Hey, I pay for the privilege every month."

"May I ask you something?"

"Sure."

"Do you actually read all of these?" I asked as I pointed to the books.

She laughed at the question. "Parts of most of them. What can I say, I'm easily distracted. Now, did you come here to discuss my reading habits, or do you want to know about Joanne Clayton?"

"I'd love to hear what you've discovered," I said, forgetting all about the books and focusing on Barbara.

She looked pleased by the comment. "It appears that there are seven people who might have wanted her dead."

"Seven? That many?"

"There may be more," Barbara acknowledged, "but I phoned a few friends in town, and those were all we could come up with on such short notice."

"Let me get something to write these down on," I said, diving into my bag for a pen and a piece of paper. They were there in case any good puzzle ideas—or, more likely, snippet thoughts—came to me while I was out. I couldn't build a puzzle in my mind any more than I could play three games of chess at the same time, but it was impossible to predict when creativity would strike.

I looked at the paper in my purse and saw that I'd scribbled, *Compare autumn with computers in next snippet.* What in the world could that possibly mean? I flipped the paper over and looked expectantly at Barbara.

She'd been watching me, and before she spoke, she took another full ten seconds to study me. "Remember, no one can know that I've fed you this information. Agreed?"

"Not even Zach?" I asked.

"No, I'm sorry, but this has to be between the two of us alone."

"My husband was the chief of police for Charlotte, North Carolina," I said with a little more stiffness than I intended. "Trust me when I tell you that he knows how to keep a secret."

"I'm sorry, but I insist," she said. I could tell from the look in her eyes that she wasn't going to back down, so anything I said would just be a waste of good breath.

I put the paper and pen back in my bag and stood. "Then I'm sorry I bothered you. I do appreciate the thought."

"Where are you going?" Barbara looked absolutely startled by my reaction to her demand. I doubted that many folks had told her no before.

"If I can't tell my husband, I don't want to know anything you've got to say. It's as simple as that."

Barbara frowned, clearly in uncharted waters. "Even if it means not finding the real killer?"

"Even then," I said as I headed for the door.

Barbara snapped out, "You can't bluff me, Savannah; I'm too good at reading character for that to work."

"I wouldn't dream of trying to make you back down. I know better. That's why I'm just going to give up and start digging around town myself."

"No one's going to talk to you," she said in a threatening voice as I headed for the back door.

"Maybe not. I guess we'll just have to wait and see."

I was at the door when she said with an air of finality, "You'll be back."

I turned to face her, and it took every ounce of energy I had to keep smiling. "Barbara, if there's one thing in my life that I stand by, it's my relationship with my husband. I'm sure I could get along fine without him, and he could probably do the same, but there's something magical about life when we're together, and I wouldn't do anything to risk that, ever, not even if my very life depended on it."

I left her with that, and as I closed the door, the frown on Barbara's face was obvious. She'd tried to back me down on one of the few things on earth that I would never budge from, and she'd lost. I'd probably pay for my disobedience, but if that meant that my reputation around town would take a hit, it was worth it.

I'd meant every word I'd said. There was nothing more important to me than my marriage, and I would never do anything that might harm it in the slightest way. The sooner folks around town realized that, the better off we'd all be.

MY PRINCIPLES WERE ALL WELL AND GOOD, BUT THEY weren't going to help me find a killer and clear my name. Now that I'd lost my first and best chance of putting together a list of folks who might want to see Joanne come to harm, I'd have to formulate a backup plan. I returned to my car, but I made no attempt to start the engine until I had a specific destination in mind. As I went over all the people I'd met in Parson's Valley over the past few years, I thought of—and just as quickly discarded—most of the people I'd ever met there. Sure, there were plenty of folks I'd share a seat with at the Saturday night buffet on Town Square, and some I'd even share a secret or two with, but I was just beginning to realize that the ones I could trust, and I mean really trust, were few indeed. I started getting depressed about it until I realized that in all the years we'd lived in Charlotte, I could still just produce a similarly small list, a few friends I could call in the middle of the night who wouldn't ask why, instead just how they could help. It was probably like that for most people, if they were ever to honestly assess the relationships with the people they came into contact with from day to day.

In the end, I managed to come up with two names of people I knew that I could trust. It was no surprise that Barbara's wasn't one of them. I suddenly realized that I'd been going about it all wrong. Certainly Barbara Brewer knew more about the activities in our little town than nearly anyone else, but that didn't mean she'd share what information she had with me; at least not without a price I refused to pay.

The two I had left would do that, and more.

And now I knew exactly where I needed to go.

It was time to get some help from a real friend.

I WAVED TO ROB HASTINGS WHEN I WALKED INTO HIS HARD-ware store. The owner was selling a middle-aged man some exotic wood from the section of his store devoted to woodworkers. It would have surprised a lot of folks back in Charlotte that one of my best friends in Parson's Valley was the heavyset widowed owner of the town hardware store, but sometimes there's no accounting for how people make a connection. When we'd first moved into our old cottage, Zach and I had discovered that there were a thousand things that needed fixing, and we soon learned that Rob had all the answers, and on those rare occasions when he didn't, he had a good idea of exactly who in our area might. Since Zach's consulting business was just starting to take off, my husband had to go where the crime was. At times, he was gone more often than he was at home, so I'd turned to Rob for help, and we'd soon developed a friendship. What had sealed it, at least for him, was the sourdough bread I baked every week, with one loaf earmarked especially for him. His late wife had made the same subtle sourdough that I did, with a hint of the flavor instead of the overpowering blast that many starters yielded. We'd soon worked out an arrangement that both of us were happy with: his advice for my bread.

After Rob rang up the man's sale and helped him to his car, he smiled at me and said, "There goes a man who appreciates history."

"What were you two discussing?" I asked.

"Wood," he answered, looking surprised by my question. "You saw us over there, didn't you?"

"I'm probably going to regret this, but what's historic about those particular boards he just bought?"

Rob retrieved another plank from the pile—one about eight inches wide, four feet long, and an inch thick. "Savannah, how heavy would you say this board is?"

I looked at its bulk. "It looks like it weighs a lot."

Then he handed to me. "Now what would you say?"

"It's surprisingly light," I admitted.

"But it's stronger than you'd ever imagine. How about the color of the wood? Does it look familiar?"

I studied the board in my hand. It was a game we sometimes played, identifying wood species, and I'd gotten to be pretty good at it over the past few years. Even Rob admitted that it was getting harder and harder to stump me. "The grain pattern looks like it could be some type of oak, but I've never seen anything in that species that color before. It's a cross between blond and butter, if I had to categorize it."

He laughed at my description.

"What's so funny?" I asked.

"I've just never heard it described that way before, but

I think you've nailed it perfectly. So, are you ready to guess?"

I looked at it again, and then handed the board back to him. "Not today. I'm afraid you've beaten me. I give up."

He didn't gloat; I had to give him credit for that. "Don't take it too hard. There are woodworkers who've been at it for decades who've never held a piece of this in their hands. It's authentic American chestnut, harvested a hundred years ago and cut with a water-powered saw blade."

"Okay, I see the history of it," I acknowledged. "What does it cost?"

"It's ten dollars a board foot," he said. "I'd say that was cheap for a piece of history, wouldn't you?"

"I would," I said as I took out my purse and put a ten dollar bill in his hand. "I'll take it."

"That's per board foot, not per board," he said as he handed the money back to me.

"Then how much does this piece in particular cost?"

He took a few measurements, entered them into a calculator, and came up with a total, but before he would tell me, he looked at me and asked, "Do you really want this piece, or are you just making one of those points you like to make from time to time?"

"Does it matter?"

He touched the wood with reverence for a few moments. "Ordinarily I'd say no; your money is just as good as anyone else's. But with this wood, it makes a difference to me. Botanists and foresters keep trying to bring back the American chestnut, but they keep failing at it. Our country wouldn't be the same place it is now without it."

"I didn't know. If there isn't anything new to harvest, then where do these boards come from?"

"Mostly old barns that are being torn down in the country. If chestnut is cared for properly, this board will be around forever."

"That's pretty amazing." I thought about it. "Tell you what I'll do. I'll come up with something special to use it for, and then I'll come back and buy it."

"That sounds like a plan." Rob took out a small adhesive label and printed my name on it. "This will be in my office waiting for you when you're ready for it."

"You've got a deal," I said as I put my purse away.

He put the board by his desk, and then Rob said, "You didn't come by shopping for chestnut, and I don't see any sourdough bread in your hands, so what can I do for you?"

"I need some advice," I said.

"That I've got plenty of, free of charge, and worth more than you have to pay for it." He turned to his sole clerk, a young man named Lee Thomas, and said, "I'll be in my office for a few minutes. Call me if you get swamped."

Lee asked, "Do you want me to start putting the barbeque grills away in the basement?"

"No, just watch the floor. You can do those later, but leave one on the sales floor."

Lee grinned at him. "Do you honestly think anyone's going to want to buy a grill this late in the season?"

"If we don't have one on display, how will they know they can?"

Lee nodded, and Rob and I went into his office. It was in sharp contrast to Barbara's, with everything put away in a neat fashion. I admired him for his sense of order, even if I didn't emulate it myself. There was a bookcase along one wall, but there were no library books on it. Instead, there was a mass of vendor catalogues, neatly organized. It didn't appear that Rob ever threw one out.

As Rob settled into the red leather chair behind his

desk, he leaned back and asked, "What kind of advice are you in the market for, Savannah?"

"I'm trying to figure out who killed Joanne Clayton," I said abruptly.

As I said it, I saw Rob's face go white, and he nearly fell out of his chair. It seemed that my friend hadn't heard the news about our fellow resident of Parson's Valley, and he was taking it harder than I ever could have imagined he would.

Chapter 5

...

"**A**RE YOU OKAY?" I WAS WORRIED THAT ROB WAS TAKING the news so hard, and I felt guilty for not sugarcoating it a little, instead of just blurting it out as I had.

Some color was coming back to his face, but I could tell that he was still shaken by the news. "I'll be fine," he said. "I just need a second to come to terms with it. I hadn't heard a thing about it."

"I didn't realize you two were that close," I said.

"We're not now," he said with a sad voice, "but we were, at least at one point in our lives. I admit that it was so long ago that it almost feels like it was someone else, but the news is tough to hear."

"Were you two ever an item?" I asked as delicately as I could. I couldn't imagine my friend ever finding Joanne attractive—not that she didn't have her share of suitors over the years. I just doubted that he'd be able to take the barbed comments she was so famous for.

"No, never," he said with a quick dismissal that I instantly believed. "She was good friends with my Becky, though."

I knew Becky was Rob's late wife. "I'm so sorry. I didn't realize."

He shook his head. "It's not your fault. My wife was gone long before you and Zach moved to Parson's Valley." Rob put a hand through his hair and appeared to try to shake off the bad news. "I'm kind of surprised that nobody told me. When did this happen?"

"Today, in Asheville. We were having tea together at Café Noir, across from the obelisk."

He looked startled yet again, and I worried for a moment about his heart. "Did you actually see it happen?"

"I might have," I said.

Rob frowned at me before he spoke. "Savannah, either you did or you didn't. It's a simple question."

"I just wish it had a simple answer. I was picking a few things up in the city, and I decided to have lunch across from Pack Square. Joanne spotted me, and then joined me at my table. Sandra Oliver and Laura Moon came soon afterward, and we all had some tea together."

"Do you know how she died?"

"She was poisoned," I said.

His face grew even paler. "Do the police think you did it?"

"I'm not sure what they think," I admitted.

"Surely Zach is going to clear you," Rob said. He had a great deal of faith in my husband's ability as a detective; a belief that I happened to share.

"He's trying, but there's only so much he can do. I've got more problems than being a murder suspect, though."

My friend looked genuinely puzzled. "What takes precedence over that?"

"Think about it," I said as I leaned forward in my chair. "I know I didn't kill Joanne, and I believe Zach will find a way to prove it. I'm just afraid that even if the killer is found, if it happens too late, my name's going to be smeared forever as a murderer. If I can nudge the Asheville police and give them other suspects, they might be able to clear my name before it's too late to do me any good."

Rob nodded. "So, that's the advice you've come to me for."

I stood. "It was, but that was before I found out you had such close ties with Joanne, even if it was far back in your past. Now I realize that it would be too painful for you to help me. I'm sorry I bothered you with this, Rob."

"Sit back down, young lady," he said. There weren't many folks who called me that, but I always let it slide with Rob. "I'll help you."

"But it's not—"

He cut me off. "There's something you should realize. Joanne Clayton was a completely different woman back then. Sometimes I think she took Becky's death nearly as hard as I did. The woman changed, I'll tell you that. I know it's hard to believe now, but before, she was fun, clever, and always willing to lend a hand. When my wife died, something died in Joanne as well. She became someone I didn't recognize anymore. She turned into a mean, spiteful, angry woman, and I gave up trying to get through to her a long time ago." He rubbed his chin, and then added, "I suppose I thought there was a kernel of goodness buried deep inside her to the very end, waiting to come back out, but we'll never know that now, will we?" He slapped his hands on the desktop, a move that startled me with its abruptness, and the ringing shot of the impact echoed in the small space. "Savannah, you and I are going to find out who robbed her of that chance."

"Are you sure you're up to it?"

"More than you could imagine. Now, you said that Laura and Sandra were at the table with you as well. Was there anyone else around that you knew?"

"She mentioned that Harry Pike came by just before I got there," I said, "but I didn't see him. I know that a lot of people around here didn't like Joanne. She burned too many bridges over the years. I don't even know where to start with possible killers."

"I'm afraid it's not going to be a short list, is it? We need to write this down so we can keep track of everyone we suspect."

I reached into my bag for paper and a pen, but he shook his head when he saw me do it. "We'll use one of my chalkboards. Every now and then I run specials, and these come in handy to announce them to my customers."

He put a board on a narrow lip on the wall behind his desk and started writing. I felt better already, knowing that I had called on reinforcements to help with my search. I had Zach working with the police, and Rob and I were going to tackle things, too.

It was a good start, but I knew that we had a lot of work to do if we were going to find a killer.

* * *

AS ROB WROTE JOANNE'S NAME AT THE TOP OF THE board, I said, "If it helps, Barbara Brewster told me that there were seven people that she knew of who wouldn't mind seeing Joanne dead."

"You already spoke with Barbara about this?" Rob asked me as one eyebrow arched skyward.

"I thought she might have an idea about where to start. She seems to have her finger on the pulse of life around here. Barbara *has* to hear things in her line of work."

Rob nodded reluctantly. "It's a good idea. Did she happen to mention any of the people who made her cut?"

I didn't want to answer him, but it was a fair question, and he had a right to know. "To be honest with you, I wouldn't let her tell me."

"Now you've got my curiosity going full steam ahead," he said. "Savannah, if you asked the woman for help, why did you refuse it when she offered it to you? I'm betting Barbara didn't take kindly to that."

"It upset her, but it couldn't be helped. She wanted me to swear that I wouldn't tell anyone what she told me."

"On the face of it, that sounds like a reasonable request," he said.

"It included Zach. That's when I walked out on her."

Rob laughed when he heard that. "Now I understand. I would have loved to see her reaction when you left. She must have been madder than a wet cat when you walked away from her. She probably threatened you as she left, knowing that woman."

"I don't know if you could consider anything Barbara said to me a threat. She wasn't happy with me, that was clear enough, but I never really gave her the chance to say much before I was gone."

"Then that was worth the price of admission alone, I'd say. Seven is as good a place to start as any. Let's see if we can match folks around town with the numbers on her list." Rob wrote down the names Sandra Oliver, Laura Moon, and then Harry Pike. After a moment or two, he added Greg Lincoln and Hannah Reed as well.

"Why them?" I asked.

"That's why you came to me second, right? Because of my knowledge of the town?"

I had never meant to hurt his feelings. "Rob, I was downtown, and when I saw Barbara's coffee shop, I didn't think twice about asking her for help. It was no intended slight on you. I promise you that."

If he had harbored any hurt because of it, it appeared to vanish with my apology. "Don't think another thing about it. I'm just glad you thought of me at all." He tapped the last two names on the board with the piece of chalk in his hand, and explained, "Greg and Joanne used to date, not that they ever let anyone in town know about it."

"If they were being so secretive, how did you find out?"

Rob shrugged. "It was purely by accident. I couldn't sleep one night last week, so I decided to take a walk around town. Joanne was sitting by herself on a park bench, and I was about to greet her when I heard a man's voice nearby. I recognized it as Greg's immediately. He's got a distinctive way of talking, and there's no doubt in my mind it was him. What surprised me was the intensity of their conversation. That's putting it mildly. They weren't chatting; they were arguing about something, and he wasn't happy when he left."

"Did either one of them see you?"

Rob looked sheepish as he admitted, "I was a little embarrassed about eavesdropping on them, so I stepped back into a doorway so I'd be out of their line of sight. I thought about asking Greg what it was all about as he neared me, but he stormed past me before I could say a word."

That was interesting news. "Were you able to hear anything specifically that either one of them said?"

Reluctantly, Rob said, "I wasn't trying to listen in on their private conversation, but I couldn't help hearing the last thing he said to her. Knowing what I know now, it really sends a chill down my spine whenever I think about it."

"What did he say?"

"He told her, 'You'll live to regret it. I can promise you that.' You know Greg; he's usually full of harmless bluster, but he didn't sound harmless that night. It might bear looking into."

"Sounds good. I'll talk to him first," I said.

"Hang on a second, Savannah. I'm not sending you out into the world with this information to confront someone who might be a killer. You need to tell your husband and let him handle it."

"I can question Greg myself," I said. Sometimes Rob had the idea that women were delicate flowers, and I did everything in my power to dissuade him of that belief whenever I could. I was a grown woman, perfectly capable of handling just about anything that came my way.

"At least take him with you," my friend insisted. "I'd never forgive myself if something happened to you because of what I said."

"Rob, are we going to have to have that conversation again?"

"Woman, I'm not kidding here," he said, his face screwed into a frown. "If Greg did get rid of Joanne, facing him alone would be the worst thing in the world that you could do. If you won't ask your husband to speak with him, or even go with you, then I'm begging you to at least take me. Between the two of us, we might be able to handle him if things go wrong."

I was tired of being sheltered. It was time to deflect Rob's attention to something else. "He wasn't even in Asheville today," I said.

"That you know of. The very least we need to do is get an alibi for the man. If we can cross him off the list, so much the better."

I bit my upper lip. "I see your point, but we can't exactly walk up to him and ask him, can we?"

Rob smiled. "We can do just that, if we handle it properly. In the meantime, let's get back to the list."

I studied the last name he'd written there. "What could Hannah Reed have against Joanne? I've never even heard the woman raise her voice in public, so it's hard for me to wrap my mind around the idea that she could possibly commit murder."

"From the books I've read on the subject, there are times when the least likely suspect is the one guilty of the crime."

"Are we talking fiction or nonfiction?" I asked. "I'm not sure mysteries should count as true research on how the criminal mind works."

"And why not? Many of the novels I've read are closer to the way the world actually works than the best true crime books."

I wasn't about to argue the point with him. "Okay, but that still doesn't give Hannah a reason to kill Joanne."

"There is a good one. I just haven't told you what it is yet."

I waited for him to provide the missing information, but when he wasn't forthcoming, I asked, "Are you going to tell me at some point, or do I just have to keep guessing until I stumble across Hannah's motive on my own?"

"I honestly don't know if I should share this with anyone, including you," he said. "Before I say one more word, I'm going to have to get someone else's permission."

"Not Hannah's, I hope."

He shrugged without committing to an answer one way or the other. "Let's just leave her name up there for now. If I can get the go-ahead, I'll tell you her motive later."

I scowled at him. "How am I supposed to figure out if she killed Joanne or not if I don't know what her motive could be?"

Rob said softly, "Easy there, Savannah. I realize that you're under a lot of strain at the moment, but we don't need the motive for now; not if she's lacking the opportunity."

It was time to give up that particular line of reasoning, since it wasn't likely that I would get anything more out of Rob about Hannah.

I stared at the list, and then asked him, "Is that it?"

"Off the top of my head, I'd say yes. I have to do a little digging, so I'm not ready to say that the list is finished by any stretch of the imagination."

"There's one other name that's not up there," I said somberly.

"I know you didn't kill her," Rob said, the closest his voice had ever gotten to angry in my presence before.

"It's not my name I'm talking about," I said.

"Then I'm waiting to be enlightened."

"I'll tell you, but you might not believe me."

He handed me the chalk as he said, "I don't need to believe you; at least not yet. Just knowing that it's possible is enough for me for the moment."

I took the piece of chalk from him and wrote down a name.

He looked at it, and then stared at me. "Is that some kind of joke, Savannah?"

"No, I actually think it's possible," I answered.

"Explain yourself," he said. "There were a great many things Joanne Clayton was capable of doing, but I wouldn't think poisoning herself was one of them. She wasn't the suicide type."

"I**T'S POSSIBLE," I SAID AS I PUT THE CHALK BACK ON THE** desk after writing the murder victim's name on the board. "She had access to her tea when she was by herself. I haven't heard what she was poisoned with, but it could be something she was able to get ahold of."

"That doesn't mean she killed herself," Rob said.

"No, but when we were together at the café, Joanne knocked my bag over and spilled everything onto the ground. I thought it was odd at the time that she didn't help me pick anything up, especially since she was the one who'd made the mess in the first place, but when I sat back up, I noticed my tea cup was askew."

"Are you implying that she was trying to poison you, and mixed up the cups by accident? That's a little far-fetched, wouldn't you say?"

"Rob," I said, "I can't think of a reason in the world she would want to kill me."

"Is that true? Are you saying that there was no motive for her to get rid of you?"

I thought about the puzzle Joanne had published, and the unlikely idea that she'd tried to eliminate her competition, but I found it too ludicrous to voice. "I'm just saying she could have nudged it when she was poisoning her own tea."

He shook his head. "It's entirely more likely that she'd poison the three of you for spite before she'd ever dream of killing herself."

"Fine. I just thought I'd throw it out there."

I started to erase her name when he said, "Hold on. There's no reason to be rash about it. I'll ask around about that, too."

"You can't do everything by yourself," I said. "This is my investigation, and I'm not about to sit back and let you do all of the work."

"Funny, I thought the police were running an inquiry of their own," he said, a twinkle in his eye.

"They can do what they want, but I'm going to ask questions, too," I said flatly. I wasn't going to let him try to charm me out of doing some digging on my own. I wasn't wired that way. When something needed to be done, I did it, with no apologies and no excuses.

"You ask the questions," he agreed, "but there's a good chance that unless I go with you, no one's going to answer any of them."

I knew he was right, though I didn't want to admit it. "When can we get started?"

He looked at the clock on the wall. "We close in ten minutes. Can you wait that long?"

"I suppose I can," I answered.

"Good enough."

As he got up, I asked, "Is there anything I can do right now while you're waiting around to close?"

"Savannah, if a broom fits your hand, I wouldn't mind you sweeping up around the place," he said.

I thought he was most likely kidding, but I decided that would be exactly what I would do. I knew myself well enough to know that otherwise I'd just sit there and fret, so why not do something productive in the meantime?

When I grabbed a broom once we were out front, it clearly confused Lee. "Hey, boss, is she working here now, too?"

"I don't know. You'll have to ask her," Rob said, as dead serious as he could be.

"Well, are you?" Lee asked me pointedly.

"For the moment," I said.

He apparently didn't like my answer. "What does that mean? I'm still the senior clerk around here."

Was he seriously concerned about sharing a workspace with me? I looked at the clock over the register and saw that we had three minutes to go before Rob locked up. "Tell you what. I'll leave when you do."

"That's fine, because I'm not going anywhere," he said, the resolve strong in his voice.

"Not even at six?" I asked.

"Do you mean today?"

I smiled as brightly as I could at him. "That's right. I'm what you'd call a temporary, seasonal, part-time employee."

He caught my smile, and then said, "Well, that's all right then. I understand now."

"Do you?" Rob asked. "Then would you mind explaining it to me?"

That just served to confuse the young man even more. "Is there a joke going on here that I'm not getting?"

"If there is, it probably isn't very funny," I said. "I'm just pitching in for a minute today, and then I'm finished and off the payroll. As far as I'm concerned, your job here is safe."

"It's not up to you though, is it?" he asked with a grin.

"You can come back tomorrow, Lee," Rob said. "After that, we'll see."

"That's good enough for me."

At six on the nose, Lee couldn't get out of the hardware store fast enough.

I turned to Rob as he was balancing out his cash register. "That wasn't very nice of me, was it?"

"Lee's a little too young and a little too earnest to get the full range of your humor, Savannah. He's a good kid, don't get me wrong, but he's got some seasoning to do first."

I smiled at him. "I'm not sure if you're complimenting me, or if that's meant to be an insult."

"I suppose some things in this life must remain a mystery to us all," he said with a slight smile.

A minute after I finished sweeping the floor, Rob looked up from the stack of cash on the counter and the register tape. "Good, it balances out on the first try. Lee is coming along nicely."

"Do you have big plans for him?"

"Are you kidding? Someday I'm hoping he'll take over so I can spend my days fishing."

I thought about saying something, and then decided to hold my tongue. After all, it wasn't any of my business.

Rob caught my hesitation, though. In some ways, he was just as sharp as my husband was. "What were you going to say, Savannah?"

"It might not hurt to tell him your plans, if you're serious about it. He seems a little jumpy about his job, if you ask me."

"I appreciate your advice, and I'll give it every consideration it deserves," he said with a smile.

I matched his smile as I said, "In other words, butt out of something that's none of my business."

"Your way is more succinct than mine, but not nearly as elegant. Now, if we're done with our bantering, let's go do a little digging in Parson's Valley and see what we can uncover."

Chapter 6

...

"**D**O YOU HAVE A SECOND?" ROB ASKED GREG LINCOLN AS we walked into his barbershop. There wasn't a soul in any of the waiting seats, or the two barber chairs near the long mirror in front. The floor was clean swept, an apron was draped on one side of one chair, and the other cutting area was completely vacant. Though the shop had, at one time, housed two men, Greg was now literally the only barber in town, and I was sure he grew tired of folks asking him who cut his hair, or if he managed it himself in the mirror.

"Sorry, my appointment book is all full at the moment," he said with a smile as he leaned against the wall. Greg was in his early forties, and I'd heard Zach say that he'd bought the place from his dad when he retired, at a steep interest rate. If Greg minded, he didn't seem to show it. He looked as at home there as if he'd had a pipe, a robe, and slippers.

"Try to fit me in anyway," Rob said, matching the light mood of the moment. He turned to me and said, "You know Savannah Stone, don't you?"

He nodded in my direction. "I've seen you around town. You're married to Zach, aren't you?"

"Guilty as charged," I said with a little of the humor my husband liked, though I realized as soon as I said it that it might not be appropriate at that exact moment. I wondered how long this playful bantering was going to last, and Rob's next question took care of that nicely. "What were you and Joanne Clayton arguing about the other night out on the street?"

Greg looked guarded, but not surprised, as he answered, "What are you talking about? I didn't have an argument with her."

"Save it, buddy. I saw it myself," Rob said. From the abrupt tone he was now using, it was clear there was no doubt in his mind about what he'd seen.

After a moment of thought, Greg finally gave in. "We never argued. Joanne might have raised her voice a time or two when we discussed things, but it was all innocent enough. Why does it concern you, anyway?" He looked a little more intently at Rob. "When did you start spying on me?"

Rob shook his head. "I wasn't spying. I was out walking around town and I saw you two together. I heard you threaten her, Greg."

The barber looked uncomfortable now. "I didn't mean it, and she knew it. You know how Joanne can be. You've known her longer than I have. Sometimes she says things just to get a reaction from folks." Greg sat up straight and asked, "Has she been spreading rumors about me in town, Rob? Let's get her over here right now. I'm certain she'll tell you I didn't mean anything by it. We're on good terms, generally. We just had an off night, that's all."

"Are you trying to say that you two were in love, Greg?"

"I'm not saying anything of the sort." He looked a little dumbfounded by the question, as if he were searching for the underlying joke attached to it. When he saw Rob was serious, he asked, "What's gotten into you? I have no idea what you're talking about."

"You hid it well, but you weren't able to fool everyone in town," Rob said. For the moment, they were both ignoring me, which was fine with me. I could get a lot more out of their conversation if I wasn't actually a part of it.

"I don't know where this is coming from," Greg said, still holding on to his denial. "I suppose I like her well enough, but love might be a little strong to describe how I feel about her." He narrowed his eyes as he asked, "Why, did she say that I loved her?"

This had gone on long enough. The pathetic look in his eyes when he asked the last question was too much to take.

I was about to tell him the truth when Rob said bluntly, "I'm sorry to be the one to tell you this, but she's dead, Greg." I studied the barber closely as he reacted to the news.

"That's not funny, Rob," he said, clearly choosing to discount the news. "If you think you're being amusing, you're really not, and I'd appreciate it if you'd just drop it."

"Ask her. She was there when it happened," he said as he pointed to me.

That wasn't exactly true, but it was close enough. "I'm terribly sorry," I answered. "She died today in Ashcville."

It was horrifying to see the transition in his face. The whisper of a smile had been replaced suddenly with open shock.

"You should sit down," I said.

"Maybe you're right." Instead of taking one of the waiting seats, he slumped into his own barber chair. "It's really true? When did it happen?"

"This afternoon," I said. "Have you been cutting hair all day?"

It was almost as if he hadn't heard me. "I just can't believe it. Not Joanne. It's not real."

"She asked you a question, Greg." Rob had an edge of steel in his voice now; there was no disguising it. "Have you been here all day?"

"Of course I have."

"Are you trying to tell me that you didn't even take a lunch break?" Rob asked him.

"Come on, Rob, you've sat in my chair long enough to know that I've shut down from eleven until noon every day the shop has been open since my dad started running the place."

I figured that would give him a decent alibi, if it were true. I'd once made it to Asheville from Parson's Valley in twenty-eight minutes by hitting every green light between and pushing it a little too fast on the interstate, but it was certainly nothing that could be counted on. When the parking situation in Asheville was figured into the equation, even with a nearby open garage to tuck a car in, I didn't see how he could have killed Joanne in the allotted time unless he'd been very, very lucky.

"That's good to know," Rob said, his voice easing up a little.

It was time for me to get involved in the conversation.

"Greg, do you know of anyone in town who might have had a grudge against Joanne?"

He looked down at his hands, and then asked me softly, "Do you mean besides you?"

"Pardon me?"

He looked at me critically as he said, "She showed me her puzzle, Savannah. Joanne told me that she was going to take every newspaper you were syndicated to away from you. We both know that she was doing her very best to ruin you, and Joanne just about always got what she set her mind to."

"She had one paper that doesn't even count," I said loudly. "It was no motive for murder."

Rob butted in and asked, "You've said your piece about Savannah. What we want to know is, was there anyone else?"

Greg frowned for a few seconds, and then said, "I know she could be abrasive at times. Most people around Parson's Valley didn't see the softer side she had. Joanne had her share of enemies."

"Is there anybody in particular you might be thinking of?" I asked.

He nodded. "Everyone knows about her public spats with Laura Moon and Sandra Oliver. Then there's the fact that she had a fight going with Harry Pike a few days ago, and she wasn't all that fond of Hannah Reed, either. I don't know. I can't think about it right now. It all makes me too sad."

"I'm so sorry about Joanne, for your sake," I said. "I had no idea about the two of you."

He nodded sadly. "She didn't want anyone around here to know about us. Joanne was afraid of the gossip mill in town, so we had to keep it quiet. There was something there, though, you know? I don't know if it was really love, but it might have developed into it, if we'd just had enough time."

I didn't know how to begin to answer that. "You have my deepest sympathies."

"If you don't mind, I need some time to be alone." He got up and walked us out of the barbershop. As we left, I watched him through the glass door as he snapped the locks shut and flipped the "open" sign to "closed." An instant later, the red-and-white-striped electric barber pole went dark, and the sign stopped turning. It was clear that Greg was done, at least for the moment.

"At least we cleared one thing up," Rob said. "Greg didn't know about what happened to Joanne."

"It appears that way," I answered.

He looked at me with surprise. "Do you honestly think that he was acting just now?"

I thought about it, and wasn't sure how to answer truthfully. "I don't know. There was something about that entire conversation that seemed, well, *rehearsed* is the best word I can come up with."

Rob clearly didn't buy it for a second. "Don't forget, the travel time between here and Asheville alone would be enough to clear him."

I shrugged. "I considered that, but it's all predicated on him leaving exactly at eleven, and getting back here at noon on the dot. If he left ten minutes early and got back ten minutes late, he could have poisoned her and no one would know he'd ever left town."

"So he stays on our list until we can prove otherwise," Rob said.

"I think so. At least for now." Another name had popped up that intrigued me. "Can we tackle Hannah Reed now?"

"I guess so," he said a little reluctantly. "Are you sure there isn't someplace else you need to be?"

"Zach's probably still in Asheville," I said. "And even if he's back in town, he's not going to want me tagging along as he helps interview suspects."

Rob grinned. "Then it's a good thing he doesn't know about Hannah yet, isn't it?"

"That's another reason we should speak with her now. If we interview her before Zach hears her name in connection with the case, he can't complain about me interfering." As I said it, I knew how ridiculous that statement was on the face of it. Even though Zach and I were on the same side, it didn't mean we always saw eye to eye on the right way to investigate a crime. He liked the slow and methodical approach, weighing and analyzing clues, and moving toward an inescapable conclusion. I, on the other hand, loved stirring the pot every chance I got to see who boiled over first. It was a little more dangerous than my husband's approach, especially when I wasn't armed with much more than the pepper spray in my purse, but it was tough to argue with the results when I made things happen.

W E GOT TO HANNAH REED'S CRAFT CORNER JUST AS she was closing the register in her shop for the night. Hannah ran a small business that specialized in all kinds of crafting supplies. Between the yarn, colored thread, candle molds, cardmaking supplies, and soapmaking kits, she had something for just about anyone who wanted to work with their hands. I loved to give homemade soap to some of my friends at Christmas, and Hannah's shop was the only place I trusted to buy my supplies. The woman was amazing, mastering every craft her store represented, until she could do just about anything there was to do in the crafting world. I couldn't imagine under any circumstances that she could be a murderer, but if living with Zach all these years had taught me anything, it was that you can't tell a killer by looking at them.

"It's not Christmas, Savannah," she said as Rob and I walked in. "Have you finally decided to branch out into candles?"

"Not yet," I said, "but soon."

She nodded, and then turned to Rob. "Robert, I don't believe that you've set foot in this store since I opened it. I have a feeling you two aren't here for supplies or tips, are you?"

"Hannah, I was wondering if we could have a word with you," Rob said. As long as I'd lived in Parson's Valley, I'd never heard Rob called "Robert" by anyone, and I wondered what their connection was, and how far back it went.

"I thought that was what we were doing." She frowned at her register tape. "I may be a fine craftswoman, but I am a dreadful accountant. One day I'm seven dollars short, and the next I'm ten over. I have no idea what happens, but things seem to get away from me over the course of the day."

After hearing that particular confession, I promised myself that I'd pay closer attention to my change the next time I came into her shop. "Have you heard the news about Joanne Clayton?"

"Yes, sadly, I have. How dreadful."

"Did you happen to hear it from the police?" Rob asked her. "Or did someone else tell you?"

She looked surprised by the question. "Why on earth would the police have any reason to share that information with me? Sandra Oliver was here picking up a book she had me order for her, and she told me then."

"Mind if I ask what the title was?" I asked gently.

She looked at me for a moment before she answered. "Actually, I do. I like to offer my clients some sense of privacy when they deal with me. I may not be protected by the Constitution, or maybe I am, but either way, it's something the people who shop here expect from me, and I don't aim to disappoint them if I can help it."

"That doesn't matter," Rob said. "I have to ask you something about Joanne. It's about what happened between the two of you last month."

Hannah's face whitened. "I'm sure I don't know what you're talking about, Robert."

"I think you do," he said.

She decided to shift the focus from herself onto me. "Savannah, have you seen the new book on soapmaking with all-natural ingredients that I just got in? It's got lots of plants native to our area that you can use in your concoctions. You should go look at it."

It was clear that I was being treated like a small child by being sent to the other side of the store, but there wasn't a great deal I could do about it. If I fought them on it, I was certain neither one of them would say anything incriminating in front of me. On the other hand, there was the question of whether or not I was going to allow myself to be dismissed so easily.

I decided for the moment to stay right where I was. "Thanks. It sounds tempting, and maybe I'll look at it later, but right now, I'd love to hear exactly what Rob was talking about."

She looked at Rob, who frowned at me. "Savannah, this is private. Do you mind giving us a minute?"

"I do," I said.

The three of us stood there for what felt like an hour, but I was certain it was only a few seconds. I saw something ease in Hannah's face, a tension that was there before that suddenly vanished. "She's a member of our community, Robert; I can't see keeping it from her. But if you don't mind, I'll tell her myself."

"Go ahead," he said. "After all, it's your story."

Hannah looked at me, took a deep breath, and then said, "Savannah, not many folks outside of Parson's Valley know this, but I had a reason to despise Joanne Clayton with all my might, though I can assure you that I wasn't the one who killed her."

"Why did you hate her?" I couldn't believe how calm Hannah was being as she talked. A thousand possible reasons danced through my mind, but I wasn't expecting the one she finally gave me.

"She was the reason my son left Parson's Valley ten years ago, and because of her, he'll never come back. I've lost him just as surely as if she'd plunged a knife into his chest and stopped his heart."

"**N**OW, HANNAH, THAT'S NOT EXACTLY THE TRUTH," ROB said softly.

She gave him a quick look of contempt. "Robert, are you questioning my word and my honor?"

"No, ma'am," he said quickly, "but I've kept in touch with Wes over the years, and he denies wholeheartedly that Joanne was behind his leaving." Rob turned to me and explained, "Wes and I were in school together."

"I didn't know that you kept in touch," Hannah said with a snap in her voice.

"There was no need to mention it to you," Rob said, clearly trying to placate her. "He calls you, too. I know it, because he tells me about it."

"My son telephones me twice a year, on my birthday and on Christmas Eve," Hannah said. "How often does he contact you?"

"We email back and forth every now and then," Rob admitted. "He's told you that he'll email you, too."

"I can't even work a cash drawer," Hannah said in exasperation. "How am I supposed to learn to work a computer?"

"I don't know what to tell you, but it's just about the only way he communicates these days," Rob said.

Hannah looked puzzled by Rob's earlier statement. "If my son didn't leave because of Joanne, then why did he go so far away?"

I didn't want to be in the middle of that conversation, but there was no way to bow out of it without being obvious.

I could tell that Rob was choosing his words carefully. "Hannah, he just got tired of living in a small town."

She didn't like that answer. "Nonsense. He hasn't found happiness in New York City, has he?"

"I couldn't say anything about that," Rob answered, though I had a suspicion that he might know. "From what I gather, he's happy enough, and how much more can any of us hope for these days?"

Hannah frowned, and I could swear she wanted to cry. "I don't want to discuss this anymore. It distresses me too much."

"There's just one more thing," Rob said. I saw him draw in a deep breath before he asked her for an alibi, and a part of me wanted to stop him, but unfortunately, I needed to hear the answer myself. "Hannah, have you been in your shop all day?"

"No, I ran some errands this morning. I didn't open until one today."

"Would you mind telling me where you were earlier, then?"

"Of course I mind. Robert, I'll ask you to leave now." She turned to me and said in a softer voice, "You should go as well, Savannah. I believe this conversation is over."

"If you tell me," Rob said, not budging one inch, "then I can promise that I'll leave you alone."

"Here's a surprise for you. You're going to do that regardless," the older woman said, showing a hint of the spunk that was just beneath the surface. "Leave my store, Robert."

They locked stares for nearly a minute, and then Rob finally turned and left without saying another word.

"I'm so sorry," I said to Hannah as soon as he was gone. "I didn't mean to be a part of bringing up bad memories for you," but it was as though I hadn't spoken. Hannah went back to her register tape, and I left her shop in silence.

Once I was outside, I said, "That was chillier than I ever thought Hannah could muster."

"To be honest with you," Rob said, "it was no more than I expected from her. She's got a mean streak very few folks around here know about, and that woman can hold on to a grudge like nobody I've ever seen in my life."

It was certainly news to me. "Before we went in there, I would have said that Hannah wasn't capable of committing murder."

"And now?" Rob asked.

"I'm not so sure. Tell me something. Why did her son really leave town, if it wasn't because of Joanne?"

"If you want to know the answer to that, you're going to have to ask him yourself," Rob said with a ring of finality to his statement that wouldn't bear further questioning.

"In other words, it's none of my business."

"I wouldn't exactly go that far," Rob said with a grin, "but I'm not saying anything else about it, either. That takes care of our list, at least the ones who aren't currently being questioned by the police. What did you have in mind next?"

I glanced at my watch and saw that it was getting late. "I'm not sure there's much more we can do tonight."

"I can believe that. Savannah, if you need me tomorrow, I'll be at the hardware store first thing," Rob said.

"Thanks, but I should be fine on my own for a while."

When he realized that I meant business, Rob said, "I'm not joking around here. If you need someone to watch your back and Zach isn't available, call me day or night."

"I will," I promised.

I watched Rob walk down the street back to his store before I headed for my own car. Why was he being so helpful, where Barbara had stonewalled me? Was it because of some sense of loyalty he felt to me from our friendship, or did he have his own reasons to want to know what had really happened to Joanne Clayton? He'd admitted himself that they'd been close once, and I had to wonder if he was looking for a little justice on her behalf.

Either way, I'd use his help if I could, but only if I had to; I wasn't comfortable risking anyone else's life in my informal investigation.

As I walked to my car, I decided it was time to head back to the cottage. With any luck, Zach would be there waiting for me, and we could compare notes about what we'd learned so far today.

Chapter 7

...

"THERE YOU ARE," ZACH SAID AS I PARKED MY CAR AND walked up the path to our front door. "I've been wondering when you were going to get home." He was out front admiring the mix of annuals I'd planted in our raised beds along the walkway, filled with flowering plants that hummingbirds were supposed to love. We'd already lost the race against time between when the flowers would bloom and when the delightful little birds started their migration south. Zach had been right to bet that the tiny birds would be long gone before the blossoms could do them any good, but I still held out hope for a bright floral display. Even if they hadn't been ready in time for the birds, I'd been watching the frost warnings and covering the beds with spun fiber cloth as protection. I was determined to enjoy at least a few blossoms before a heavy frost killed the delicate plants.

"I'm surprised you beat me home," I said.

"Is it a good surprise, or a bad one?" he asked as he wrapped me up in his arms. There was a chill in the air; though nowhere near freezing, I was still glad to have him hold me.

"It's always a good thing," I said as I buried my head into his chest.

"Always?" he asked as he stroked my head.

"Well, almost," I admitted. "There's no chance you cooked something for dinner, is there?"

"Sorry, I haven't been here long myself. We could always have chili," Zach said. One of the few things my husband could cook was chili, and whenever he was stuck at home without anything to work on, he'd make batches and batches of the stuff. I'd freeze it, and we'd pull some out whenever neither of us felt like cooking that night. I wished he'd learn to make something else, but he claimed that his chili had special powers to intensify his thought process, and I was in no position to dispute it.

In all honesty, I wasn't all that thrilled about having chili tonight, but then again, I was also too tired to cook anything myself.

"Chili sounds great," I said.

"Excellent. While it's defrosting, you can tell me about what you've been doing since we split up."

I nodded, but I wasn't going to give up my hard-won information without a little equal exchange. "Only if you promise to bring me up to date on what you've been doing, too."

He frowned for a second. "Savannah, I can tell you most of it, but there are a few things I'm not in any position to reveal. I'm truly sorry about it, but I owe that much to Captain North."

"But you'll tell me everything the second you can, right?" I asked as I pulled out a container of chili and popped it into the microwave.

He nodded and put his hand over his heart. "I promise."

My husband was, above all else, a man of his word. "That's good enough for me. Where should I start?"

"How about the second you left me in Asheville?"

"Hey, you told me not to be that specific anymore."

"I know," he said with a laugh. "Can I help it if I missed you?"

"I missed you, too, though sometimes I wonder why," I answered with a smile.

As he set the table, I started sharing with him everything I'd learned since we'd been apart.

He stopped me when I told him about Barbara. "You could make her that promise, you know."

"Zach, how am I going to keep anything from you? She should have known better than to ask me." The microwave stopped, so I stirred the chili a little before resetting it. After it was busy doing its job again, I looked at my husband and asked, "Should I have told her, and then kept what I found out to myself?"

"It seems fair to me. After all, I'm going to have to hold a few things back from you," Zach said as he put a glass of milk in the freezer while the chili finished warming through. He loved his milk nearly frozen, though it hurt my teeth when I tried to drink it that cold.

"That's different," I said.

"Why? Because I'm working with the police?"

"No, that's not it." I thought about it for a minute, and then said, "I suppose I could have agreed, but what it boils down to is that I don't like someone else dictating my behavior to me."

"I know that more than anyone else would," he said with a smile. "Still, if your investigation stalls, you might have to make that promise after all."

"Why don't I burn that bridge when I get to it," I said. "Besides, I don't think I'm going to need her help."

He looked surprised by that response. "You're certainly not going to do this by yourself."

"I won't," I said. "I enlisted someone else to help me in my cause."

"Really?" he asked as he got out the saltine crackers and the cheddar cheese. "Who's playing Watson to your Sherlock Holmes?"

"Rob Hastings," I said as I checked the chili again. It was almost ready.

"I would love to know how that came about," Zach said.

"Think about it, Zach. Who knows more about what's going on in town than Rob does? I mean, besides Barbara Brewster."

He nodded as he sliced off a few pieces of cheese. My husband was a purist when it came to his chili, but I liked to add a dollop of sour cream to mine—something he frowned upon but had finally stopped commenting about. "That's a good point. Was it tough convincing him to help you?"

"As a matter of fact, he dove right in," I said as I served the chili in nice ceramic bowls we'd picked up on a trip to Charlotte once.

"No offense, Savannah, but why would he be so eager to give you a hand? I know you two are friends, and I heartily approve, but he should have more motivation to stick his neck out than because he likes you."

"I was surprised, too, but because of something I haven't told you about yet. It seems that Joanne was best friends with Rob's late wife, Becky, before she died. Rob thinks Becky's death is what turned Joanne so sour to the world. He told me that he'd always held out some hope that Joanne would someday recover from her foul mood, and I think he was angry that she didn't get the chance."

He shrugged. "Okay, I'll buy that. Did you two have any luck? I'd be interested in getting Rob's take on all of this, since he knows the principals better than we ever will."

I nodded as we sat down at the kitchen table to eat. "The first thing we did was speak with Greg Lincoln and Hannah Reed."

The names clearly surprised him. "I know Rob must have had a reason to interview the two of them, but I can't imagine what it could be."

"Believe me, I was surprised, too. Evidently Rob saw Greg arguing on the street with Joanne a few nights ago. It turns out that the two of them were dating, and they had a fight about something. From what Rob said, it was all pretty intense."

Zach stopped eating and frowned at me, so I asked him, "What's wrong?"

"I'm having trouble picturing Greg and Joanne together," he admitted. "It's not an obvious match, is it?"

"Take my word for it and stop before you can picture it," I said, and then took another bite. Despite the frequency of having my husband's chili, it honestly was pretty good. "The toughest part is not picturing it once it's stuck in your head."

"I think I'll quit while I'm ahead, then." He took another bite, and then asked, "Did he say what they were fighting about?"

"Greg claimed that they'd had a little tiff, and that they had them all of the time, so it was no big deal."

Zach took a bite of chili, and then asked, "Did you believe him?"

"No," I said flatly. "His whole story sounded rehearsed to me."

He nodded. "I trust your instincts. What about Hannah? What possible reason could she have for killing Joanne?"

"We went to see her at her shop, and she told us she believes that Joanne ran her son out of Parson's Valley, though Rob told her point-blank it wasn't true. Apparently he's been corresponding with Wes on the Internet, and Hannah's son claims he's happy in New York."

"But Hannah didn't buy it?"

"Not only didn't she believe him, the woman practically threw us out when Rob said it."

Zach nodded. "That might bear looking into as well. She sounds pretty touchy about the whole thing. Is there anything else to share tonight?"

"That taps me out. Now it's your turn."

As I took a healthy bite of chili, Zach said, "Some of this I can't tell you, but I can fill in some of the questions you are probably asking yourself about now. We spoke with Sandra, Laura, and Harry today ourselves. It turns out they all had grudges against Joanne."

"They actually admitted that to you and Captain North?"

"Not exactly," he said with a slight laugh. "They took turns talking to us about one another. It was one long afternoon and early evening of finger-pointing and cross accusations. To tell you the truth, it made me want to take a shower just to clean myself up after we were through. If that's what friendship boils down to, I don't know who needs it. Still, it was interesting to listen to them."

"I'm still waiting. What did you hear?"

He took a last bite of chili, chased it with a sliver of cheese, and then drained the rest of his milk before he spoke again. "The gist of it is that Laura believes that Joanne stole something valuable of Sandra's. Sandra thinks that Harry and Joanne were in some kind of real estate scam together. To wrap it all up, Harry pointed out that Laura Moon stands to inherit Joanne's estate now that she's gone."

"How is that possible?" I asked. "I didn't even realize they knew each other that well." A sudden thought struck me. "They aren't related, are they?"

Zach looked pleased with my conjecture. "It turns out that Laura was Joanne's third cousin, and evidently, she's the only one Joanne was willing to trust with her money, not that we can find much of an estate."

"There's at least the house," I said, remembering where Joanne lived. It wasn't as nice as our cottage, but it was located in the middle of the town's historic district, so it might be worth something on the real estate market.

"Maybe, maybe not. We're not sure if Joanne owned it free and clear, or if there's a mortgage on it," Zach said. "North's got a forensic accountant going over Joanne's books, so we should know something about that soon."

"Have you heard what the exact cause of death was yet? Poison is kind of a broad explanation, isn't it?"

"I'm really sorry, but I can't tell you that right now."

I bit my lip, and then said as graciously as I could muster, "That's okay. I understand."

"As a matter of fact," Zach said as he picked up his empty bowl and glass and moved them to the sink, "I'm not allowed to say that we'll have the results in the morning, and that it might just turn out to be a natural poison, instead of a manufactured one."

"What does that mean?"

He grinned. "You know, it's amazing how many toxic plants there are in our part of the world. I bet your friend at the Asheville Botanical Gardens could give you a list."

"Are you saying I should go see him?"

"I'm not making any suggestions at all, Savannah, but if you were to make the trip, you might want to wait until we know something more concrete. But like I said before, I really can't talk about it."

"Can you at least tell me if I'm still a suspect in Captain North's mind?"

He stretched, and then my husband said, "I can't say what's going on in her head, but if I were running the investigation and I didn't know you, there wasn't anything I learned today that would take your name off the list."

"Got it," I said. "So, I need to keep a low profile while I'm digging, is that what you're saying?"

"It couldn't hurt," Zach said. "That chili was excellent, but I feel like some dessert."

"Have anything in mind?" I asked as I rinsed the dishes and put them into the dishwasher.

"Chocolate cake would be nice."

"I agree. I hope you feel like baking one, because I sure don't."

My husband laughed, a sound I couldn't ever imagine growing tired of. "I could, but then it would probably be inedible, wouldn't it? Is there any chance the bakery in town is still open?"

I glanced at the clock and saw that it was nearly eight. "Not even close; Emma closes at four."

Emma Parson was descended from the folks who founded Parson's Valley. She'd told me once over scones that she'd inherited a good deal of land on her eighteenth birthday, along with a check that had more zeros than I was certain I'd ever see in my lifetime. She'd taken a small portion of it, gone to culinary school in Chicago, and then promptly come home to open her bakery. The town might have thought that was odd, but when she donated half her remaining fortune to the city of Parson's Valley to be used exclusively for the benefit of its citizens, folks seemed to be willing to accept her even with all of her eccentricities. She told me once that she had held on to every square inch of the land she'd inherited, so she wasn't as crazy as some might think. I loved hanging out with her, and if my waistline wasn't constantly expanding from the contact, I might have seen her even more often than I did.

"If we can't go there, what are we going to do?" he asked, for a split second sounding like the petulant little boy he must have once been.

"Why don't I make pudding?" I asked.

"No offense, but that's not nearly as good as cake."

"We can go to the grocery store in town, or drive into Asheville for some. It's up to you."

"Pudding sounds great," he said after a moment's hesitation. "To be honest with you, I'm beat."

"So am I." I laughed as I got the stand mixer out from its nook. "I thought you'd agree homemade would be better."

* * *

AFTER THE PUDDING WAS MADE AND CHILLING IN THE refrigerator, Zach and I walked outside to our front porch and sat in a pair of oak rocking chairs we'd bought the minute we'd moved in. It allowed us a view of some of our acreage and our garden, and at night, we could see the glory of the evening sky through the naked canopy of branches above us.

I asked Zach, "What's your plan for tomorrow, or do you have one yet?"

"The toxicology results are supposed to be in by ten, so I imagine I'll find a reason to be in Asheville around then. After that, we'll just have to see where it leads us. North is willing to allow me to tag along for now, and I'm going to take advantage of it before she changes her mind. What about you?"

"I thought I might take Barbara up on her offer to help me dig into this," I said.

"Why the sudden change of heart?"

I shrugged, though I doubted he could see it in the darkness. "You said you wouldn't mind if I kept any secrets about the case from you, and if it means clearing my name of suspicion, I can swallow a little pride and let Barbara have the upper hand with me."

"I've been thinking about that, and to be honest with you, I wouldn't do it," Zach said softly. I couldn't see his face in the shadows, but his tone of voice was enough to get my full attention.

"Why not?"

"We have to live in this town long after the investigation is over," he said after a moment's hesitation. "Barbara Brewster's help probably comes at too high a price for you to pay. Besides, you're doing fine as it is."

"With Rob's help today," I said, "we got some folks to

talk to us, but Barbara implied that we were considered outsiders, and without her, we wouldn't discover anything, no matter how many questions we asked."

"Maybe not," Zach said as he stretched out a little in his chair. "They were all certainly willing to speak with me today."

"Don't forget, you were with a state police investigator," I said. "That might be a factor, too."

"Maybe, but you have a way with people, Savannah. They'll open up to you if you give them a chance."

"I hope you're right," I said as a chill breeze came up. It was time to go back inside. "Tell you what," I said as I stood, "I'll serve the pudding if you start a fire."

"That's the best idea I've heard all day," he said as we walked back in.

I wasn't sure what tomorrow might bring, but for the moment, I was determined to enjoy every moment I could with my husband. Life was too short not to grab the seconds that were presented, and I wasn't about to squander a single one of them if I could help it.

THE NEXT MORNING, I WOKE TO THE SMELL OF FRESHLY brewed coffee. When I opened my eyes, I saw that my husband was waving a mug of it near my nose.

As I reached for it, he playfully pulled it away.

"Hey, that's not fair."

"It's time to get up. You have a lot of digging to do today, remember?"

I thought about my unofficial investigation and grabbed my robe as I climbed out of bed. Zach surrendered my coffee, and after I'd taken a large sip, I asked him, "Exactly how long have you been awake?"

"You don't want to know," he said with a smile. He leaned down and kissed my forehead as he added, "I'm heading into Asheville. I'll call you when there's something I can't tell you."

"I can hardly wait," I said as he left.

With Zach gone, I decided that the puzzle I'd been working on was going to have to wait. If I had to, I could get my syndicator to run one of the extras I submitted from time to time. Neither one of us liked to deplete the surplus on hand, but there were times when it couldn't be helped. When things settled down with Joanne's murder investigation, I'd do my best to build the supply back up to a comfortable level of puzzles, but in the meantime, I had more digging to do.

The only problem I had was that it was hard to figure out where to begin. Though Rob and I had been fairly straightforward with our questioning so far, I'd hidden behind his status as a lifetime resident in town and the owner of one of Parson's Valley's most loved businesses. Would people open up to me about what they knew without Rob's presence?

It was time to find out, but first, I needed some space to think. We were close enough to town to walk to it in under thirty minutes if we weren't in any hurry, and Zach and I liked to make the stroll sometimes on lazy Saturday afternoons when the weather was nice. It would be perfect today. As I started out, I noticed that most of the leaves had dropped from the trees, but a few stragglers still held on, hoping for promises of spring. I marveled at the beauty of the glory of the mountains we were surrounded by. In the other seasons, the framework of the peaks was hidden by a vast array of leaves, but as they dropped, the character underneath was suddenly revealed. Each time of year had its own charm for me, but none more than late autumn. When we'd lived in Charlotte, Zach and I had been close enough to visit the mountains whenever his job allowed it, which was never enough for me. I knew in my heart that I had been destined to live here at some point in my life, and though the way we'd gotten here had been horrific, I was happy to at least be where I belonged, with the man I loved. Enough of that, though. I needed to come up with a plan, and my steps were leading me closer and closer to the heart of Parson's Valley.

I was nearly to town, still with no idea who to approach next, when a pickup truck pulled up beside me. That in itself wasn't all that odd—our area was populated with the vehicles, and Zach kept threatening to get one himself— but the man inside it surely was. It was one of the last folks I wanted to see at the moment, but someone I definitely needed to talk to.

I just hoped I could get him to answer my questions.

Chapter 8

...

"CAN I GIVE YOU A LIFT?" HARRY PIKE ASKED ME FROM THE cab of his truck. It was at least twenty years old, and had gone through a hard life at that, with scrapes on its sides and a hood with more peeling paint than the original gray. I couldn't imagine what the interior looked likc, but it was hard to be all that choosy this time. Ordinarily I would have refused the offer as a matter of course, not because of Harry, but because once I started a walk, I liked to finish it. This time it was different, though. It would hopefully give me the perfect opportunity to get him to answer some of my questions.

"That would be great," I said as I climbed into the cab. I had no idea what condition the original material of the seats was in, since the entire bench seat was covered with an old blanket.

"Where are you headed?"

That was a good question. For some reason, Brewster's Brews popped into my head. "I thought some coffee might be nice on a chilly morning like this. Do you have time? I'd love to buy you a cup."

He laughed. "Savannah, it's just a mile away. You don't have to pay me for the lift."

"Then how about the company?" I said.

"Fine, but only if we get it to go."

"Don't you want to warm up a little inside? Or do you have a problem with Barbara?"

Harry rubbed his chin, and I saw that he'd missed shaving today. In fact, the closer I looked at him, the more I realized that his entire appearance was disheveled. His eyes were reddened, and his hair hadn't seen a comb in days, either. "How are you doing these days, Harry? Is everything okay at the nursery?"

"We've still got trees for sale, if you're in the market after that blow of a storm we had," he said, "but the bedding plants are all gone. Things are finally starting to slow down a little, and I've got to tell you, I could use the rest."

We got to the coffee shop, and as Harry stopped the truck, I asked, "How would you like your coffee?"

"Strong and black," he said. "I didn't get much sleep last night."

"Got it," I said. I went into the shop, bought two coffees to go, and as I did, I looked around for Barbara. Normally at her post by the cash register, she was conspicuously absent at the moment. Was it because of me, or was I just being paranoid? I grabbed the coffees and went back outside, only to find Harry's truck was gone.

That was odd. Where would he go, knowing that I had coffee for him?

I started to walk down the street when someone pulled up beside me. It was Harry.

"I thought you skipped out on me," I said as I got back into the truck after handing him his cup through the open window.

"No, I figured I'd circle the block while I waited. Barbara hates it when people park in front of her shop. She's threatened to sic the law on me more than once in the past."

"She wouldn't have known if you'd been driving a parade float. She wasn't in there."

He looked surprised by the news. "You don't say. I didn't think she ever left that post of hers where all of the action is."

"I was a little surprised myself," I said as I took a sip of my own coffee. "Would you like to find a place to stop and enjoy this, or are we going to just drive around and drink?"

He shook his head sadly. "Sorry, I'm not myself today, Savannah. I'd be happy to pull over as soon as I find a spot."

I took a chance and said, "I'm guessing that it must have been tough on you seeing Joanne just before she died."

Harry looked sharply at me. "Savannah, what did you hear? Has that husband of yours been talking about me?"

"I didn't hear it from Zach; Joanne told me herself. When we had tea, she said she bumped into you at the café just before I got there."

He suddenly stopped the truck and hopped out without commenting. Was that going to be the entire sum of our conversation about Joanne? I wasn't sure what he was doing, but then I watched as Harry sat down at a bench that overlooked Town Square, decorated for autumn with hay bales and stacks of pumpkins. It was charming, there was no doubt about it, but Parson's Valley held its own share of secrets, regardless of how homey and pleasant it might look to an outsider.

"Were you two that close?" I asked when I joined him, knowing that I was probably pushing it. I really had no choice if I wanted to learn anything new.

"A long time ago we were," he said, and then took a long sip of his coffee.

"Harry, were you just business associates, or was it something more than that?"

"What makes you ask me that?" He was staring at me with bloodshot eyes, and I had to wonder if he'd been on a drunken bender since he'd heard what had happened to Joanne.

"I understand you two had some business dealings together."

"Who told you that?" he asked me, not looking in my direction as he spoke, but staring straight ahead now. I felt like he was hiding something, but I didn't have a clue what it might be.

I answered him truthfully. "I thought everyone knew about it."

"That's the trouble with folks around here. Sometimes they just think they know things."

"So, you weren't doing any real estate deals together?"

He shrugged. "We owned some property together from time to time. Most of the time we made money, so it worked out fine for both of us."

"But there was nothing current you were working on?"

He didn't answer, taking another drink of coffee instead. Finally, Harry said, "Savannah, I know what you're going through. Folks have been looking at me oddly since they heard what happened to Joanne. You must not have been the only one she told yesterday that she'd seen me. It's only natural to want to find out what happened to her, but you need to be careful. Not everyone is as forgiving as I am about poking and prodding into people's business."

I started to say something when he hoisted his cup one last time, and then abruptly stood. "Thanks for the coffee."

All I could do was call out, "Anytime," before he got into his battered old truck and drove away.

That was one of the oddest conversations I'd ever had with anybody in Parson's Valley.

But I was sure there were more like it to come.

AS I FINISHED MY COFFEE, I KEPT WONDERING ABOUT Harry's reactions to my questions. He'd deflected or flat-out refused to answer some of them, and didn't give me any specific details at all, when I thought about it. He was hiding something; I grew surer of that by the minute.

But what?

Harry might not have told me what I wanted to know, but I knew one place where I could get the facts, and not someone else's shading of them. I walked to the courthouse and took the steps down into the basement where the Register of Deeds was located. I'd been there before, doing my own title search on the cottage we'd bought. It wasn't to confirm that the property was for sale; our real estate lawyer took care of that. I had been more interested in who had owned it before us, and I'd spent a day there going through the records, tracing the land's ownership all the way back before the country had even been born. It shouldn't be that hard to track Harry Pike's purchases and sales, and see if he and Joanne had anything pending.

When I got there, I was amazed by the change in the place. Gone were the thick green and gray ledgers that had recorded every transaction for generations. In their place was a series of computer terminals, all with colorful screens.

"Hello," I said as I walked inside.

A young woman with auburn hair and striking blue eyes greeted me. "Good morning. My name is Tina. Is there anything I can help you with today?"

"When did you change all of the records over to computers?" I asked.

"We've been tackling it gradually since the start of last year. It's slow progress, but it's going to make life so much easier for everyone once we're finished."

"Where does your progress stand now?" I asked, not sure that this particular application of technology was a good one.

"We've got the last eleven years on electronic file," Tina said proudly.

That would most likely be enough for me. "Thanks."

"I'll be glad to help you with your search. I know it can seem a little intimidating at first."

I didn't want anyone looking over my shoulder as I worked, or to even know what I was doing. I had learned early on that living in a small town came with its own set of caveats, just as large cities like Charlotte had, though they were mostly different from each other.

I approached a far terminal with its display swiveled away from the counter, and studied the system. There wasn't anything romantic about searching these records, at least not compared to reading through spidery writing when I had traced our property's past owners, but it was a great deal quicker; I had to acknowledge that. I typed in Harry Pike's name and was amazed by the number of transactions he'd made over the past eleven years. I'd always thought he was a simple nurseryman, growing trees, shrubs, perennials, and annuals for sale, but I was beginning to discover that he was some kind of land baron as well. With his beat-up old pickup truck and his common clothes, it was tough to tell that his net worth was most likely one of the highest in town. There was a synopsis of his transactions that might come in handy, so I hit the print button on the computer. Nothing happened, so I hit it again.

Still nothing.

Tina walked over to me, and I reached out and hit the power button on the display. I wasn't sure if she was connected to the computer in any way, but I didn't want to take any chances.

"Did you want both copies?" she asked as she neared me.

"Pardon me?"

Tina smiled. "We have to charge five cents a copy, so when you print a document, it comes to our desk. I held up the printing cycle to be sure you wanted duplicate copies."

"Can you see what I'm printing?"

She nodded. "We can, but we don't look at what you're printing, just the number of documents, and their reference numbers."

"I just want one," I said. "Thanks for asking."

She smiled. "It will be waiting for you up front."

As Tina walked away, I had even less faith in the system than I had before. It had been foolish to turn my monitor off. If anything, it just gave Tina more reason to snoop. Whether she'd been trained not to notice what I'd been doing or not, I still didn't like it. Someone looking over my shoulder electronically was somehow worse than if I'd been able to feel her breath on my neck.

I couldn't stop my hunt, though.

The next search was for Joanne Clayton's name. Joanne had only three transactions in the past eleven years. She'd bought her home, and she'd sold a little piece of land out in the middle of nowhere, but the third parcel was the one that interested me. The owners listed were Joanne Clayton and Harry Pike, and they'd bought a parcel of land in the heart of Parson's Valley for nearly half a million dollars. There was no record of a sale after that on the property, which meant that the two of them had owned it together on the day Joanne had died.

I hit the print button again, and then kept exiting screens until I was back at the starting position.

Sliding a dime across the counter to Tina, I waited for my copies. She collected them, and then took my money from me. "Would you like a receipt for that?"

"No, I'm good," I said.

"Come back anytime," she said.

"Absolutely," I replied, though I couldn't imagine the circumstances that would bring me back. I'd found what I'd been looking for.

The only problem was that I had no idea what it meant.

A S I LEFT THE COURTHOUSE, MY PHONE STARTED QUACK-ing at me, a signal that my husband was on the line. He'd objected to my ringtone from the beginning, but I loved it, and while I had reservations about it from time to time when it announced itself at the most inappropriate moments, I wasn't about to change it. Whenever Zach took himself too seriously, I reminded him of it, and most of the time, it brought him straight back to reality.

"Hi there," I said. "I was just about to call you."

"Did you find something?" he asked. I could tell from the tone in his voice that he was in no mood to joke around.

"Zach, something's wrong. What happened?"

"We got the toxicology report," he said. "It was a natural poison, just as the medical examiner suspected. There was an air of almonds around Joanne when they processed the body."

"What was it specifically? It sounds like cyanide poisoning to me. Can you tell me anything else?"

He lowered his voice. "I'm not really supposed to, but I need your help, so I don't have much choice."

"I'll do whatever I can," I said. "You know that."

He lowered his voice, and then said, "I need you to go to Asheville to the Botanical Gardens and ask your friend there about plants that have cyanogenic glycosides."

"That's what killed her?" I asked, suddenly chilled by the poisonous agent having an identifiable name.

"Yes, but the lab's list of plants in nature that possess them is too long to narrow down, at least with my limited resources. We need to know what's found locally that contains them. Can you do that for me?"

"I'll get right on it," I said. "Do they have any idea exactly when she was poisoned? It might help knowing that when I talk to Jay."

"The report said that most likely it wasn't before

eleven in the morning, and not after two that afternoon, but that leaves a pretty big window of opportunity for someone to slip something in her drink."

"I'm on my way right now," I said as I hung up on Zach. I could make it to the gardens in thirty minutes when I got back home to my car, if luck was with me. I just hoped Jay, the garden manager, was there.

HE WASN'T.

"Do you know when he'll be back?" I asked the volunteer behind the desk at the Botanical Gardens Welcome Center. I'd driven through the big black iron gates and had been lucky to find a parking space near the front.

She frowned, and then leafed through a few papers. "Sorry, but he didn't say."

"Will it be today, do you think?"

"Oh, I doubt that," she said with a shrug. "He had a suitcase with him when he left here two hours ago. Let me make a call."

She got on a walkie-talkie and asked, "Jim, do you have any idea when Jay will be back?"

"Two weeks," a voice replied.

"Thanks."

She looked at me and said, "Two weeks."

"Yes, I got that. Is there anyone else I can speak with who's knowledgeable about local poisonous flora?"

She nodded. "Jim is taking over for Jay while he's gone. He's from the Botany Department at UNC Asheville." I knew that the campus for the university was nearby, so I suppose it made sense.

"Is there any chance I might speak with him? It's important, or I wouldn't ask."

"Hang on a second. I'll check," the woman said.

After she made the request, Jim told her, "I'm trimming the American beautyberry up on the trail. If she wants to talk to me, have her come over here so we can do it while I work."

I got directions, thanked the volunteer, and exited the center, heading down the path on the left that I'd taken countless times before. I descended the slight hill and walked over to the concrete table and chairs where I often picnicked when I was in the mood for a touch of nature. Oddly, something crunched underfoot, and I looked down to see a host of broccoli florets, and all for the most part untouched. How odd.

I kept walking on the path, crossed the green wooden bridge, and made a left at the Memorial Rock Outcrop, where many delicate native species were planted. I found a thin, young, bearded man with a pair of garden shears in his hands, studying a bushy plant that had clearly taken a beating recently. It was still quite attractive, despite the carnage, sporting purple-clustered berries along its stems and serrated green leaves emerging from the groups.

"It's lovely," I said as I studied it behind him.

"You should have seen it a few days ago," he said sadly. "Jay and I are trying to decide how to trim it." He pointed to a shattered tree nearby. "It came down in a storm and nearly took out the entire bush."

"I have a suggestion, if you're interested," I said.

"Anything's welcome at this point," he said.

I studied the bush again, and then said, "If it were me, I'd leave it exactly like it is."

"But it's damaged," he protested, as if I'd just suggested he light a match and try to set the remnants on fire.

"Don't get me wrong; I'd trim the dead branches," I

said, "but I wouldn't do anything to the overall shape. I never saw this bush before, and I think it's glorious, no matter how lovely it was before the storm. It's a matter of perspective, don't you think?"

He looked at it again, and then shrugged. "You may be right. I'll leave it alone for now."

"I have a question for you," I said.

"I'll answer it if I can."

"I saw a lot of broccoli florets on the ground by the stone bench across the creek. Is it some kind of experiment in modern composting or something?"

He grinned. "Nothing so scientific. If I hadn't been working in the creek nearby, I would have been baffled as well. One of our visual media arts students from the university wrote a script for her class, and she was filming it with her classmates."

"What was it about, the power of broccoli?"

He laughed, and I loved the easiness in it. Jim sounded like a man completely comfortable in his own skin. "I suppose that's exactly what it was, in its own way. Emily, that's the student, showed me a final cut of the film to explain their insane behavior. It was a spoof on the old black-and-white horror movies. Her premise was that the only thing that would stop a zombie attack was broccoli, since nobody likes it. At least that was her punch line. I happen to love the stuff myself, but she had a point. It was all pretty hilarious." He snipped a dead branch, and then stood back to examine the result before he spoke again. "But I'm sure you weren't looking for Jay to answer the great broccoli question for you."

"No, but it's a delicate subject, and I'm not sure I should involve you in it."

He scratched his chin. "Well, I'll say this for you; you certainly know how to build suspense. Tell you what. Why don't you ask your question, and I'll decide if I want to answer it or not?"

"That sounds fair," I said. "It involves a locally available plant or tree that has cyanogenic glycosides in its bark, leaves, or berries."

He whistled. "That's some serious poison you're talking about there."

"Then you won't help me?"

"Why not? You can find that information in any library," he said. "What you do with the knowledge is completely up to you. Let's see, if I wanted high doses of cyanogenic glycosides, I'd probably use wild cherry or black cherry."

"They're really poisonous?"

He grinned as he said, "More than most folks know. In the wrong amounts, the seeds, leaves, twigs, and even bark contain quantities of amygdalin and prunasin."

"But not cyanogenic glycosides?"

"That's what they are," he said, his enthusiasm for death and destruction filling him, for some reason, with great glee. "When they're ingested, they transform into highly toxic hydrocyanic acid."

"What would that do to you?" I asked, not sure I wanted to know the outcome of the poisoning.

Jim thought about it, and then finally said, "Let's see, you could have respiratory failure, spasms, go into a coma, or even die from it."

"That's pretty powerful," I agreed. "Is there anything else that might have the same result?"

He nodded, and then pointed to a nearby harmless-looking plant. "You don't want to eat any of these leaves, especially if they've wilted or have been cut. The same thing could happen with them, and this plant is found nearly everywhere around here."

"What's it called?"

"One of the other symptoms I didn't mention is losing your voice. That may be why they call it chokecherry."

I WAITED UNTIL I WAS BACK IN MY CAR TO PHONE ZACH. IT just didn't seem right talking about death among all that beauty. I'd known nature had a bite at times, but it was amazing how deadly a common-looking plant could be. Jim had studied them around the campus extensively, and was writing a paper on the many ways that flora could kill.

"Hey," I said when Zach answered. "I got word from an expert that the most likely culprit is either wild cherry, black cherry, or chokecherry."

"Would the dried leaves be dangerous?" he asked.

I remembered Jim's lecture, and said, "Absolutely."

"Good job, Savannah. That explains the delivery system. Someone slipped some powdered leaves into her tea. From the sound of it, just about every suspect on our list had access to the poison that killed her."

"So, it's a dead end," I said, suddenly deflated by my news.

"Not necessarily. It took someone who knew what they were doing to even pick the right leaves."

"That's something, I guess," I said as a feeling nagged at the back of my mind. I lost it just as quickly as I'd had it. I knew the worst thing to do was focus on the missing information until it came back to me. If I ignored it, I would most likely have my answer soon enough.

"Is that all?" I asked Zach. "Since I'm in Asheville, I'd be glad to investigate anything else for you."

"No, that's it for now. You can come back to Parson's Valley anytime you'd like."

"I'm on my way," I said as I drove out of the parking lot. I tried my best to ignore my subconscious and the nagging feeling that something was hiding from me, hoping the information would pop back up, but I didn't have any luck.

It would come to me; I was certain of that.

I just hoped it wouldn't be too late to help our investigation.

INSTEAD OF GOING HOME, I PARKED BY THE COURTHOUSE once I got back to Parson's Valley, and I was trying to figure out what to do next when a voice startled me out of my thoughts.

"Savannah, I need to talk to you," someone said through my open car window.

Chapter 9

...

I LOOKED UP TO SEE LAURA MOON STARING DOWN AT ME, and from the expression on her face, she wasn't going to tell me that I'd won Yard of the Month from the local garden club.

"What can I do for you, Laura?" I asked as I got out of my car. I didn't like the way she'd been looking down at me, and I wanted us to be on an equal level if we were going to have a conversation that I wasn't all that anxious to have in the first place.

"Why did you do it?" she asked pointedly. "What did Joanne ever do to you, anyway?"

"I could ask you those very same questions," I said as calmly as I could manage. "Do you think there's a chance in the world that you would like that any more than I'm enjoying your accusations?"

"Of course not," she said, "but I didn't kill her."

"Neither did I," I said a little more emphatically.

"You were still there when Sandra and I left Asheville."

"For two minutes," I replied. "I got out of there just as fast as you two did. Anybody could have poisoned her, including the two of you."

"The only difference is that I know that we didn't do it."

"Are you that sure about your friend?" I wasn't trying to sow discord, but I was honestly curious.

"Of course I am," Laura said, but I saw something in her glance downward that told me I might have hit too close to home.

"I'm assuming that you've already heard that Joanne was poisoned, Laura. Word gets around fast in a small town, doesn't it?"

"For your information, the police told me as soon as they found out. I was her next of kin, you know."

"That's what I heard, but to be honest with you, the news kind of surprised me. I didn't realize that you two were that close, let alone family. I couldn't tell anything by the way you acted toward each other yesterday at Café Noir."

"We had drifted apart, but lately we were getting to know each other again," Laura said softly. "She didn't approve of my friendship with Sandy, and Joanne never made any apologies for expressing what she felt. Still, we were beginning to work things out, and then someone stole that opportunity from me, and I want to know who is responsible."

"So do I," I replied. "Why do you think I'm running all over town making everyone uncomfortable with the questions I'm asking? Why do you just assume that I was the one who poisoned her?"

"She told me she sold her first puzzle and that she was going to show it to you," Laura said haltingly, as though she was beginning to lose faith in her theory that I was the killer.

"That's no motive for murder. Inheriting her estate might be considered one, though."

"There's not much of an estate," Laura said with a hint of wry laughter in her voice. "She'll probably have more bills than assets by the time I'm finished, and I get the privilege of spending the next six months sorting through it all."

"At least she owned some property," I said.

"Are you talking about her house? From what she told me, she'd mortgaged it to the max. Face it, there's nothing left."

"Then she must not have shared everything with you," I said.

"What are you talking about?" From the way Laura was looking at me, I had no doubt that she was in the dark about Joanne's land deal with Harry Pike. I debated sharing the information with her, but I knew that she'd find out sooner or later. And then another thought struck me. Why not tell her now and see how she reacted?

"Check the courthouse records," I said. "That's what I did. Joanne had a great deal more money than you think."

"I'm sure you're mistaken," she said. A point suddenly occurred to her. "Why were you snooping into Joanne's life, anyway? What motive would you have to do that?"

"I'm going to solve her murder myself and clear my name in the process, Laura, whether anyone else likes it or not. I would have thought you'd be delighted to have someone working to find the real killer, so those of us who are innocent won't stay under a cloud of suspicion."

"I want to find her killer more than you do," Laura said plaintively.

"Then I suggest you visit the courthouse, and then look me up," I said. "The records are all there. You just have to know the right questions to ask."

Laura stared at me a second, and then said, "What can it hurt?" as she turned and headed toward the courthouse basement.

In all honesty, I hadn't expected such a burst of loyalty toward Joanne from Laura, and it surprised me. I could think of a few reasons she might be feeling it, though. If she hadn't killed her cousin, she could sincerely be regretting the times in the past that she'd fought with Joanne, and the moments still ahead of them that she'd now lost.

Laura's reaction to Sandra's name when I'd mentioned it had shown a flicker of doubt in her eyes. I was curious to see if Sandra had equal doubts about Laura, and there was only one way to do that. I'd spoken with all of the suspects save one anyway.

It was time to find Sandra, and see if her motives for murder were any stronger than mine or anyone else's on my list.

S ANDRA OLIVER WAS AT HER DESK WHEN I WALKED INTO the law firm where she worked as a receptionist. She looked startled to see me. "Savannah, what are you doing here? I don't have you on my appointment schedule for today."

"That's because I'm not on it," I said. "I was hoping to speak with you for a few minutes, if you have the time."

"Sorry, I'd love to, but I'm awfully busy at the moment," she said.

I looked around the empty waiting room. The furniture was at least two decades old, and mismatched at that. The carpet was starting to fray on one edge, and the curtains hadn't been cleaned since the Reagan administration. It wasn't the most prosperous place in town, if the furnishings were any indication.

"Is that so? Is Nathan in his office?" Nathan Haggerty was a brash young lawyer who'd come back to Parson's Valley after graduating from Duke Law School. He'd received offers from some big firms, but he ultimately decided small-town law was what he wanted to do, so he'd bought out a dying law practice from his uncle and was trying to make a go of it. He and my husband had become good friends since we'd moved to town, though the two of us weren't all that close.

"He's gone, but I have work of my own to do," she said.

I couldn't argue with that, but I still wanted to speak with her. "Surely you get a break sometime during the day. This won't take long, and then I'll be out of your hair."

"No, I'm sorry, but I can't," she said, clearly not sorry at all.

"That's fine," I said as I turned back toward the door. "I just thought you had a right to know what I heard about you. I wanted to give you the benefit of the doubt, but I'll go ahead and let Zach know. Don't say I didn't come here and try to get your side of it first." I was bluffing, but I had to believe that Sandra couldn't tell. At least that was what I was counting on.

"What did you hear?" Sandra asked, her voice nearly shouting now.

"It's okay, really. I understand all about your situation. You're a busy woman; I get it."

"I'm due for a break after all," she said as she stood from her desk chair. "I can give you five minutes."

"That should be all I need. May we go outside, or do you need to stay here and answer the phones?"

"Don't worry about it. If we get any calls, the machine will pick up," she said as she walked me to the door.

Once we were outside, I had plans to get her talking about Laura and her relationship with Joanne, but Sandra was clearly not interested in anything but my bluff.

We were barely out onto the porch when she stopped and looked at me. "What did you hear, Savannah?"

"I understand that Joanne stole something valuable of yours," I said.

She looked at me sharply. "Where did you hear that? Is your husband reporting back to you, or have you been listening in on his telephone conversations?"

"I wouldn't dare. No one knows how sacred he holds those values more than I do," I said, neatly skirting the question. It was a favorite trick I'd picked up from Jenny. If you don't like the question, ignore it and answer one of your own. At the very least, it confuses the daylights out of people, and they rarely call you on it. Now, if she'd only allow me to deflect from her real question. "Is it true? Did Joanne steal something from you?"

"No, of course not. It's nonsense. What have I lost of value?"

"I was hoping you could tell me," I admitted.

"There was nothing. If you don't believe me, you should speak with Laura about it."

"I already did," I said.

That scored. Sandra looked long and hard at me before she spoke. "When did that happen?"

"Right before I came to speak with you," I said. It was true, every last word of it. If she made her own inferences from what I said, I couldn't be held responsible, could I?

"Are you saying Laura told you about something?" she asked.

I just shrugged. "It doesn't really matter how I heard it, does it?"

"It matters to me," she said.

"Why? You already denied it ever happened."

She was stewing about telling me something; I could tell by the way she pursed her lips. If I just gave her enough time, maybe not more than a few minutes, I had a feeling she'd volunteer something I needed to hear.

Just as she was about to break, I heard a familiar voice behind me. "Savannah, are you harassing my receptionist?"

It was Nathan Haggerty.

"Hello, Nathan," I said. "Sandra and I were just chatting."

Sandra looked as though a spell had been broken within her. She glanced at her watch, and then said, "If you'll excuse me, I have work to do."

Once she was back inside, Nathan looked at me curiously. "Why do I have the feeling I just interrupted something?"

"Beats me," I said, not wanting to drag the young attorney into the investigation if I could help it.

He let it go. "How's Zach doing with the Clayton investigation?"

"How did you hear he was working on the case?"

Nathan laughed. Every time I looked at him, I had to fight the urge to ruffle his hair, but just because he was young didn't mean that he wasn't more than competent. I'd have to watch my step around him, or I'd end up telling him everything.

"Come on, give me a little credit. You were seen with the victim not long before she died, and you've got a motive to kill her. It doesn't take a Herculean effort to figure the rest of it out."

"As a matter of fact, he is working with the Asheville police on the homicide, but it's nothing official."

"I heard about the chief's embezzlement. I was kind of surprised they didn't offer the job to Zach."

"They did," I said, "but he turned them down. There's a Captain North from the state police serving as acting chief for the moment."

"That wouldn't be Gretchen North, would it?" He had a wry smile on his face as he asked the question.

"I'm not sure. Why, do you know her?"

He whistled softly under his breath. "Only by reputation. She's supposed to be the best there is."

"Do you mean besides my husband?"

Nathan laughed with genuine emotion. "Of course, that's exactly what I meant." His cell phone rang, and as he answered it, he looked at me and said, "Excuse me."

After a brief conversation, he put the phone away and said, "Sorry, but I have to go. Tell Zach that we need to go fishing again before he forgets how to bait the hook."

"You can tell him yourself, but I will give him your love."

Nathan made a face. "Don't do that; he'll think I've gone soft. Give him my regards, instead."

"You men are something else. I feel all warm and fuzzy inside just hearing it," I said.

Nathan smiled, and then ducked into his office. I hadn't managed to shake Sandra up enough to talk to me in detail, but I had a feeling that if I took another run at her later, I might have more luck.

In the meantime, I'd spoken with everyone in Parson's Valley that I needed to, at least for the moment.

It was time to head back home and organize my thoughts concerning everything that I'd learned so far.

I WALKED INTO THE COTTAGE, FLIPPING THROUGH THE MAIL as I went. It was mostly bills, but I found a long envelope with my name on it among them, and I tore into it. My syndicate was a little erratic in my pay schedule, but the envelope was unmistakable. I pulled out the check, and realized that it would be quickly devoured by the bills already sitting on the counter.

Such was the life of a midlist puzzlemaker.

I threw the stack of letters on the coffee table and saw Joanne's puzzle still sitting there from the day before.

Picking it up, I glanced at it to see how difficult she'd made her first puzzle. I could remember my first one, as complicated as I'd ever made one. I had been petrified that everyone would be able to figure it out instantly. Instead, I got several complaints about how hard it had been, and after that, I'd lowered my sights a little. At least Joanne hadn't made that mistake, too. As puzzles went, it wasn't bad. I liked the way she'd used threes as a theme in one of the logic puzzles, and I was surprised that she'd been able to come up with it. It was a little more sophisticated than a neophyte's puzzle should be, with patterns appearing within the puzzle beyond just the solution.

I kept staring at it long past when I should have chucked it into the recycling bin.

There was something familiar about it.

And then it hit me.

There was every reason in the world it should look memorable to me.

I was pretty sure that I was the one who'd created it.

ZACH, I'VE GOT A PROBLEM," I SAID A FEW MINUTES LATER when I called my husband's cell phone.

"Did someone threaten you? I told you to be careful nosing around town, Savannah."

"That's not it," I said, "but it's still bad news. It turns out I may have had more of a motive to kill Joanne than we first realized."

"What are you talking about?"

I took a deep breath, and then plunged into it. "Do you remember the puzzle she published in the Asheville paper?"

"I'm not likely to forget it. Why?"

I tapped the paper with a finger as I explained, "I took a good look at it today, and there was something about it that looked really familiar. It should. I created it two years ago."

There was a long pause, and then Zach asked, "Savannah, I don't mean to be obvious, but how can you be certain? There have to be a limited number of ways to come up with those puzzles. Isn't it possible it's just a coincidence?"

"Not a chance," I said.

"How can you be so sure?"

I tried to keep the exasperation I was feeling out of my voice. "Zach, a puzzle has the creator's fingerprints all over it. It just takes a trained eye to see it. This is one of mine. I dug through my files and found the original. She didn't change a thing on hers. The empty spaces are identical, along with every solution. It's mine. There's no doubt about it."

"Who have you told about this?"

"Nobody. The second I discovered it, I called you. Why?"

I could hear him take a deep breath on the other end of the line, and then he said, "Don't share this with anyone just yet, okay?"

I thought about that for a few seconds. "Isn't that concealing evidence? You can't just bury this. Your principles are too important to you, Zach."

"Savannah, don't be stupid. Do you honestly want North to think you killed Joanne? Don't worry, I'll handle it."

"How do you propose to do that?" I knew my husband loved me, and that he'd do just about anything in the world for me, but I couldn't let him cover up information on an active case, no matter how bad it would make me look.

"I'll come up with something. In the meantime, put that paper and your original puzzle in a safe place. We might need them both."

"I'll take care of it, but I don't like this one bit."

"What do we gain by telling North right now? It's only pertinent if you killed Joanne. You didn't, did you?"

"Of course not."

"Then we're not even obstructing justice, as far as I'm concerned."

I whistled into the phone. "Are you listening to yourself, Zach?"

"Good-bye, Savannah."

After we hung up, I wondered about Zach's decision to conceal this new evidence from Captain North, but I had to trust his instincts about it. What he'd said made sense. I hadn't committed the crime, so there was no reason the state police captain needed another motive for me to have done it. Was that really true, or was I starting to slide on the slippery slope that had already gotten Zach? As I sat there, I realized that acting rash would only get me in trouble, so I decided to do what my husband had asked me to, at least for the moment. I took both papers and stashed them in our fireproof safe in the master bedroom closet. Why anyone would want to steal them was beyond me, but I trusted my husband's gut feelings.

After the safe was locked, I made myself a cup of hot chocolate and sat outside. I'd started to reach for the tea bags automatically, but the thought of Joanne's poisoning was enough to stay my hand. The more I thought about one of my puzzles being pirated, the madder I got. I couldn't believe the nerve Joanne had exhibited, stealing something I'd created and taking credit for it as her own. I felt betrayed by the action, and more than a little angry. I wouldn't kill her over it, but I was certain that if she were still alive, I'd do my best to publicly berate and humiliate her with the truth. Hadn't she realized that, or did Joanne think she was so clever that I'd never uncover the truth? It had been the height of arrogance to steal my puzzle, but even brasher was that she'd waved it in front of my face.

If I was being honest about it, I knew that I'd heard of worse motives for murder in my life.

There wasn't anything I could do about that at the moment, though. I was just going to have to forget my own motive and continue to look for whoever had killed Joanne.

I was torn from my thoughts by the sound of a car coming up the drive. For a second I thought it might be Zach coming home, but instead, it was Rob's pickup truck. It was easily recognizable, since he used it for deliveries and it had the hardware store's name embossed on both door panels.

"Hey, mister, you've got the wrong house. I didn't order anything from the hardware store," I said as I stepped off the porch to greet him.

"I wouldn't be too sure about that," he said as he held up a replacement doorknob for one of my kitchen cabinets that I'd asked him about weeks ago.

I laughed as I took it. "I nearly forgot about this. What did it cost me, two dollars?"

"Sorry, they went up to two fifty," he said.

"I might be wrong, but isn't it a little expensive to make a delivery on something this small?"

He shrugged. "I was out this way delivering a load of pine straw to Steve Waverly, so I thought I'd drop this off to you while I was here. What have you been up to today?"

"Oh, a little of this and that," I said.

"Don't hold back on me, Savannah," he said with a grin. "I'm still a member of the investigating team, right?"

"I hate getting you involved," I said.

"I believe we've already gone over that." He glanced at my mug. "Is that coffee?"

"Hot chocolate," I admitted.

"Even better. I've got some time before I have to head back, and I'd love a cup if you've got it to spare."

"Come on in," I said.

"If it's all the same to you, I think I'll stay out here and enjoy one of these rocking chairs. I don't get to sit and rock nearly enough."

"I'll be back in a minute," I said.

I made his cocoa, and freshened mine up with a dash more of the hot chocolate while I was at it.

Rob was rocking away when I handed him his mug. "Thanks." He took a sip, and then smiled. "That's outstanding. You know, you and Zach have done a wonderful job with these flowers."

I looked at the raised beds, and their nearly spent buds. "We have vegetables, too, but I love surrounding myself with blossoms and blooms."

"Don't tell anyone, but I do, too. My garden feeds my body, but my flower beds feed my soul."

I smiled gently at him. "I never realized you had a poet's heart, Rob."

He shook his head. "I wouldn't say that, exactly, and I surely wouldn't spread it around town. After all, I've got a reputation to uphold."

"Don't worry, I won't give you away."

"Good," he said as he took another sip of cocoa. "So, what's new on the murder investigation?"

"I don't even know where to begin," I said.

"Start anywhere, and I'll stop you if I've heard it before."

I started to tell him about the conversations I'd had so far without him, but I held back on mentioning my visit to the Asheville Botanical Gardens, and what I'd discovered there. I didn't think Zach would want me to tell anyone about the poison that had been used to kill Joanne, so I decided to err on the side of caution until I discussed it with him first.

After I was finished recounting what I could, Rob whistled softly under his breath. "Do you realize something? If we're right, you've talked to a murderer in the past twenty-four hours."

I hadn't really thought of it that way, but what he said was valid. "I'm still no closer to knowing who did it than I was before."

"I might be able to help you with that," he said a little smugly.

"Go on. You've got my attention."

Chapter 10

∎ ∎ ∎

"**W**OULD IT HELP IF YOU HAD A CHANCE TO GO through Joanne's house without anyone looking over your shoulder?" Rob asked. "Could there be a clue hiding there about what happened to her?"

"There might be, but I doubt Laura would let me near the place, even if Zach approved of it."

"You have to get his permission to snoop?" Rob asked softly.

"When it comes to getting actively involved in one of his investigations I do. I wouldn't do it any more than he would pick up a pencil and change a number in one of my puzzles. There have to be some boundaries."

Rob thought about that, and then nodded. "I can see that. Assuming he gives you the green light, would you like to look around her place?"

I took another sip of cocoa, and then said, "I'm not at all certain that Laura would appreciate me doing that. If she's Joanne's nearest living relative, she's not going to just invite me in."

"Maybe not, but you could come with me," Rob said with a grin.

"How did you get the magic key?"

He took a sip, and then said, "That's closer to the truth than you know. A magic key is exactly what I've got."

"What are you talking about?"

He held a key up and waved it in the air. "Laura came by an hour ago and gave me this key to Joanne's house. She's paying me to change all of the locks in the place, and to give the new keys just to her. She seems concerned that someone's going to get in there without permission."

"Couldn't you get in trouble for bringing me along?"

"Not if you're my helper," he said. "Have you ever thought about moonlighting at the hardware store for real? You were teasing with Lee yesterday, but we could make it official. I can only hire you for one job, and there won't be any salary or benefits attached, but it's yours if you want it."

I smiled despite the serious nature of our investigation. "How can I turn down an offer like that? When are you going to do it?"

"As a matter of fact, I'm heading there right now," he said. "Laura's paying me double time for a rush job, and I wasn't about to turn her down."

"Let me grab something first, and then I'll need to call Zach."

"I'll be right here waiting," he said.

I called my husband, and he answered on the second ring. "Savannah, did you put those papers in the safe yet?"

"The second we hung up," I answered. "Let me ask you something. Have you been through Joanne's house yet?"

"I didn't get a chance to go myself," he admitted. "North had it checked out while we were interviewing suspects. I would have loved to go through it, too, but she's already released it to Laura Moon. Why do you ask?"

"I've got a chance to snoop around a little right now, but I didn't want to step on your toes."

I could hear him taking a deep breath before he asked, "How did you manage that?"

"Oddly enough, I've got a part-time job. No, that's not right. A temp position is probably closer to the truth."

I told him what Rob had in mind, and he said, "Is he sure he wants to put himself on the line like that?"

"I told you before, he's doing this for his late wife, so who am I to say no? What do you think?"

"Be careful, don't take anything, and don't get caught," Zach said.

"That's what I like: directions I can follow."

He laughed at that. "When's the last time you followed anyone's directions that didn't involve a recipe?"

"Hey, there's always hope."

"Savannah," he said, his voice growing serious for a moment. "Be careful, okay? Never forget the fact that we're dealing with a murderer here."

"How can I?" I asked, and then hung up.

I grabbed my digital camera from the closet. After I brought up the pictures in storage on its memory card, I found that the last photo on it was one of Zach working in the garden, a look of serene happiness on his face. I checked the battery level, and then let out a low moan. I'd forgotten to recharge it since my trip to the Botanical Gardens. It had just a small charge left on it.

I hoped it would be enough.

Tucking it into the pocket of one of my oversized jackets, I went outside to tell Rob that I was ready to go.

"What did your husband have to say about our little excursion?" Rob asked as he got out of his chair.

"We're good to go," I said. "Hardware Store Apprentice Stone reporting for duty, sir."

He laughed, and then said, "Just get in the truck, Savannah."

As we drove to Joanne's house, I said, "Zach had a good point when I told him what we were up to. You don't have to do this, you know. If Laura finds out I was in Joanne's house, she can tell everyone in town that you aren't trustworthy, and it could do some serious damage to your business."

"Most folks have known me their entire lives," he said. "I'm willing to take the chance that they'll believe my word over hers." He paused, and then added, "Besides, what's life without a little spice in it? Do you have any idea what you're looking for at Joanne's place?"

"Not really. I'm kind of hoping I'll know it when I see it."

Rob smiled slightly as he shook his head. "I've always admired that in you, Savannah. You're not afraid to tackle something without any plan ahead of time whatsoever."

"If I waited for a sound strategy every time I acted, I'd never get anything accomplished," I said.

He shrugged. "I'm sure you have a point there, but I've always been a big planner, myself."

"Don't worry, keep hanging around me and there's hope for you yet."

He drove to Joanne's place, and as we pulled into the driveway, I got that same nagging feeling I always got when my life's path crossed with someone who was recently dead. There was something eerie about it, but I did my best to suppress my emotions. This wasn't the time to let my feelings rule me. It was an opportunity that I was certain I wouldn't get again, and I was determined to make the most of it.

J OANNE'S PLACE WAS FAIRLY MODEST FROM THE OUTSIDE. The grass had been mowed recently, and the leaves were neatly bagged and sitting by the curb for pickup. I doubted Joanne had done it herself. She didn't seem the type to enjoy yard work, or any other type of work for that matter. The ranch-style home was neatly painted and well cared for. With Joanne, I knew that appearances mattered a great deal to her.

My place was quite a bit more lived-in, at least from the exterior. If there was a choice between style and substance, I always chose the latter.

We walked up to the front porch, Rob with his toolbox and me carrying the replacement locks. So far, to any prying eyes in the neighborhood, I was acting out my part in this charade.

Rob unlocked the front door, and we stepped inside.

The furniture was nicer than I'd been expecting, especially after hearing Laura protest that Joanne didn't have any money. There were several pieces of furniture that were more expensive than anything I'd ever owned, and I saw some original artwork hanging on the walls that had to be worth more than our cottage, if the quality of the paintings was any indication.

"What do you know? It's as neat as a pin," Rob said.

"And much nicer than I'd been led to believe."

He looked surprised by that comment. "What are you talking about?"

"When I spoke to Laura, she told me that she doubted there would be enough cash to pay off Joanne's bills, and she said this place was mortgaged to the hilt. Looking around here, I'm guessing that she was mistaken."

"I don't know if she was wrong or she just flat-out lied to you, Savannah. I know for a fact that the car Laura is driving around town came from Joanne."

"How could you possibly know that?" I asked. "Their kinship was supposed to be some big secret."

"To most folks, it probably was, but you have to remember, Joanne and I knew each other for what felt like forever."

I ran a hand over the surface of a walnut end table. "Laura had to know I'd find out the truth eventually. What was the point in playing all of this down?"

"Maybe she was embarrassed about all she's going to get. Then again, she could have been just trying to throw you off her track," he said as he examined the doorknob. "I can do all of this in half an hour, if everything works out."

"Does that ever happen?"

He grinned at me as he took out an electric drill with a screwdriver bit chucked in it. I hadn't been working with Zach on the cottage without picking up a few things here and there. "Do you really need my help, or was it just an excuse to let me satisfy a little curiosity?"

"Okay, I'm willing to admit that I can handle this by myself," Rob said. "Why don't you go look around and see what you can turn up? Just do me one favor, okay?"

"Anything. All you have to do is ask."

"Put everything back where you found it, and we're good."

"I can do that," I said. I started walking around Joanne's house as Rob went to work removing the old doorknob. I didn't have a lot of time, so it was important that I got busy right away.

THERE WAS NO INDICATION THAT THE POLICE HAD DONE anything but a superficial search of the house as far as I could tell. Either Captain North was a very thorough investigator, or she didn't believe the clue to Joanne's death could be found in her house.

Either way, I had my work cut out for me. Thirty minutes wasn't a lot of time to dig into someone else's life. I went to Joanne's bedroom and started looking inside drawers. The thought of leaving fingerprints behind worried me a little, since they'd be difficult to explain, but I couldn't imagine it ever coming up. I found Joanne's bank statements in one of her dresser drawers, and I pulled the top one out. In that money market account alone she had nearly fifty thousand dollars. There shouldn't be a big problem paying off all of her bills, despite what Laura had told me. I took a photo of the statement, and then turned to the recording section of her checkbook. I didn't even have time to read the pages; I just snapped a photo of each one with the intention of going over the individual entries later. After I returned her financial records back to the drawer where I'd found them, I started looking around for other things, personal items that might give me some indication of who might want Joanne dead.

As I searched, I found three letters she'd been writing tucked away in a big book of Impressionist artists lying on the nightstand by the bed. None of them were addressed yet, but each note held variations of the same theme.

You should be more careful with your secrets. I found out, and if you don't watch your step, everyone else in Parson's Valley is going to know, too.

How odd. I doubted that she was blackmailing anyone, since there was no mention of money in any of the letters. Apparently Joanne was threatening someone—or possibly three someones—to straighten up. Were these three drafts written to the same person, or was Joanne threatening to expose three different people's misdeeds? I took a quick photograph of all three and then put the letters back where I'd found them.

On her dresser was a framed photograph of Joanne taken in the mountains. From the look of it, it had been snapped somewhere on the Blue Ridge Parkway, a scenic drive that traced the Appalachian Mountains from North Carolina to Virginia. I always thought that it was odd when people kept pictures of themselves around their homes.

When I opened Joanne's closet, I nearly lost my breath when I saw how many shoes the woman had. I personally didn't get the fascination with owning a thousand shoes, but I knew a lot of women did. I had a sturdy pair of boots for hiking and gardening, three pairs of tennis shoes, three pairs of three-inch heels, and two pairs of flats, one in black and the other brown.

It was clear that Joanne believed that she could never have enough shoes. Row after row after row of shoes were stacked, some in their boxes and some in the open air, halfway to the ceiling. She could barely get her skirts and blouses inside the closet. I opened a few of the boxes at random, but they contained only shoes.

I was about to close the closet door when I noticed that one of the boxes away from the door had been shoved in upside down. It was tough to notice it at first, but once I did, it was a glaring error in shoe filing. I leaned down and pulled the box out, careful to keep the lid on tight so nothing would fall out. I flipped it over and began to replace it among its brethren when I realized that the box felt heavier than a pair of heels should be.

Carefully lifting the top, I held my breath as I stared inside. Unfortunately, before I could take more than one quick peek, I heard a woman behind me asking, "What are you doing here, Savannah?"

It was Laura Moon, one of the last people in Parson's Valley I wanted to see at the moment.

"**I** CAME TO HELP ROB," I SAID.

"I know; he tried to stop me from coming back here. I was under the impression that I'd hired him to change the locks. Is he shoe shopping, too?" she asked, staring at the box in my hands.

"No, I confess I came back here on my own. I had to use the bathroom, and when I saw the bedroom door open, I couldn't resist a peek inside. Joanne had fabulous taste, didn't she?"

She walked up and reached for the box in my hands. "This is the first time I've seen her closet myself."

I handed the shoe box to her, but as she tried to take it, I "accidentally" let it slip before she could control it.

As the box turned over and the lid fell off, a shower of tens and twenties drifted down to the floor.

"What is this?" she asked, the expression of shock on her face no doubt matching mine.

"Don't ask me. It's not my money. I'm just as surprised as you we found it."

We both stared at the cash lying scattered on the bedroom floor, and then Laura asked me in a hushed voice, "Savannah, how much do you think there is here?"

"I have no idea, but that's not what I'm wondering."

"Where it came from?" she asked as she started gathering it up.

"That, too, but what I'm really curious about is whether any more of the boxes have money in them."

"That's a good point," she said as a genuine smile crossed her lips. As Laura knelt down, she saw that I still wasn't moving. "Are you going to just stand there, or are you going to help me look for more?"

"I'd be glad to help," I said. Apparently Laura had already forgotten her displeasure at finding me in Joanne's bedroom. It was amazing how money could do that. We started going through the boxes one by one, but there were no more hidden caches of money.

As we both sat on the floor among the carpet of shoes, Laura said, "I'd be lying if I said I wasn't a little disappointed there wasn't more."

"It was like a treasure hunt, wasn't it?" I looked at the cash Laura had counted. "How much was in there?"

"A little over eleven thousand dollars," she said.

"That's still not bad then, is it?"

She shook her head. "Not bad at all." When she turned to look at me, she added, "Savannah, I need a favor."

I wasn't exactly in a position to refuse her any reasonable request at the moment. "What can I do for you?"

"Do you think there's any chance that we can keep the discovery of this money between the two of us? I don't know how I'm going to handle it yet, and I don't want the rumors to start up that Joanne had millions stashed around the house."

"It was just over eleven thousand," I said.

"Sure, we both know that's the truth, but the exaggerations of it will play out so much better around Parson's Valley, don't you think?"

I had one caveat. "I'm not comfortable lying to my husband, even if it is only a lie of omission."

Laura nodded. "I understand completely, and I wouldn't expect anything less from you." As she stored the bills back into the shoe box and closed the lid, she added, "I plan to tell him about it myself. I know he can be discreet."

"How could you possibly know that?" I asked.

"He was an important man in Charlotte," Laura said. "When he came by with that state trooper to question me yesterday, I could tell he was a man who could keep a secret. I'm not wrong, am I?"

"No, you sized him up pretty well. As a matter of fact, there are a lot of things I'd like to know that he won't tell me, either."

"Then you can tell him what we found, and that way we can figure out what to do with this cash. I know I'm her only beneficiary, but I want to make sure I handle this the proper way." She paused, bit her lower lip for a second, and then added, "Tell you what. Why don't you call him right now? He can come over, and we can figure out what to do about this together."

"That's a great idea," I agreed just as Rob poked his head into the bedroom. It was clear from his expression that he hadn't known what to expect, but finding us sitting on the carpet among all of those shoes wasn't one of the scenarios that had played out in his mind.

"Is everything all right here?" he asked.

"We're fine," I said.

"Did you finish installing the new locks?" Laura asked.

"I've got your new keys right here," he said. Laura and I stood, and I noticed that she had the box of cash tucked under one arm. I didn't blame her. If it had been me, I'd have held on to it tightly myself.

"Do I need to sign something, or should I pay you now?" she asked as she took the keys from him.

"No, I'll just bill you for it."

If it had been me, I might have paid him out of the bounty we'd just found, but Laura didn't even try. "That's fine, then. Thanks for coming and doing that so quickly," she added.

"I was happy to do it." He turned to me and asked, "Savannah, are you coming?"

"If it's all the same to you, I think I'm going to stick around awhile," I said. "Thanks anyway."

I could see the burst of curiosity on his face, but he quickly disguised it. "Good enough. I'll catch up with you later."

"Bye now," I said.

After he was gone, I got out my phone and hit the speed dial for my husband. It was time to bring Zach up to speed on what Laura and I had discovered. There would be a chance to share the notes I'd found with him later.

For now, we had a cash flow situation that he needed to know about.

Chapter 11

...

"**H**EY THERE," I SAID WHEN MY HUSBAND PICKED UP HIS cell phone.

"What's going on, Savannah?"

"I need you over at Joanne's house as soon as you can get here."

"Nothing's wrong, is it? Did something happen?" he asked, the concern in his voice coming through loud and clear. I was glad that I'd called earlier and given him a heads-up about my intentions. That way I wouldn't have to explain in front of Laura why I was there, or what I'd been doing. I looked over and smiled at her as reassuringly as I could, and she smiled back at me, a good sign.

"Everything here is fine. As a matter of fact, we need to discuss something with you."

I could hear a bit of hesitation in his voice. "We? Savannah, talk to me. Is Rob all right?"

"As a matter of fact, he just finished installing the new locks and left." It was clear that I was going to have to explain more than I would have liked to over the phone, because I couldn't continue to be vague about the reason we needed Zach there with us. I should have known better than to try to stonewall him. "I was here helping Rob, and on a trip to the bathroom I noticed a shoe box turned upside down in Joanne's closet. Laura came in around then, and when we looked inside it, we found a box of cash."

"You and Laura were searching the place together," he said slowly.

Not precisely right, but close enough. "That's right. Can you break free and come over here right now? We're not sure what we should do with it."

"I'm on my way. How much exactly are we talking about here?"

"A little over eleven grand," I said.

"I'll see you in six minutes."

I hung up and told her, "We're all set. Zach's on his way."

Laura nodded, and then looked around at the litter of shoes and boxes on the floor. "Should we clean this up before he gets here?"

I nodded as I took in the sight. "We could probably organize it a little better, but he's going to want to look into every single one of these boxes for himself."

"Okay. The least we can do is put the lids under the boxes so he can look inside easier, and we can match the shoes with the boxes."

I wasn't sure we had to be that organized, but at least it would help pass the time.

As we worked, Laura paused and looked intently at me as she said, "You were really serious when you told me before that you were looking into Joanne's murder, weren't you?"

I was startled by the question. "It's likely it's the only way I'm going to clear my name."

"Are you that concerned with the police, even with your husband working with them?"

I shook my head. "It's not law enforcement I'm worried about as much as it is the folks in Parson's Valley. The longer this is all hanging over my head, the harder it will be to get anyone's trust back when it's finally over."

She seemed to think about that before she commented again. "So, you decided to snoop around Joanne's place."

"Hey, I really was ready to help Rob if he needed it," I explained. "If you're going to get mad at anyone, it has to be me. Rob had no idea what I was up to."

She looked at me curiously, and then she asked, "Savannah, were you under the impression that I was angry with you?"

I shrugged. "You weren't all that happy when you found me in Joanne's closet."

She nodded. "True, but that's mostly because I wasn't expecting to find you. How can I be that upset when you helped me find this money? If you want to know the truth, I probably wouldn't have checked a single shoe box. I would have donated them to Goodwill or the Salvation Army or even had a yard sale, and I might never have known about that cash. I should be thanking you for helping."

"You're most welcome," I said with a smile.

"So let me get this straight. You've been questioning folks all over town since Joanne died. Isn't everyone going to know what you're up to?"

"I certainly hope so," I confessed.

She nodded. "Then they'll understand that you're trying to clear your name. That's pretty clever." After a moment's pause, she asked, "I'm a suspect, too, aren't I?"

There was nothing I could do but nod. "Anyone who had contact with Joanne in Asheville is," I said. "Naturally, we're both on that list. I don't want a black cloud hanging over me, and I'm guessing you don't want to be a murder suspect, either. It's pretty unpleasant."

"Believe me, I know what you mean," she said. "This whole thing is driving me crazy. I thought we were best friends, but Sandra's not even talking to me anymore, did you know that?"

"Why on earth not?" I asked.

"She thinks it's my fault that she's a suspect, too, since I'm the one who suggested we go shopping in Asheville yesterday."

"That's ridiculous," I said as I heard someone knocking on the front door. "She's probably just scared and upset. She'll get over it."

"I hope so."

There was another knock on the door, and I got up to answer it. As I did, I glanced at my watch. Zach had made good time.

"Would you talk to her for me?" Laura asked as she joined me and we walked out of the bedroom with the shoe box full of cash.

"I can try," I said.

I was pleased to see my husband, but he seemed more interested with Laura than he was with me. "Is that it?" he asked as he pointed to the shoe box held reverently in her hands. I noticed he'd taken the time to put on a pair of latex gloves as he'd walked to the door.

"It is." After seeing his gloved hands, Laura said, "There's no reason to worry about the fingerprints, is there? Savannah and I both touched it, and I'm sure Joanne did as well."

"You can't be too careful," he said. "May I?"

"Absolutely," she said as she handed the shoe box to him.

Zach lifted the lid off and looked at the money inside. "That's a lot of cash," he said. "Any idea where she got it?"

"I wish I knew. She could have been selling things on eBay for all I know," Laura said. "Do you think it's significant?"

"It's hard to say. It might be," Zach said.

"Or it might not be at all," I said. I explained to Laura, "My husband has a tendency to overanalyze things at times."

"Savannah, you don't need to apologize for me." He put the lid back on the box, and then handed it to Laura. "You need to call the attorney handling Joanne's estate and give this directly to him."

"You mean I can't keep it?" she asked, clearly startled by his advice.

"If what I've just heard is correct, it's yours anyway. You are the sole beneficiary, aren't you?"

She nodded. "I was surprised when I found out, but it's true."

"Then you should be fine. All I'm saying is that you don't want there to be any gray areas."

"I don't really even have an attorney," she admitted a little reluctantly. "I found the will among some of her papers, and I took it to the courthouse this morning so there wouldn't be any delay. I'm the executor and sole beneficiary, so they told me I could handle everything myself."

"In that case, you should turn this cash over to yourself as soon as possible," Zach said with a slight grin. "I honestly don't see a problem doing that, but we need to tell Captain North about it right away."

"I understand, but could she confiscate it?"

Zach frowned. "No, I don't see how she could. Still, it might help her to know that Joanne had some cash squirreled away. It might mean something."

"Then it's significant?" Laura asked.

I piped in. "Laura, Zach believes that all information is useful. I'm not sure I don't agree with him, but the money's yours."

She nodded. "We had a joint checking account, so I'll probably just stick it in there so I can pay her bills."

"That would be the prudent thing to do," Zach said.

"Good, it's settled, then."

Laura turned to me and said, "Savannah, I might not have even found this if it weren't for you. May I give you a reward?"

I thought about the cash, but there was something else in that room that I wanted more. "I couldn't take any money," I said.

She was about to accept that when I added, "But I wouldn't mind that book on art Joanne had. I love the Impressionist period."

"It's all beyond me," she said. "If that's what you'd like, by all means, go on and take it. It's yours, with my thanks."

"Would you like me to stay and help you clean up?" I offered.

"Thanks, but I can handle it from here. Besides, you lost your ride earlier, remember?"

"True." As I looked around the room, I said, "If you

change your mind and would like some help, all you have to do is call."

"Thank you for that," she said. "I appreciate it more than I can say."

After Laura saw us out, she locked the door behind us. No one who wasn't invited was going to get in now that the locks had been changed.

"That was nice of you," Zach said as we walked out to his car.

"I couldn't believe how it turned out. One minute I was snooping through Joanne's things and being caught red-handed by Laura, and the next I was helping her look for more cash. I don't even think she remembers catching me."

"That's not what I'm talking about." After we were in his car, he tapped the book in my hands before he drove away. "She would have given you cash, but you took this book instead. I didn't even know you were that interested in Impressionism."

"I am, but that's beside the point. There's something in here that you need to see."

Zach smiled at me. "Savannah, I was a fan of Monet and his friends long before you were. I doubt there's anything in there that I haven't seen before."

I opened the book and removed the three letters I'd found earlier. "Want to bet on that?"

ZACH PULLED OVER THE SECOND I EXPLAINED TO HIM what I'd found.

He studied each letter carefully in turn, and then said, "I can't say whether these are three drafts of one letter or three versions. Either way, she was a bit of a busybody, wasn't she?"

"It might be what got her killed," I said.

"People don't appreciate it when other folks go digging around in their closets." He grinned at me as he said it. "And yes, I mean that figuratively and literally, too."

"I make no apologies for what I do," I said.

"Yes, I know that. It's part of your charm."

He kept reading the letters, and then made a U-turn as he pulled out. We were now heading away from home, instead of toward it.

"Where are we going?"

"I was going to tell North about the money tomorrow morning, but she needs to see these as soon as possible. Good work, Savannah."

"I do what I can," I said as we drove to Town Hall downtown where the police captain had set up a temporary office while she was in Parson's Valley.

AFTER CAPTAIN NORTH FINGERPRINTED THE LETTERS and took a set of my own to eliminate them, she came back into the office where we'd been waiting. There was a dour look on her face. "I knew it was a long shot. There were just your prints and the victim's," she said.

"That's kind of what we expected," Zach said.

As the captain examined the notes, she asked, "How did you happen to find these?"

"I just opened the book, and there they were."

She looked at me a moment before speaking again. "Savannah, you know full well that I'm asking you why you were in Joanne Clayton's bedroom this evening in the first place."

"That's easy," I said with a smile. "I was helping Rob Hastings install new locks at Joanne's house."

She took a deep breath and then let it out before she spoke again. "I was under the impression that you were a puzzlemaker, not a locksmith. And you work at the hardware store on the side?"

"Tell her why you were really there," Zach said.

I didn't have much choice at that point. I had to admit that my cover story didn't really bear up well under close scrutiny. "I wanted to snoop around Joanne's place to see if I could figure out who killed her."

"That's what I suspected," she said. The captain turned to Zach and asked, "And you approve of this behavior?"

"I'm not ashamed to say that I even encouraged it, and you should, too," he said. "There are things that Savannah can find out that we might not be privy to. Folks around here will talk more openly with her than they will with either one of us."

I wasn't certain about the validity of that statement, but I was in no position to dispute it.

"Did you allow her to assist you on cases when you ran the city of Charlotte's police department?" Captain North asked.

"Of course not. That was different," Zach said.

"In what way?"

"She didn't have a stake in any of them. This case directly involves her, and I'm not the officer in charge of the investigation. We can use what Savannah finds, if we just let her help."

"That's out of the question. Frankly, given your reputation, I can't believe you are even suggesting it."

"Well, believe it. Look what was missed by the officers investigating the scene: a box of money and an incriminating set of notes that might have been written to one person, or possibly three."

Captain North didn't look all that pleased with Zach pointing out the ineffectiveness of the police search. "I wasn't at the scene investigating the victim's home, but you can be sure I'll have a word with the officers who were there."

Zach kept frowning at her. "You have to admit, both of these clues could turn out to be valuable."

"That's beside the point," she said, raising her voice. "I can't have an amateur meddling in my investigation. This has to end, right here and right now. Understood?"

I wasn't exactly certain what to say to that. Fortunately, I didn't have to say anything. Zach turned to me and asked, "Savannah, would you mind stepping out for a minute? I want to talk to Captain North cop to cop." My husband looked at me with a plea for me to comply in his expression, and I decided this was not the time to disagree with him.

"Go ahead; take all of the time you need. I don't mind a bit." That was one discussion I had no problem missing out on. "I'll be outside if you need me."

I walked out into the bracing autumn air, knowing that winter was just around the corner. I loved the snow—it gave everything a clean and refreshed texture—but autumn was still my favorite time of the year. Even with the trees nearly barren of their leaves, there was something in the crispness of the breeze that suited me as it rattled through the stragglers still clinging to their old perches.

I stood under a pin oak, its brown leaves all still in place, and listened to the wind. I wasn't certain how long I stood there looking up as the leaves moved in unison with each gust, but I was surprised when I heard someone call my name. I hadn't even been aware that anyone could see me.

When I looked toward the sound of the voice, I saw

that it was the coffee shop owner. "Barbara, what are you doing out here?"

To my surprise, she actually smiled at me—something I hadn't been expecting, given our last conversation where I'd walked out on her.

"I always take a walk around town this time of evening," she said. I had a hard time believing that. When I took a stroll, I wore tennis shoes, blue jeans, and an old jacket, but Barbara was wearing a dress and a pair of flats. Still, to each her own.

"It is a glorious night, isn't it?" I asked.

"I think so. I've been meaning to speak with you, Savannah. I may have been a little abrupt with you when you came to me for help yesterday."

"Not at all. I understand your position completely. You were right to ask that I keep our conversation private. I'm just sorry I couldn't make you the promise you asked me to."

She shrugged slightly. "That's what I've been mulling over. You could have easily lied to me, you know. That way you could have had my input and told your husband afterward. I would have never known."

"Probably not, but I would have, and that's all that matters. I won't give my word if I have no intention of keeping it," I said.

"I can't tell you how much I admire your candor. I've changed my mind. I'll help you," she said.

This was almost too good to be true. Barbara could let me in on the secrets of Parson's Valley like no one else could, even Rob. I still had to be sure she understood my position before I accepted any aid from her. "Even if I tell Zach everything we talk about?"

"As long as it's just him, I can live with that. I have to trust a former police chief's discretion. What do you say?"

I looked around, but there was still no sign of my husband. That didn't mean he wouldn't show up soon, though. "I can't do it right now. I'm so sorry, but Zach is going to be here any minute."

Barbara laughed. "I didn't mean right now. Why don't you come by first thing tomorrow morning? We can have a cup of coffee outside if it's nice, and I might have some solid information for you by then."

"Are you saying you don't mind being seen out with me?" That, too, was a turnaround from her previous position.

"Of course not," she said with a smile.

I wasn't about to let it go that easily, though. "The reason I ask is because before we were meeting in your back room like a couple of anarchists plotting to overthrow the government."

"It's nothing as dire as all that," she said. "We have every right to chat in public as much as anyone else does. I'll see you in the morning."

"I'll be there," I said as she started to stroll away. "And, Barbara?"

She paused and looked back at me.

"Thank you."

That brought out a hint of laughter in her voice. "You're welcome. We're going to have fun."

Zach came up and joined me a few seconds after she was gone. "What was that all about?"

"Were you spying on me?"

"No, to be honest with you, I was mostly just ducking Barbara. Was it my imagination, or did I actually see her smiling?"

"You weren't mistaken. She wants to meet in the morning so we can talk about Joanne's murder."

He looked steadily at me as he asked, "Did you promise not to tell me anything you learned?"

"No. As a matter of fact, she told me I could tell you everything, as long as you were discreet. Why does everyone think you can keep a secret but I can't? I'm beginning to be a little offended by it."

"Don't let it bother you too much."

I shrugged. "I'll try. How did it end with the captain?"

"She's not happy about what you're doing, but she's not going to throw you in jail for it, either, so I suppose that's some type of progress."

"How does she feel about you?"

He frowned. "That's a different story altogether. Can we talk as we go back to the car?"

"That's fine with me. What should we talk about? The weather's just about perfect, isn't it? Do you think we'll get much snow this year? I think we should plant more trees out back; what do you think?"

Zach laughed as he said, "Slow down, woman. I wasn't looking for random topics. There's something specific that I want to discuss with you."

"Sorry, I thought you were trying to fill some kind of lag in the conversation. What's up?"

He took his time telling me, so I knew it was most likely something I wasn't going to like. "I need to take you home so I can tag along with North when she goes to Joanne's to interview Laura in twenty minutes."

"How did you manage that?" I asked.

"A little bit of flattery and a whole lot of groveling," he said with a grin.

"Okay," I said simply.

"It can't be as easy as that, is it?" he asked as he stared openly at me.

"I'm not all that difficult to get along with," I said. "I'm just amazed you got her to agree to your presence during the interview."

"It was close, but I managed to convey the impression that Laura wouldn't talk to her without me there as well. I didn't really leave her much choice."

"Who knows?" I asked as my husband drove me home. "You might just be right. Laura trusts you, but I don't think she's too fond of any other law enforcement personnel."

As we drove the familiar roads, I asked, "What does she hope to accomplish by talking to Laura? She really wasn't much a part of Joanne's life. Captain North knows that, doesn't she?"

"I have no idea, but it took a major miracle to get to tag along, so I'm not going to blow it."

He pulled up in our drive, and I got out.

"I might be late," Zach said as he drove away.

That meant there was no real reason for me to stay home, now that I had my own transportation.

I had time to do a little more digging on my own, and I was going to take full advantage of it.

First things first, though. I knew what I'd told Laura, but I needed to see Rob and bring him up to speed on what I'd found out at Joanne Clayton's house. I also needed to let him know about my new arrangement with Barbara. It was only fair, and I wanted his take on why she'd so willingly given in on her earlier demand.

I'd been stirring the pot as hard as I could, and it appeared that things were finally starting to happen.

Chapter 12

...

ON AN ORDINARY EVENING, THE HARDWARE STORE
would already be closed, but given the state of our
local economy, Rob had started to stay open later on certain nights to try to help his bottom line. For once, I was
happy that he had to, since we needed to talk.

When I got there, the parking lot was nearly deserted.
I walked inside and looked around for Rob, but I couldn't
find him anywhere. I walked over to Lee, who was putting out a display of snow shovels. "Any idea where your
boss is?"

"Hey, Savannah. The last time I saw him, he was outside with a customer in the bedding plants."

"This late in the year? I'm amazed that anyone would
wait this long to plant anything."

Lee shrugged. "You know my boss. If we've got it in stock, Rob's going to sell it."

I started to go out the side entrance to where Rob kept his plants for sale. From early spring to mid-autumn, he offered flowers and vegetables of all kinds to his customers, but the area was rather barren at the moment.

I spied him through some dead ferns hanging from baskets and was about to speak when I realized that his customer was still there.

I couldn't believe it when I saw that he was talking to Harry Pike, one of the suspects on my list. From the clouds on Harry's brow, it was a good bet that they weren't discussing the chances a dried-up tomato plant had of producing a crop this year, either. There was clear and obvious tension between the two men.

But I had no idea what it could be about, so I tried to get a little closer to hear.

Harry said, "I'm not telling you that, so stop asking."

Rob replied, "Do you honestly think you have any choice? Talk to me, Harry. I'm not messing around here."

Harry said something I couldn't hear, so I took another step closer. Too close, it turned out, as a terra-cotta potted fern slipped off the hook and plummeted to the concrete, shattering the pot it had been in.

Both men looked at me as though I'd fired a shotgun at them, which, on reflection, was probably what the pot had sounded like when it had exploded on the ground.

"Hey, Savannah," Harry said as he quickly scurried away.

I walked up to Rob and said, "Sorry about killing your pot. I'd be glad to pay for it."

"Don't worry about it, Savannah; it was cracked anyway."

"What were you and Harry talking about? And don't try to say it was ferns, because I know better. I saw the look on his face when you pressed him. You were asking him about Joanne, weren't you?"

Rob knelt down and picked up most of the major shards of pottery after he threw the dead fern on a compost bin in one corner. He looked almost relieved as he admitted, "Harry knows something. I'm sure of it. I was just about to get it out of him when that pot fell."

"Sorry, I didn't mean to sabotage your investigation. Why didn't you wait for me, though?"

"You were busy at Joanne's," he said. "Harry came by unexpectedly, so I decided to take a chance and talk to him without you."

"I wish you wouldn't do that," I said as I got a broom and started sweeping up the remnants of the soil and the pot as Rob finished with the pottery pieces.

"I'm not going to apologize," he said with a smile. "I saw an opportunity, and I took it."

I knew arguing with him about it was just a waste of breath. "If you have to go out on your own, at least keep me posted on what you find out. Can you do that much for me?"

"If you return the favor."

"You know I will," I said as I finished with the broom.

Rob looked at me with a smile on his face as he asked, "What happened at Joanne's, anyway? I was expecting Laura to scream at you when she found you snooping around in the bedroom, but when I came in later, you two were acting like old buddies. I don't understand how you were able to manage that."

"It might have helped that I found a box full of money," I said.

Rob's eyes lit up. "Are you serious? How much did you find?"

"A little over eleven thousand dollars," I said. "But keep it to yourself. No one's supposed to know." I realized too late that I'd promised Laura to keep her secret. I just hoped it didn't come back to bite me later.

I wasn't expecting the level of his disappointment at my discovery. "It's not exactly a fortune, is it?"

"I wouldn't turn it down if someone gave it to me. Would you?"

"Of course not," he said. "Was there anything else?"

The letters were an entirely different story. They were now a part of the police investigation, and I felt hesitant about sharing that particular bit of information with him. I was about to tell him no when my phone rang. It was squawking ducks, so I knew it had to be Zach. "Hang on."

"Hey, what's up?" I asked as I answered my phone.

My husband's voice was somber as he asked, "Have you said anything to anyone about the notes you found?"

"No. I just told Rob about the money."

Zach let out a breath, and then said, "That shouldn't be a problem, but the captain wants to keep the existence of the notes to the three of us. Laura doesn't know, either, does she?"

"I didn't mention it," I said.

"Good enough. That's it. I've got to go."

I said good-bye to dead air, and looked up to find Rob staring at me curiously. "What was that all about?"

"He wants us to keep the money found between ourselves. I probably wasn't supposed to mention it to you, but we made a deal. Can you keep the secret?"

"Of course I can," he said. "Was there anything else?"

"Just something unrelated to what we're doing," I lied.

I owed a great deal more loyalty to my husband than I did to Rob. I tried to sound disappointed when I added, "That's too bad. I thought the money was a real clue."

"I don't know," Rob said. "I keep a fair amount of cash on hand in a safe myself. It's just natural given the volatile times we live in. What did Zach say about it?"

"He's not sure that it means anything yet, but he doubts that it has any real significance."

"But we can keep digging into the case?" Rob asked.

We were on delicate territory now. "I have to say that until the officer heading the investigation tells me personally to stop what I'm doing, I'm considering it a green light to keep snooping."

"Then I will, too. Who's next on our list? Is there anyone else we should speak with, or should we focus on the suspects we have so far?"

"There's something else we need to discuss first," I said.

He didn't look at all pleased by my statement. "Whenever a woman tells me we need to talk, it's never good news, is it?"

"It's not that," I said as I put the broom away. "Barbara has had a change of heart, and she's decided to help as well."

Rob looked a little deflated by the information. "Did you promise to shut Zach out on what you find?"

"No," I said carefully, "but he's the only one I can tell. I'm sorry. I'm not trying to exclude you, but I had no choice. I appreciate all you've done, but if you want to drop out, it's okay with me."

"No," he said after a few moments of thought. "I think you did the right thing. Barbara can be a help, but so can I. I say we keep going."

"It's a deal." I was relieved by Rob's acceptance of another coconspirator working on the case.

"What's next?" he asked.

I thought about it, and tried to come up with a viable suspect we could talk to. Maybe it was time to speak with Sandra again and see why she'd suddenly had a falling-out with Laura. It might reveal more than she wanted us to know.

WHEN WE GOT TO NATHAN'S LAW OFFICE, THERE WAS a sign on the door saying that it had already closed. It had been a long shot, but one worth taking.

"We could always try her at home," Rob suggested.

I stifled a yawn. "Let's save it for another day. I haven't been sleeping well, and I'm beat. Do you mind?"

He looked clearly disappointed as he said, "No, that's fine with me."

I had a sudden hunch that my friend was putting on a show. "Rob, don't talk to her without me."

He shrugged. "If I run into her, I'm not going to ignore the woman."

"You know perfectly well what I mean. Sandra can wait until another day. Surely there's got to be something else you can do this evening."

"Nothing comes to mind," he said.

I suddenly felt a little guilty having someone to go home to, even if Zach wasn't there at the moment. Rob must have been lonely, given the years since his wife had passed away. "I'm sorry; I didn't mean anything by that."

"Go home, Savannah," he said with a slight smile. "I'll stay out of trouble so you can go and get some rest."

"It's a deal," I said. I dropped him off at the hardware

store and drove back to the cottage. Darkness was already creeping in, but I knew that the worst of it was just beginning. Sometimes I loved daylight saving time, but there were moments when I wished we'd leave time alone. It always took me a few weeks to get my internal clock matched back up with most of the rest of the country, and I found myself admiring those pockets of resistance that had refused to go along with the majority.

Zach's car was still gone; no real surprise there. I parked out front and walked up onto the porch. The motion detector in the porch light switched on for one minute, giving me time to dig my keys out of my purse and unlock the door. I had lobbied for a longer delay before it shut itself off, but Zach had insisted that a minute was plenty of time.

I grabbed my keys as I looked at the front door.

There was a note taped there.

In block letters, it read, DROP IT OR DIE.

It was short, to the point, and emphatic, with a promise attached if I disobeyed.

It seemed that I'd managed to get under someone's skin.

I started to pull it off the door, then changed my mind, staring at it as I tried to figure out who I'd goaded into threatening me.

I MUST HAVE BEEN STANDING THERE MOTIONLESS FOR AT least a minute, because the light snapped itself off. I was about to move to activate it again when a pair of headlights came up the drive. I couldn't make out who it was, but I wasn't sure I wanted to broadcast my presence on the front porch. I felt vulnerable standing there alone and unarmed, but if I moved, I'd give the visitor light to see me by. That would make me an easy target in case they decided to come back and put their threat into action.

I held my breath as the car approached, and when I finally realized that it was Zach, I started toward him. The light came back on, and I was caught in his headlights.

The note fluttered in the breeze as I ran across the drive toward my husband.

As Zach got out of his car, I nearly knocked him over with my flying tackle. He held me for a few moments, and then he asked, "Savannah, what's wrong? Did something happen?"

As I buried my face into his chest, I said, "I'm so glad you're home."

"What is it? What's going on?" he asked as he stroked my hair. It was clear from his tone of voice that he was worried about me.

"Someone left us a note on the door," I said.

"Let me see it."

He finally broke our hug and walked toward the house.

After he read the note, Zach shook his head. "We're dealing with an amateur; there's no doubt about it."

"Why do you say that?" I asked as I stared at the note.

"Anybody with any experience wouldn't have warned you first." Zach took a pair of gloves and a plastic bag out of his pocket. He was always prepared, something that I teased him about from time to time. After taking a photo with his cell phone, Zach collected the note, careful to preserve the tape. Once it was secure, he said, "If they'd been pros, they would have been waiting for you in the bushes when you drove up and taken care of you without announcing anything as dramatic as this."

I searched wildly around for a few moments, knowing all the while that I was being paranoid, but still not able to help myself. "If they were trying to scare me, it's working. Can we go inside?"

"You can drop your end of this investigation; you know that, don't you? Why don't you go visit one of your uncles? I know either one of them would be thrilled to see you." One lived in Hickory, and the other stayed in Charlotte most of the time, so visiting either one would get me away from Asheville, Parson's Valley, and a murderer who wasn't pleased with me, but I couldn't bring myself to do it.

"I'm sorry. I'm just not made that way," I said. "I might not like being threatened, but I'm not letting anyone run me off." I tapped the bagged note in his hand. "Besides, I'm clearly getting to someone."

"Any idea who that might be?" Zach asked.

"I have a suspect list," I admitted.

"I would have been surprised if you didn't," he said with a reassuring smile. "Why don't we go inside where it's warm and talk about it."

Zach checked the door, saw that it was still locked, and then led me in. I noticed that he wasn't easy until he was certain that the visitor hadn't made their way inside our home.

"Aren't we going to call Captain North and tell her about this?" I asked as we walked into the living room together.

"To be honest with you, I'm still not sure what I should do about it. We're on precarious ground here, Savannah. On the one hand, she probably has a right to know, but on the other, the only thing telling her would do would be to rub her nose in the fact that you're digging into the murder investigation. It took everything I had to get her to allow me to keep tagging along. Something like this would end every last shred of her patience with both of us."

"Then we keep this to ourselves," I said.

"For now." Zach put the note on top of the bookshelf in our living room. "I'm starving. How about you?"

"As a matter of fact, I am. Are you offering to cook?"

"Given my limited range, I am."

I laughed, happy for the opportunity to do so. Zach recognized the tension in me, and he also realized the best way to break it.

"No chili," I said.

"That limits what I can offer you, then," he said.

"Then I'll cook," I said with a smile. "I don't have time to make a full dinner, but how about some chicken noodle soup and grilled cheese sandwiches?"

"Is the soup going to be homemade?" he asked.

"Would I serve you anything else?"

"Is the cheese cheddar?"

"Yes, I know what you like."

"I don't like those little processed squares," he added.

"I'll save those for mine. Is there anything else, your majesty?"

"Nothing I can think of, but I'll get back to you if I think of something."

I laughed as I started the soup. Zach was doing his best to wipe away the remnants of my fear, and he was doing a great job. That was one of the advantages to being married so long to the same person. We could read each other most of the time as though we were holding up big signs.

I found a great deal of comfort in that, and I knew that Zach did, too.

* * *

AFTER WE ATE, ZACH GOT OUT A WHITE LEGAL PAD, READY to take some notes.

"Let's start with your list of suspects," he said.

"Okay. Let's see," I said as I consulted my mental list and started ticking names off with my finger. "We've got Laura Moon, Sandra Oliver, and Harry Pike to start with, and we can't forget Greg Lincoln and Hannah Reed, either."

"Hang on, I'm writing as fast as I can." After a minute, he finished and looked up at me. "Is that it?"

"So far," I said.

I was expecting to go on to motives and alibis after that, but Zach surprised me by asking, "Who else has taken an interest in the case?"

"Besides us, and Captain North, you mean?"

"I can put all of us on the suspect list, but I don't think that would be very productive, do you?"

"Not so much. Let's see, I guess Rob's name would have to go there."

"And Barbara's, too," he said as he wrote her down.

"I came to her first, remember?"

"Funny, I thought I saw her approach you today."

"You did," I admitted.

"Then it shows interest, especially after you turned her down so thoroughly. Anyone else?"

I tried to think of everyone I'd spoken to recently about Joanne. "Not that I can think of."

"Then we'll leave a little room at the bottom, just in case. Now, we need to tackle motives."

"I've got them for just about everyone," I said.

"You've been busy, haven't you?"

"I have my moments," I admitted.

Zach's writing hand paused.

"Is anything wrong?" I asked.

"I was just wondering, is there any chance we have any ice cream left?"

I couldn't believe it after all he'd eaten. "Are you honestly still hungry? We just ate."

He frowned slightly. "There's nothing wrong with a little dessert."

He had a point. "I suppose I might have a little room myself."

I started to get up when he said, "You stay here. I'll get it. After all, that's the least I can do, and I mean it."

"You could always do dishes, if you wanted to be really helpful."

He nodded. "You're right. I haven't done them in a while. Let's skip the ice cream and I'll get right on the dishes." We'd discussed installing a dishwasher in the cottage since we'd moved in, but it wouldn't be an easy, or inexpensive, fix, so for the time being, we were hand-washing our things.

"I don't mind doing them later," I said.

"Nope, I've made up my mind. You write while I wash. Let's go work on this in the kitchen."

I wasn't about to try to discourage him anymore. "Okay, that works fine for me."

"You aren't putting up more of a fight than that?"

I grinned at him. "Not today."

As he filled the right bowl of the sink with warm, sudsy water, I took his legal pad and started to write.

"Hey," he protested, "I don't mind doing these, but you wouldn't mind doing that out loud, would you?"

"Sorry, I got carried away," I said.

"I get it. I know how you are. What have you got so far?"

I started reading from the list. "Harry's got a land deal with Joanne that's worth a great deal of money; Joanne supposedly stole something of value from Sandra—"

He cut me off. "Any idea what that's all about? She wouldn't tell us a thing when we interviewed her."

"No. She denied it to me as well. Rob and I were going to try to talk to her this evening about it again, but she and Nathan were already gone when we got there."

"You two are a regular team on this, aren't you?"

"What's the matter—jealous?" I asked.

"Maybe a little," he said as he moved a glass to the other sink to rinse it. "You do seem to be spending a lot of time together lately."

"We're working on the case," I said. "You're kidding, right?"

"Mostly I am," he conceded. "Is there anything wrong with wanting to keep my wife?"

"Not in my book," I said as I gave him a kiss. "I have no desire to be with anyone else."

"Me, either," he said. After washing a bowl, Zach said, "I'd love to know what Joanne took from Sandra."

"It could be important. We need to ask her again."

Zach considered that, and then said, "Maybe you should ask Laura. After all, she's the one who told us about it in the first place."

"That's another thing," I said. "Laura told me at Joanne's place today that Sandra isn't speaking to her anymore."

He paused with a plate in his hand. "That's odd. I thought those two were inseparable."

"Apparently so did Laura."

"Okay, let's move on. How about Laura herself?"

"She's due to inherit everything Joanne owned, but according to her, that won't be much of anything after the bills are all paid, even though I find that hard to believe, given what I've seen so far. Hang on a second, she knows about the land deal with Harry Pike. That changes everything."

"We need to dig a little deeper into what she knows, and when she learned it," Zach said. "The timing of it all could mean everything. If she knew about the money and property beforehand, it could change everything."

"I'll try, but money is always hard to discuss."

"You can do it, Savannah. I have faith in you. Besides, you already have an in, there."

"You're talking about the money we found, aren't you?"

"I am. That eleven grand just might be the key to this whole thing," Zach said. "Where do you suppose it came from?"

"I've been trying to figure that out since we found it. Could she have been saving it over the years?"

My husband frowned. "A shoe box isn't much of a vault, is it?"

"I don't know. It's better than putting it under her mattress."

Zach rinsed another bowl and put it in the drying rack. "I still can't believe the police missed it. North couldn't understand it, either."

"None of them are as competent as the great Zach Stone," I said with a grin. "But then who is?"

"True, it's a high bar I set when I was an officer of the

law," he said, laughing. "What other reasons do you have that might lead to murder?"

"Greg had a lover's quarrel with Joanne before she died, and Hannah believes that Joanne ran her son out of town forever. Those could both be pretty strong motives."

"I hope if anything happens to me they don't find so many folks with a motive for murder," he said.

"Don't worry, I'm certain they'll focus their investigation all on me," I said with a smile.

"You would be the most likely suspect," he said.

"Hey!"

"Statistically speaking," he added with a chuckle.

"Now that we have our list, what do we do next?"

"Aren't we forgetting something?" he asked as he finished rinsing the pot I'd made the soup in.

"No, I think you got them all," I said as I looked around the kitchen.

"Suspects," he said. "Do we have motives for Barbara and Rob?"

I decided to go along with him. "Well, Rob said Joanne had been friends with his wife. Maybe there's an old grudge there."

"It's possible. How about Barbara?"

"I don't have anything yet, but we're meeting in the morning to discuss the case, so I'll see what I can come up with then."

As Zach let the water drain out of the sink, I said, "You know what? I'm in the mood for ice cream after all."

"Sorry, but the kitchen is now officially closed."

"You're kidding, right?" I asked as I reached into the cabinet for a clean coffee mug. I liked to use them instead of bowls, trying to fool myself into believing that if I used a smaller vessel, I'd have a reduced portion as well. It rarely worked, though. I usually ended up just filling the cup more than once.

"I'm not washing that," he said.

"Relax, I'll rinse it when I'm through and take care of it tomorrow. Care to join me?"

"When you put it that way, how can I refuse?"

Chapter 13

...

ZACH WAS GONE BY THE TIME I GOT UP THE NEXT MORN-ing, something that wasn't out of the ordinary most days, but especially when he was wrapped up in a case. My husband had an obsessive quality to his personality, and it had bothered me when we'd first started dating, but I knew better than to ever try to change it. That was one of the reasons I loved him now. He could put an intense focus on whatever he cared about, and fortunately, one of the things he cared about most in the whole world was me.

I made myself a quick breakfast, and then got into town a full two minutes before I was due to meet with Barbara. I had no idea why she was so eager to help me with my investigation so actively all of a sudden, but I was going to do my best to find out.

I had just walked into Brewster's Brews when Barbara herself greeted me at the door. "Savannah, I'm so glad you could make it," she said as she showed me to a table by the window. It also happened to be somewhat isolated from her other customers. I wasn't sure whether she was doing it for my sake, or hers.

"Thanks," I said, startled as she took my coat and laid it on one of the free chairs at our table. When I sat down, I found a coffee waiting for me—just the way I liked it— and a fresh cranberry scone. "I don't know what to say."

"Think nothing of it. I want to apologize for my rudeness before. There was no reason for me to act the way I did."

"It's not necessary. You had every right to make the request that you did. I just can't lie to my husband."

"That's an admirable trait," she said. "I shouldn't have tried to punish you for it."

What was going on here? "Barbara, is everything okay?"

"Everything's absolutely perfect," she said. "Why do you ask?"

"You have to admit that your change of heart was pretty sudden," I said, and then took a sip of her delicious coffee.

"Are you questioning my motives?" Barbara asked softly.

"Absolutely," I said, making my voice match hers.

I wasn't sure how it was going to end up for a few seconds, but suddenly she smiled. "I've underestimated you, and that's something that I rarely do. You're stronger than you seem to be at first glance, aren't you?"

"I don't know about that. I just like to know the motives behind the actions that people take."

Barbara thought about it for a few seconds, and then said, "I guess I just hate the fact that something's been going on in my town, and I didn't have a clue it was happening."

"I didn't realize Parson's Valley belonged to you," I said with a smile.

She laughed at that. "It doesn't—I know that—but I still feel overprotective toward it."

"And that's it?" I asked.

She shrugged. "Okay, I'm nosy; I admit it. You intrigued me with your request for information, so I started doing some digging on my own despite our misunderstanding. I found something out in the process."

"What's that?" I asked, honestly curious about her reply.

"It's harder to sit on information someone else could use than I ever would have imagined. Will you indulge me?"

"I'd love to hear what you've uncovered," I answered.

The gleam in her eyes was bright as she lowered her voice and said, "I've got some information that's going to interest you. I guarantee it."

"I'm listening," I said as I took a bite of scone. It was delicious, and I had to wonder if Emma Parson had made it in her bakery. I was glad the baker's name hadn't come up in my investigation so far. It was good to have someone I liked that I didn't consider a suspect in a murder case. She was the other person I knew I could rely on, but thankfully, I hadn't had to ask her for help yet. How nice it would be if I didn't have to involve both of the folks who helped make Parson's Valley home to me. I'd already dragged Rob straight into the middle of my mess, but so far, Emma was safe.

Barbara said, "To begin with, I understand you've been

speaking with Greg Lincoln. That's very astute of you, Savannah. Not many folks in town knew what was going on between him and Joanne." It was clear by her praise that she herself had known all along.

I didn't want to tell her that I'd gotten Greg's name from Rob. It wasn't that I wanted the credit. I was more concerned with keeping his role in my investigation as neutral as I could. "Do you have anything on Greg?"

"I know for a fact that he was absent from the barbershop for at least ninety-five minutes on the day Joanne was murdered. That would give him plenty of time to drive to Asheville, kill her, and make it back here."

That didn't jibe with what I already knew. "He told me that he takes an hour for lunch every day, no more and no less."

Barbara nodded. "That's normally true, but I've been asking around, and Kyle Peeler complained that Greg was closed when he went by for a trim at ten thirty, and I saw him myself fiddling with his keys at five minutes after twelve."

"That's interesting," I said. If it was true, she was right. That kind of timeline would give Greg plenty of time to kill Joanne and get back to Parson's Valley to open up for the afternoon.

"Is there anything else?" I asked after taking another sip of coffee.

"Oh, we're just getting started," she said. There was a tone of joy in her voice that was unmistakable. Barbara was having the time of her life. No wonder she was being so nice to me. I was sure she was just about to the bursting point with all of her information, and she had no one to tell it to who could truly appreciate it but me.

"Okay, go on," I said.

She looked around the room a second, and then added, "I understand you've been trying to figure out what Joanne stole from Sandra."

That caught me by surprise. How good were her sources, anyway? It had been the right decision to come to her in the first place for her knowledge and her contacts. "How could you possibly know that?"

Joanne grinned at me. "I can't really divulge that information, but I've got a good idea what it means, if you're still interested."

"You know I am," I said eagerly. "I'll take whatever I can get. I'm not that choosy."

"Good. Two years ago, Sandra was seeing a married man in Edgemont. No one was supposed to know about it, but I heard through the grapevine that he offered to leave his wife and marry her. Joanne got wind of it and went to the man's wife first. In the guise of doing the right thing, she told her all about the affair. The woman confronted her husband, and then threatened to go after sole custody of their children if he followed through with his plans. He couldn't handle that, so he dumped Sandra and ended up staying with his wife. Sandra was furious when she found out what had happened, and she hasn't softened her position of wanting Joanne dead ever since."

"So she didn't steal anything material," I said. "Joanne stole Sandra's future, at least in her mind."

Barbara looked deadly serious as she said, "Think about it. Is there anything worse you could take from someone else?"

"Hang on a second," I said. "I heard them talking the day Joanne was murdered. Sandra was cool to her, but she was still cordial. It's hard to believe that there was so much bubbling just beneath the surface."

"Think about it, Savannah. What would she have to lose by being gracious if she planned to kill Joanne later? I'm surprised she wasn't grinning from ear to ear."

That definitely gave me something else to think about. "Okay, I'll look into that as well."

One of Barbara's employees came over to us and said, "Sorry to bother you, but that machine is on the fritz again."

"I'm busy, Juney," she said.

"It's going to mean that we'll lose some business," the woman said.

"Then we'll just have to deal with it. This is more important."

Juney clearly had a hard time believing that was possible. After she returned to the counter, I said, "We can do this later if you'd like."

"Savannah, it's not going to get any slower in here than it is right now. I've got two more things to tell you before you go, but I'll have to make it quick."

"I appreciate it."

"Happy to help." Barbara lowered her head a little as she added, "Laura has been acting like she didn't realize that Joanne had money, hasn't she?"

"That's the impression I've been getting, yes," I admitted.

"I've got a feeling that she knew exactly how much Joanne was worth, though I can't say whether or not she knew that she was going to inherit *everything*. I'm pretty sure she knew that she was getting *something*. I just don't have any hard evidence to support it."

"What else have you got?" I asked as I saw that the place was starting to really fill up.

"I know he's been helping you dig around, but I also

know for a fact that Rob Hastings always blamed Joanne for his wife's death."

"What are you talking about? I haven't heard that before."

"Nobody ever wanted to say it, but it was true then, and it's still true today. Watch your step. You might have more on your hands than you realize by taking him into your confidence." She looked back at the counter, where Juney was waving frantically to her. "I'm sorry, but I really do have to go, Savannah. I hope I helped."

"More than I can say. Thanks again, Barbara."

She was beaming as she left me, but I was more troubled than ever. If I accepted everything she told me as fact, it raised some serious questions about the people I'd been talking to about Joanne. The real question was if I could believe everything she'd said. Was Greg's barbershop really closed longer than he'd admitted, giving him ample time to kill Joanne and get back into town? Did Laura know Joanne had money? It could be an excellent motive for murder. Could Sandra have blamed Joanne for ruining her life with her lover? And the most disturbing question of all was whether Rob blamed Joanne for his wife's death. I knew he thought about her all of the time. If what Barbara had told me was true, it would give Rob the perfect motive: avenging his wife's death.

That brought another question to mind.

How had Rob's wife, Becky, died?

I had to find out before I spoke with him again. If it was true that it was something he could blame Joanne for, it could be time for some hard questions soon.

* * *

I'D HAD ENOUGH HEARSAY AND INNUENDO. GOSSIP SEEMED to be all my investigation was fueled by, with an errant fact thrown in here and there. It was time to ignore what people were telling me and focus on what solid and provable information I could collect. I considered going to Zach for help in finding the cause of death for Becky Hastings, but I knew he was already skating a thin line with Captain North. Since I couldn't access police records, it might be time to tackle the local newspaper's archives to see what I could find there.

WHEN I GOT TO THE OFFICE OF OUR BRANCH OF THE main newspaper, it was dark inside, and there was a sign posted on the door.

It read, "Sorry for the inconvenience, but due to budgetary cutbacks, this office has been absorbed into our parent newspaper in Asheville. *Parson's Valley News* will now be consolidated into one section of the *Asheville Daily News* until further notice. Thank you."

It appeared that we no longer had a local paper. Given the state of the newspaper business, it was a sad statement, especially for me, since that was the exclusive method by which my puzzles were delivered to the world. I'd been considering trying to branch out into other means of distribution, but so far my tentative inquiries had been met with stony silence.

If I couldn't dig into the newspaper's archives, I knew another place I could go. I headed over to the library to see if I could get some information there.

And when I walked up the steps, I saw that the hours it was open to the public had been reduced as well. Its doors were locked and its stacks darkened, and I wondered what that said about our civilization when our access to information seemed to be solely controlled by a blind and uncaring Internet that many times presented fact and fiction in the exact same light. Content generated online could be from learned professionals with decades of study and experience in their field, or from one lonely guy sitting in a basement somewhere wearing a tinfoil hat to protect him from thought-rays from outer space. The problem was, at times it was difficult, if not impossible, to tell the two sources apart.

There was one place I could go where I still had hope. If it turned out to be another dead end, I'd have to find Zach and get his help after all.

THE COUNTY HALL OF RECORDS WAS ON THE OPPOSITE side of the building as the Register of Deeds. One dealt with property and chattel, while the other covered the people who inhabited our county. There was a great deal of history there, if the searcher only knew the right way to gather information.

At least they were open. I studied the computer terminal for a few minutes before a gruff middle-aged man with a salt-and-pepper beard approached.

"You know what you're doing?"

"I haven't got a clue," I said with a smile.

He stopped and grinned at my confession. "At least you admit it. They say that's always the first step. What exactly are you looking for?"

"A death certificate for someone who died several years ago."

"Yeah, we have those on file in the system." He tapped a few keys until a new screen came up. Instead of asking me for my information so he could enter it himself, he said, "Type the name here, and anything else you know about the person. That will do a search of our stored archives."

"I'm afraid that the name is the sum total of my information."

He nodded. "That should still be good enough, unless it's a variant of John Smith you're looking for."

I started to tell him Becky's full name when he held up one hand. "Keep it to yourself. I don't want to know."

"You seem to have a remarkably low sense of curiosity," I said.

He shrugged as he replied, "I've learned over time that the less I know, the better off I am."

"So, you're trying to achieve a state of blessed ignorance, is that it?" I said it before I realized how it must sound to someone else. I had that problem sometimes, saying things before the gatekeeper in my head could act to shut them off or let them on through.

He wasn't offended at all. "You've got it. Let me ask you something. Do you have flotsam and jetsam of useless information from life floating around in your head? Something like your eighth grade locker combination, or the telephone number of your best friend from high school who moved away from home decades ago?"

"Of course I do. Everyone does, don't they?"

He looked around the room at the ledgers and the computer monitors. "Now multiply that by a thousand, and you'll see what I'm up against. I was genuinely interested in every search that was made here at first, but I soon learned that if I was going to survive this job, I'd better learn to block most of it out."

It was the most curious personal philosophy I believed I'd ever heard. "If you feel that way, why do you continue to work here?" I wasn't being nosy; I was actually interested in his answer.

"It's a great job," he said with a smile, "as long as I can keep not caring about the results."

I finally got it. "You know what? I believe I understand."

"Good for you. Now type in the name you're searching for, and hit the print button if you have any luck. I'll get the printouts at the desk, but I can promise you, I won't look at the results."

"I didn't think for a moment that you would," I said.

I didn't even wait until he was back at his desk before I typed Becky Hastings's name into the search engine. There were no hits at all, which puzzled me until I realized that Becky was most likely just a nickname. I tried Rebecca Hastings, and this time I hit pay dirt.

There were three hits from the search, and in them, the collection appeared to sum up her life with important dates: her birth certificate, a marriage certificate, and the final death certificate. I had the outline of her existence in three documents, the broad strokes of a portrait that wouldn't tell me much about who the woman had been but that might shed some light on what had eventually become of her.

I skipped the birth certificate and the marriage license and went straight to the death certificate.

It took a few seconds as I scanned the document, but then I found the entry I'd been looking for: the cause of death.

I couldn't believe it.

It appeared that Becky had died from accidental poisoning.

The coincidence that it matched Joanne's murder was too big to ignore. It appeared that whoever killed Joanne might have done so to avenge Becky Hastings's murder, and there was no one in the world who had more incentive for that than my partner in crime, Rob Hastings.

It was time Rob and I had a serious conversation.

"ROB, I KNOW IT'S NOT YOUR FAVORITE EXPRESSION IN the world, but we need to talk," I said as I confronted him at his hardware store ten minutes later. He was waiting on Myron Feeney, a white-haired senior who had the biggest garden I'd ever seen in my life. That fact alone wouldn't have been odd, but Myron was a widower with no children. He donated nearly all of his produce to some of the poorer mountain folks who lived on the edges of Parson's Valley, which made him a saint in many people's eyes.

Myron laughed after I said it. "That's never a good sign when a woman tells you that, Robert. Look at the storm clouds brewing on her brow. You must have done something wrong."

"I usually do," he said. "Myron, will you excuse us for a minute?"

"I'm just about finished shopping, anyway. If you'll take a bit of advice from an old man, it has always been my experience that whatever you've done, it's best if you apologize up front and get it out of the way."

"Bye, Myron," I said. I tried to match his smile with one of my own, but I could barely bring myself to do it.

After Myron went up front so Lee could check him

out, Rob asked, "What's wrong, Savannah? You look upset."

"I get that way when people withhold information on me," I said.

"What are you talking about?"

I looked around the store, and saw that it was fairly crowded. "I don't want to have this conversation in front of everyone here," I said.

"I'm sorry, but I can't just leave Lee here all by himself. Can this wait?"

I didn't like it, but there was nothing I could do about it. "I guess it's going to have to. When can you talk?"

He glanced at the people in his hardware store. "If we don't get another rush, I should be free in about fifteen minutes. You can wait in my office until then, if you'd like."

I had no interest in staying there. What had once been a warm and inviting place now felt cold and detached from me. "No thanks. I'll be outside."

I walked out, and Myron said good-bye to me in the parking lot as I passed him. He was fumbling with his truck keys as he said, "Take it easy on him, Savannah. You might not know it, but this is a hard time for Robert."

"Why's that?" I asked as I stopped beside him.

"Two days ago was the anniversary of his wife's death," Myron said softly. "He always gets a little sad this time of year."

"Did you know her?" I asked.

He nodded, and I saw a wistful look in his eyes. "Rebecca was a charming woman. She's been missed by a great many folks over the years, I can tell you that."

"Then you knew her well," I said, pushing him.

"As a matter of fact, I did. Why do you ask?"

Maybe it would be easier getting the information from Myron than probing Rob about the circumstances of his wife's death. "It might seem like an impertinent question, but trust me when I tell you that I have a reason to ask."

As Myron stowed his goods in the back of his pickup truck, he asked, "What can I help you with?"

"How exactly did Becky die? I know it was accidental poisoning, but that's all the information I have. I was going to ask Rob about it, but it might be too painful for him to discuss, especially given the time of year."

Myron shivered a little. "It's always been a source of distress for him. What was so sad was that it could have been so easily prevented."

"What do you mean?"

Myron leaned against his pickup, and I could really see his age in his hands and his face, but most of all in his eyes. "Rebecca believed in everything natural long before it became a fad or a trend. She made her own soap, would always rather walk than drive, and did just about everything she could to leave a small footprint on the planet. One of the things she prided herself on was her herbal tea. She used to go to the Botanical Gardens in Asheville and pick out plants for her brews. While she never had any formal training, she'd become quite an accomplished botanist."

I was starting to see where this was going. "Until one day she collected the wrong plant?"

Myron nodded. "She and a friend had been out gathering all day, and they made a tea with some leaves from the wrong plant. Her friend got sick, but Rebecca reacted more violently to the chemicals in the brew, and she died before they could do anything to help her."

"It must have been horrible," I said.

"It wasn't pretty." Myron scratched his chin, and then added, "It's odd that you'd ask about Rebecca this week."

"Because of the anniversary of her death?" I asked.

"No, because of what happened in Asheville. The friend she gathered plants with that awful day was Joanne Clayton."

Chapter 14

...

"**Y**OU'RE NOT SERIOUS," I SAID.

"I wish I weren't, but it's true enough. Why, is that significant?" Myron looked honestly perplexed by my question.

"Joanne Clayton was poisoned as well," I said.

"I didn't hear that. Are you certain of your information?"

"I'm positive," I said, having a hard time believing that there was still so much I didn't know.

"I'm sure it's just a coincidence," he said. "I've known Robert his entire life. He isn't capable of murder."

"Not even to avenge his wife's death?"

Myron frowned. "No one ever blamed Joanne, including Robert. He knew his wife's nature. She could be a little reckless at times. Besides," Myron added after a moment's consideration, "it's not like Joanne didn't get sick herself."

"She didn't die though, did she?"

Myron shrugged. "No, but it was touch and go for several days, and I know for a fact that Joanne was weakened for a good many weeks from drinking the tea herself. I believe in my heart that Robert accepted it as an accident."

"How can you possibly know that with any certainty?"

"He told me so himself, just after it happened." Myron seemed to chew on the new information, and then added, "Besides, if Robert was going to exact his revenge, he wouldn't have waited so long to do it. If he suspected Joanne of murdering his wife, he would have shouted it from the rooftops, not waited patiently all these years to strike back. No, I'm sorry, but I could never believe it."

"Believe what?" Rob asked from behind me. How had he managed to approach us so quietly?

"I didn't hear you," I said.

"Soft-soled shoes," he said, pointing to his treads. "It's the only way standing on concrete all day is tolerable for me. What are you two talking about?"

"The past, with all its glory and tragedy," Myron said. As he got into his truck, he said, "If you two will excuse me, I've got work to do."

He drove away in a hurry, and Rob frowned at me. "You said something to spook him, Savannah. What were you two discussing?"

I had two options: I could lie to him, or I could tell him the truth and take my chances. It was broad daylight and there were dozens of folks out and about. I couldn't imagine a safer place to confront him about what I'd learned, though I wouldn't have minded having Zach standing right behind me.

"Rob, why didn't you tell me that your wife was poisoned?"

He looked startled by my question. "I just assumed you already knew," he said, clearly puzzled by my tone.

"We didn't live here when it happened," I said. "You know that."

He shrugged. "Sometimes it feels as though you and your husband have lived in Parson's Valley all your lives. I wasn't trying to hide anything from you, Savannah. In fact, I've been sort of waiting for you to bring it up yourself. It's a strange coincidence, isn't it?"

"I know it must be painful for you, but I'd really like for you to tell me what happened," I said.

His shoulders slumped slightly. "From the look on your face, Myron already did. Becky picked the wrong plant to make into tea, and it killed her." His voice was cold and flat as he said it, as if he were reciting a poem he'd memorized back in grade school.

"Joanne was with her when she died," I said. "You never mentioned that, either. Rob, surely you must realize that you had more reason to want her dead than anyone on our list! I've heard a rumor that you blamed Joanne for Becky's death, but you haven't said a word about it to me. I had to dig through the courthouse records to find out the truth."

"Savannah, have you been investigating me?" he asked, the outrage thick in his voice.

"I've looked at everyone who had a motive for murder," I said firmly. "Besides, I'm not about to let you blame your righteous indignation on me. I wouldn't have had to go digging into your life myself in the first place if you'd just been honest with me from the start."

"I don't like your tone of voice, or what you're implying." There was an edge there now, nothing soft and friendly about the way he was speaking to me. Perhaps I should have waited for Zach before I confronted Rob after all. "I didn't blame Joanne for what happened to Becky then, and nothing's changed my mind since. I had no reason to kill her."

"But you can still prove that you were in your hardware store all day when she was murdered, right? At least tell me that much."

He shook his head. "No, I was over at the Asheville Hardware Store picking up some supplies. I ran low on carriage bolts, and I have an arrangement with them there. They sell me whatever I need at cost, and I do the same for them. It's a courtesy, really."

This was beginning to look worse and worse for him. "Did you see Joanne while you were in town?"

"I did not," he said flatly, "and frankly, I'm insulted that you could even ask me that."

"I don't blame you. They're hard questions," I agreed, "but they have to be answered."

He shook his head. "Savannah, I thought you knew me better than this. I never expected you to accuse me of murder."

"I'm not," I said. "I'm just trying to get to the truth. Did Joanne ever write you any letters or notes?"

"Of course not. What kind of question is that?"

"I'm not exactly sure," I said.

"You'd better make sure, before you come around here again accusing me of murder."

As he started to walk away, I called out, "I'm still gathering facts."

"Well," he said as he stopped and turned to me, "you're

going to have to do it without me from here on out. It should go without saying, but I'm finished helping you."

After Rob was gone, I thought about what he'd said, and what he'd left unspoken. Would I feel different now if he'd told me from the beginning about how his wife had died? Could that have made a difference in my mind? I'd never know, because he'd held out on me, something that made me immediately suspicious of him. When I thought about enlisting him in my cause, it made my skin crawl a little. Had he really been trying to help me as he'd claimed, or had he volunteered to give me a hand so he could stay close, in case I stumbled onto the truth? What would he have done then? If Rob was the killer, I might have gotten a dose of poison myself.

I was still standing in the parking lot, and was so lost in my thoughts I nearly screamed when I heard my husband call out to me.

"Why are you so jumpy, Savannah?"

"What are you doing here?" I asked as I tried to collect my breath.

"I had a suspicion that you'd be over here." Zach looked at me closely, and then added, "You look as though you've just seen a ghost."

"Or a killer," I amended.

"What are you talking about?"

I brought him up to speed on what I'd discovered, and he nodded briefly as I talked. "That's good work."

"You didn't know about how his wife died?" I asked.

"I never had a clue. I need to tell North as soon as I can."

I suddenly felt bad about just blurting out what I'd discovered. "It doesn't mean he killed her," I said.

"It's not exactly a ringing endorsement, either, is it? North needs to talk to him herself and form her own opinions."

He got out his telephone, but before he could call, I put a hand on his arm. "Hang on a second," I said.

"What is it? Is there something else I need to know?"

"I just had a thought," I said, spinning it out as I went along. "What if the killer knew Rob's history with Joanne? Wouldn't poison be the perfect way to divert suspicion from anyone else? The timing is too spot-on to be coincidental. It's all just a little too neat, wouldn't you say?"

"Sometimes murderers think they're being clever when in actuality they're begging to be caught."

I still couldn't see it. "Would he really poison her all these years later?"

"I'm not saying that he did it," Zach said. "But the investigating officer needs to know about this. Thanks for bringing it to my attention."

He finished dialing, and I heard him in deep conversation with Captain North. It seemed that Rob was going to be getting a visit in the next few minutes because of me, and if our friendship had been hurt before, I was certain this would kill it completely. I hated it, especially if he wasn't guilty, but if it was collateral damage, there wasn't a thing I could do about it.

That didn't make it go down any better, though.

After Zach finished his call, he said, "She's coming here, and we're going to question him together."

"Zach, what if he didn't do it?"

"Then he'll have to get over it. Once he settles down, Rob will have to realize that this wasn't personal."

"That's kind of the point, though, isn't it? It doesn't get much more personal than accusing someone of murder."

He hugged me briefly, and then said, "Savannah, you know the risks connected with digging into a case. The fact that we live here just makes things that much harder. It's a great deal simpler accusing someone that you don't know of murder." He paused, and then added, "Maybe this is the time to stop your investigation."

"I'm in too deep already," I said. "I'll see it through, one way or another."

CAPTAIN NORTH DROVE UP TWO MINUTES LATER. WHEN she got out of the cruiser, she walked straight over to me. "I appreciate you bringing this to my attention. If I've been a little hard on you in the past, you should know that I was just doing my job."

"I don't think Rob did it," I blurted out. I couldn't handle looking at Zach, afraid of what his reaction to my outburst might be.

"Nobody said that you did," the state police captain said gently. "I'm not going in there accusing him of anything. It's important that we get the facts before we leap to any conclusions." She turned to Zach and said, "You can sit this one out, if you want to. I know you have to live in this town long after I'm gone."

"If you don't mind, I'd like to come in with you."

"I owe you at least that much," she said.

I waited out front as they went inside, wondering what I'd just done to Rob. If he was a murderer, which I highly doubted the more I thought about it, it was necessary, but if someone was using the circumstances of his wife's death to commit murder and blame it on him, I'd done him a huge disservice, one I was not certain he'd ever be able to forgive. Waiting was torture, but I wasn't about to budge until they had finished speaking with him.

TWENTY MINUTES LATER, THE HARDWARE STORE'S FRONT door opened and Captain North and my husband came out. She nodded to me but didn't say a word as she got into her cruiser and drove off, leaving me with Zach.

"What happened?" I asked.

"He denied everything. What did you expect, a full confession? We both know that only happens in the movies."

"Do you think he did it?" I asked, barely able to bring my voice above a whisper.

"I'm not in any position to say right now," he said.

"Cut the attitude, Zach. I'm asking you for your opinion, not what your cop's instincts are saying."

"How do I separate them, Savannah? Every conclusion I reach is based on my years of experience as a police officer. I can't just turn it off and on like some kind of switch."

"You've got to think something, one way or the other. I'm not asking for proof, just an opinion."

He shrugged, took a few moments, and then said, "I'm not entirely certain what I'm basing it on, but in my personal opinion, he had nothing to do with Joanne's murder."

I hadn't realized that I'd been holding my breath until I let it all out in a rush. "I can't tell you how relieved I am to hear that."

"You shouldn't be," he scolded me. "I have nothing to go on other than my instincts."

"I trust your gut over physical evidence and eyewitnesses any day of the week," I said.

"It's too bad Captain North doesn't share your high regard for my intuition," he said with a wry smile.

"Does she actually think he did it?"

"I wouldn't go that far, but I do believe he's shot to the top of her suspect list. She pushed him pretty hard in there, but he never wavered."

"Then we've got to help him," I said.

"Savannah, if I were you, I'd steer clear of the man until this is all settled. He's in no mood to talk to you right now."

"But I can make it better," I said plaintively.

I started to go back inside when Zach gently grabbed my arm. "How are you going to do that? I said that I didn't think he killed her, but I could be wrong. Until we know for sure, I want you to treat him as though he were covered in barbed wire, do you understand?"

"The longer this rift lasts, the harder it will be to heal," I said a little reluctantly.

"Then it's just going to have to be hard," Zach said. "At the moment, there's nothing you can do about it."

"I guess you're right," I said, "but I don't have to like it."

He laughed at that comment. "Welcome to my world. Do you have any more ideas that I don't know about?"

"More than I can list," I said. "Right now, I think just about everyone in town had a reason to want Joanne dead. It's a pretty sad testament to her life that it ended like that, isn't it?"

"She chose to be the way she was," Zach said. "Nobody made her into the person she'd become." There it was: that hard edge that my husband hid so well most of the time. His world was nearly devoid of gray, seeing mostly in black and white. That stance had eased somewhat since he'd retired, but it was still there, and we both knew it.

"We don't really know that, do we?" I asked.

"I suppose not," Zach replied, "but I'm not going to waste any time worrying about it. It's getting close to lunch," he said as he looked at his watch. "Do you have any plans?"

"Actually, I'm as free as a bird," I said. "Where would you like to go?"

"Someplace that has pie," Zach answered. "For some reason, I'm in the mood for pie."

"Is that going to be the main course, or do you have the self-control to wait until dessert?"

Zach was about to answer when his cell phone rang. After a few brief comments, he said, "I'll be right there." After he hung up, he said, "Sorry, North needs me."

"Is there a break in the case?" I asked, hoping beyond any reason that this ordeal was about to be over.

"No, she has another lead she wants to follow up on, and she thinks I might be able to help her."

"What is it?"

"I couldn't say," Zach answered.

"You aren't allowed to, or you don't know?"

He grinned at me. "A little of both, I guess. See you later."

And then he was gone before I could get anything else out of him.

It appeared that I was destined to have lunch by myself.

* * *

AT THE MOMENT, I JUST DIDN'T FEEL LIKE BEING AROUND people. I made myself a sandwich back at the cottage and started thinking about Rob, and all of the other folks from Parson's Valley that I'd interrogated about Joanne's murder recently. It was a good thing that I had no ambition to run for mayor, because I doubted I could get more than two votes at the moment. I hadn't made anyone happy with my investigation, and someone had even gone so far as to threaten me. I decided it might be time to take another look at the note I'd gotten, so I reached up to the top of the bookshelf in our living room to take it down and read it again.

The only problem was that it was gone.

I GOT OUT A CHAIR AND CHECKED AGAIN, JUST TO BE SURE I hadn't shoved it back when I'd checked on it, but all I found when I looked was a disturbed layer of dust. Besides telling me that I had to be a little more thorough the next time I dusted, it also told me that at least it had been there at one point and that I hadn't imagined it. But where could it be now? Was there a possibility that Zach had moved it? I checked every tall spot in the house, dragging the chair around with me as I went, but I had no luck finding a trace of it.

Even though I knew Zach was working with Captain North, I took a chance on calling him in case he'd moved it.

The phone went straight to voice mail, which meant he'd turned his phone off. I left my question for him, hung up, and then resumed my search.

I had my head under our bed when my phone started quacking.

"Hey," I said, a little out of breath from scrambling around for my phone.

"No reason to panic about the note," he said. "I've got it."

"Why? Did you change your mind about showing it to Captain North after all?"

"I did," he admitted. "I would have told you about it, but she called before I had a chance."

"It's not a problem. What did she say?"

"She thinks there's a chance it's legitimate, but mostly she's not reading a whole lot into it."

I thought about the implications of that statement. "That's not very reassuring, is it?"

He paused, and then said, "I took a shot. At least she knows now."

"You're right, there's always that."

My phone beeped, and I said, "I've got another call. Can you hang on a second?"

"Sorry, I've got to go. Talk to you later."

He hung up, and I hit the button for call-waiting.

I wasn't sure who I expected to be calling me, but I was still surprised to hear my Uncle Barton's voice on the other end of the line.

"How nice to hear from you," I said after he identified himself. "I was just thinking about you the other day."

"Good thoughts, I trust," my uncle said.

"Always. How's business?"

"Busy, tedious, and at times consuming," he answered. "In other words, just about the same as always."

"But still profitable, right?"

"Always." He laughed as he said, "Savannah, I miss being around you."

"I know, sometimes Charlotte seems a world away. I

don't even get to Hickory very often, and it's half the distance from us that you are."

"No need to worry. Thomas is doing well," Uncle Barton said.

"Have you spoken to him recently?"

"We talk every Thursday afternoon," he said. "I thought you were aware of that."

"It's news to me. That trip to Alaska really brought you two closer, didn't it? I'd love to go someday myself."

"What a brilliant idea. Why don't we go now?" he asked.

From anyone else, I would suspect they were teasing, but my Uncle Barton had the means to drop everything and fly across the country at a moment's notice.

"To Alaska? I can't pick up and leave everything like you can."

"I don't see why not. You're self-employed, so you can create your puzzles wherever you are. It's absolutely beautiful there. You'll love it."

I was tempted, there was no doubt about that. Still, I had some very real responsibilities here. "Sorry, but I can't."

A hint of determination came out in his voice. "Can't, or won't?"

"Zach and I are into a situation here in Parson's Valley," I explained. "I'm needed here."

"I'm sure your husband can handle things on his own. He strikes me as being quite capable," my uncle said. "We can invite Thomas as well. He'd probably welcome the opportunity to return to Anchorage himself. Did I tell you about the nature preserve we visited when we were there? It's an incredible place."

"I'm certain it is," I said. "May I ask you something?"

"Anything," he said. "You know that."

"Why the hard sell on me taking a trip with you all of a sudden?"

"It's not that sudden," he said after a moment's pause. "I've made the offer several times, and yet you continue to turn me down."

"Something I'm sure you're not all that used to," I said. "Think of my refusal as being good for your soul, a lesson in humility."

"My soul is just fine, thank you very much."

There was a pause, and he added, "It would be great fun, Savannah, I can promise you that."

Suddenly, I had a suspicion about what was driving his suggestion we take a trip. With a firm edge in my voice, I asked, "Zach called you, didn't he?"

He hesitated, and then said, "In the spirit of full disclosure, I phoned him first."

"But he told you to get me out of town." It wasn't a question, because there was no doubt in my mind that was what had happened.

It was clear that my uncle knew when he was beaten. "He suggested it, and I heartily agreed that it was an excellent idea."

"It is, but it's going to have to wait. There's been a murder here, as I'm sure my sweet husband told you, and I'm implicated in it. I'm not going anywhere until we find the killer."

"Then let me hire a private detective to work the case for you. Savannah, I have more money than I'll ever be able to spend in twenty lifetimes. Let me spend some of it on my family. I'd never be able to forgive myself if something happened to you because I was hesitant to act."

"Thank you, I do appreciate it, but I'm fine." I didn't

need a private detective muddying the waters. It was hard enough to get folks to talk to me. If we brought in yet another foreign presence, I had a feeling the information flow would shut down completely. I'd already alienated Rob, and possibly more folks in town than I realized. I couldn't afford to do any more of that.

"Are you certain?" he asked.

"I am, but that shouldn't keep you from going back to Alaska. I know you loved it up there, too."

"As a matter of fact, I'm looking into acquiring some property there."

That surprised me. I had been under the impression that my uncle's holdings were restricted to the southeastern part of the country. Alaska was many things, but part of the southern United States was not one of them.

"Are you going to buy a hotel there?"

He chuckled. "No, I'm not looking to acquire any new business properties at this moment. The last time I was there, I was looking at a lodge for my own use; and yours, too, of course. I was hoping to get your approval before I bought it, and that's the complete truth. Your blessing in this means something special to me."

"Then you have it," I said. "I know how great your taste is. If you like it, I'm sure I'll fall in love with it, too."

I could hear my uncle take a deep breath on the other end of the line. "If you won't come now, will you at least promise to join me there for a vacation when this is all over?"

"Zach and I would love to," I said. In actuality, my husband had been itching to go to Alaska since he'd been a boy, but life tended to get in the way of his plans. He had two loves in his life: his job and me.

"I'll hold you to that. We'll invite Thomas as well and

make it a party." He hesitated, and then added, "At least tell Zach I tried, would you?"

"I will," I said. "Should I expect a call from Uncle Tom next?"

Uncle Barton chuckled softly. "Do you mean he hasn't called you yet? I doubt he would offer you Alaska, but I'm surprised he hasn't tried to get you to Hickory."

"I'm sure it's coming," I said.

After we hung up, I figured I'd go ahead and be proactive, so I called my other uncle while I was in the mood to deal with their foolish, if well-meaning, intentions of getting me out of town.

Uncle Tom picked up on the first ring and said, "Savannah, I was just getting ready to call you."

"I figured you were, so I thought I'd save you the dime. Uncle Barton already struck out, so you can save your breath," I said with a laugh. "I'm not leaving Parson's Valley."

"Good enough," he said simply.

"What, no pleas to get me to join you? No tries at tempting me with trips, or anything else I can't refuse?"

He chuckled before he replied. "Savannah, I've known you since you were born, something Barton has lost out on, to his eternal regret. I've seen you dig in your heels before, and I know when it's time to let it go."

"Thank you, Uncle Tom. I love you."

"I love you, too. Take care of yourself."

"Right back at you."

After we hung up, my spirits were suddenly lighter than they had been just a few minutes earlier. Those two men and my husband were the only real family I had left in the world, and hearing their voices never failed to do me a great deal of good.

Now it was time to figure out who I needed to talk to next to look for information that would help me solve this crime.

That question was answered for me when the front doorbell rang, and I couldn't believe who was standing on my porch when I opened the door.

Chapter 15

. . .

"**C**AN I HELP YOU?" I ASKED SANDRA OLIVER AS I STEPPED out onto the porch.

"Savannah, I'm sorry to bother you, but I need to speak with you," she said. "Do you have a minute?"

She was still on my list of suspects, so I wasn't all that excited about inviting her into my home where no one could see us. The least I could do was stay out on the porch where there was a possibility that someone might come past, even if there wasn't much chance of it happening, given the location of our cottage.

I had an idea about how to balance it more in my favor. "Of course. I just have to make a quick call first."

"I can wait out here if you'd like," she said.

"No, I don't mind staying on the porch while I make my call." That was actually part of my plan. I wanted her to hear me call my husband, since it was another line of defense. She might not attack me if she knew my husband was aware of her visit.

I hit the speed dial for Zach's number and got his voice mail instantly. He clearly didn't want to be disturbed, but that wasn't going to stop me from using him as a backup. "Hey, it's Savannah. I can't make it just yet. I'm talking with Sandra Oliver at the house. See you soon. Love you. Bye."

After I hung up, I said, "Sorry about that, but he worries about me if he hasn't heard from me in a while."

She looked at me a little wistfully. "I envy you that. Your husband must really love you."

"Have you ever been married, Sandra?" It was a leading question, and I knew I might be pushing her too far in a direction she didn't want to go, but I needed to know if Sandy's wounds were still raw, open and sore enough to precipitate a murder.

"I came close once," she said after a pause. A tear tracked down one cheek as she said it, but I wasn't even positive that she realized it. "Actually, that's why I'm here. There's something I need to get off my chest. I know I've been avoiding giving you an answer, but I'm tired of hiding."

"Go on," I said as I took one of the rockers and motioned for Sandra to sit in the other one.

"It's true that I had a problem with Joanne. That's what you were asking about at Nathan's office, wasn't it? You wanted to know what she'd stolen from me, and I wouldn't tell you. I'm here now to do just that."

"What happened, Sandra?" I could tell the woman was still in some serious pain.

Sandra stared out into nothingness for a full minute

before she spoke. I knew that it was important not to rush her so she could tell me at her own pace. Finally, when she spoke, it was almost as though she was talking to me through a dream.

"I felt like I had a real chance at happiness once upon a time, and Joanne ruined it. I was so mad at her back then, I might have done anything to punish her for what she'd done to me." The sincerity in her voice was unmistakable as she added, "But I didn't kill her."

"Why should I believe you?"

Sandra shook her head and stared at my flower garden, not trusting herself to speak right away. "I don't know. It's true, though. I was in a great deal of pain for six months after it happened, and I might have threatened her once then, but I got over it after a while. It was clear to me that it was too late for me to have a life with Ray. The damage was already done."

"He was married, wasn't he?"

She nodded. "He kept telling me that there wasn't any love in his home, but that he was staying with his wife for the sake of their kids. Do you know how I finally got over him?"

"If you don't mind telling me, I'd be happy to listen."

With a touch of sad laughter in her voice, Sandra said, "Six months after he dumped me, he took up with someone else on the side. The funny thing was that it only took him a week to decide to leave his wife for her. They lasted a few months, and he moved on to the next heart to break. When I found out, I actually thanked Joanne for saving me from ruining my life."

"Did anyone else know about this?"

"Just Laura," she said. "I used to confide in her about everything. But that was before."

"Before what?" I asked when she didn't finish her sentence.

"Before all of this happened with Joanne, of course."

I was curious about her reaction. "How did that affect you two?"

Sandra looked at me steadily. "How can I be certain that she wasn't the one who killed Joanne? Laura has to be on your suspect list, Savannah."

I wasn't sure I wanted to admit that I even had one, let alone tell her who was on it. "Do you know something I don't?"

"Think about it. She gets Joanne's money, doesn't she? Isn't that reason enough? We were there at the café together in Asheville, and she could have slipped something into Joanne's tea just as easily as you or I could have. I had to break off our friendship, but I didn't tell her why."

"You don't have any proof though, do you?" I was very interested in hearing her answer to that particular question.

"No, not even a gut feeling," she confessed. "But I couldn't be sure, you know? Who wants to spend the rest of her life looking over her shoulder? It's no way to live."

"Ending all of your friendships isn't, either," I said.

Sandra stopped her own rocking and stared at me. "Do you really want to give me advice on maintaining a friendship, Savannah? I heard you tipped the police off that Rob probably killed Joanne, and the last time I checked, you two were the best of pals."

"Where did you hear that?"

She laughed with a hint of resignation. "Parson's Valley is a small town. Not much happens around here that everybody doesn't find out about sooner or later. All it would take would be one customer in the hardware store when your husband and that state trooper went in to talk to him, and soon enough, the entire town knows what happened."

"I just learned that his wife had been poisoned," I said as calmly as I could. "Zach had a right to know, and I won't deny that I'm the one who told him."

"Hey, don't get me wrong. I'm not blaming you. I just don't want you accusing me of doing something you did yourself. None of us can be too careful; do you know what I mean?"

I couldn't argue with that, but it brought another question to mind. "If you honestly feel that way, aren't you taking a chance coming here alone?"

She averted her eyes, and I had a suspicion I knew why she was willing to risk it. "You told someone where you'd be, didn't you? Was it Nathan?"

Sandra whirled around and looked at me. "How could you have possibly known that?"

"We all have our little secrets, don't we?"

Sandra nodded. "I don't think you're a threat, not after hearing about some of the folks around town who are vouching for you, but it doesn't hurt to be careful."

I was happy that she'd found someone to speak on my behalf, and if she told me names, I'd bake them each a cake. "Okay then, did anyone else know that you'd made your peace with Joanne?"

"I doubt it, but you could always ask around," Sandra said as she stood. "I'm glad I got that off my chest. I didn't want to say anything in front of Nathan about the dismal history of my love life. We just started seeing each other, and I didn't want him to get the wrong impression about me."

"Is it the smartest thing in the world to date your boss, Sandra?"

She smiled and shrugged as she looked at me. "Look

at you, giving advice left and right. It might not be smart, but have you looked at the dating pool in our town lately? There aren't exactly a lot of options, and Nathan is smart, he's nice, and he's good to me. But there's one thing even better than that."

"What's that?"

"He isn't married," she said. "Thanks for chatting with me, Savannah. I honestly do feel better now."

"You're welcome. Thank you for coming out."

As she started to leave, I asked, "Did Joanne ever write you any letters, Sandra?"

"What are you talking about?"

"I'm just curious."

"Not that I remember," Sandra said. After she was gone, I had a feeling that something had been staged about her revelations to me. Had she rehearsed in her mind because she'd been nervous, or was it because she had a motive besides enlightening me? Sandra had certainly painted herself as the victim after sleeping with a married man, so I wasn't sure I could believe the way she portrayed everyone else. In the end, Laura was probably better off without her friendship.

I knew who I needed to speak with next. Sandra and Laura might be fighting, but I was on good terms with both of them. I needed to confirm Sandra's story. If I could, it might allow me to strike her name off my list of suspects.

It would be nice to take one off, instead of adding another one to it.

"SAVANNAH, WHAT BRINGS YOU HERE?" LAURA ASKED AS I knocked on Joanne's front door a little later.

"I was looking for you," I admitted as I held up two

to-go cups of coffee. I'd swung by Barbara's to load up on some java, and thankfully she hadn't been around, so I didn't have to tell her what I'd been up to since we'd last spoken. I wasn't ready to give anyone a progress report just yet. "Do you have a second?"

"I can spare a minute or two," she said as she took one of the cups from me. "Thanks, I've been dying for caffeine, but Joanne is all out. Do you mind if we talk out here on the front steps? I need to get out of there for a little bit just to catch my breath."

"That sounds great to me," I said, though I'd been hoping to go back inside the house for another look. There was a chance I'd missed something important in my first abbreviated search of the house, since I'd been interrupted so quickly by Laura yesterday. There were several piles of things on the porch, so the steps were the only place we could sit.

"What's all of this?" I asked.

"Most of it is for Goodwill," she replied. "I've put all of the trash out back for collection. You can't imagine how much accumulates over the course of someone's life."

I saw the picture frame I'd spotted inside on her dresser on the pile for her charity donation, and asked, "Are you getting rid of that, too?"

"I have dozens of photographs of Joanne," she said. "If you'd like it, you're welcome to it. You don't even have to keep the picture. It's a nice frame, and if I had room for it, I'd probably take it myself."

"Thanks. I think I'll take you up on that," I said as I retrieved it from the pile. "Did you happen to find any stationery while you were cleaning up?"

"No, as far as I knew, Joanne wasn't a big letter writer."

We sat on the front steps, and Laura seemed to really

enjoy the coffee I'd brought her. "What did you want to talk about?" she asked me.

"It's about Sandra," I said.

"I don't really want to discuss her," Laura said, and I could see her spine stiffen a little as she spoke.

"I understand you two had a falling out, but there's something I need to know. It's important, or I wouldn't ask."

"Okay, I don't see what it can hurt," she finally conceded. "I'll answer it if I can."

"Is it true that she thanked Joanne for breaking up her relationship with the married man she was seeing?"

Laura looked at me for a few seconds, and then nodded. "Yes, but I'm surprised she told you about it. That was her deep, dark secret. I thought I was the only one who knew."

"About the affair, or the thanks?" I asked.

Laura chuckled slightly. "Probably a little bit of both. It wasn't exactly her proudest moment, going after a married father like that. I tried to tell her that she was wrong, but she wouldn't listen to me."

I took a sip of my coffee, and then I said, "Thanks for being so honest with me about it."

"It's okay. I don't mind, not really. Can it be my turn now?"

I was more than a little confused by the question. "Your turn for what?"

"To ask you something."

"Fire away. I'll answer it if I can."

I wasn't sure what was coming next, but she surprised me anyway when she asked, "Do you have any idea why Sandra won't speak to me? It's kind of tearing me up inside, if you want to know the truth."

I knew, but did I really want to tell her and give the

young woman more pain than she already had? "I'm not sure I should say anything."

"That's not fair," Laura said. "I told you what you wanted to know. I thought we had a deal."

"I'm not holding anything back. It's just that I'm pretty sure you're not going to like the answer."

Laura took another sip of coffee, swallowed it, and then took a deep breath before she said, "Go ahead. I can take it."

She asked for it, and I had no right to sugarcoat it. "She's afraid there's a possibility that you might have killed Joanne for her money," I said.

"Why would she think that? I didn't know she had any money, and if I did, I never dreamed I'd inherit any of it."

"Sandra seemed to think you did," I went on. It was time to take a stab in the dark. "Do you have any bills you can't pay?" I didn't like going after her when she'd just been so helpful to me, but I really didn't have any choice. It might just yield me a more honest answer than when she had her guard up all of the way.

"Who doesn't?" Laura replied as she nodded slightly. "The money is going to be tremendously helpful, and I'm not denying it, but I had no idea there would be any, or that I'd be the one getting it." She took a last sip from her cup, and then put it on the step between her feet. "I can't believe she thinks I'm capable of killing another human being."

"Don't be too hard on her," I said. "I just accused someone close to me of the same thing as well."

"Don't worry about it, Savannah. Rob will get over it," Laura said.

"You've heard already?"

She nodded. "It didn't take long for word to get around. Nobody I know believes that Rob is capable of murder."

"Is there any chance that anyone in Parson's Valley is saying the same thing about the two of us?" I asked.

"Well, about me, maybe," she said with a faint smile. "I've lived here my entire life. Your history isn't as well known as mine, so some folks have probably already convicted you without a trial."

"I never realized that it was such a big issue being an outsider here before," I said.

"You probably never would have found out if this murder hadn't come up. Folks around here have a tendency to pull together when there's trouble, and nothing's more serious than murder."

"All the more reason I have for finding the killer, then," I said.

"I hope you do," she said as she stood up. "It's been eating away at me since it happened. I should have been nicer to Joanne, and now I'll never have the opportunity to make things right between us."

"We all have our missed opportunities," I said.

"True enough, but that doesn't mean we shouldn't try harder." Laura stretched, and then added, "I'd love to stay and chat, but I've got a ton of work to do if I'm ever going to finish."

"I could help you," I said, at the moment not caring about clues as much as wanting to help someone in need.

"Thanks, but I've got it under control, even if I do complain about it. I've almost got it licked." She stretched again, and then added, "The coffee was great. Feel free to stop by anytime."

After I collected my frame and left Laura, I thought about what she'd said. She'd confirmed what Sandra had told me about thanking Joanne, so it appeared that Sandra's name could be struck off my list of suspects.

At least that was some kind of progress.

But I had too many more names there to make me feel all that good about any of it.

I T WAS TIME TO HAVE ANOTHER CHAT WITH HARRY PIKE. I drove to his nursery, hoping to find him in his office. His assistant was on the telephone when I walked in, so I stayed in the shadows outside the door until she got off. The place offered no privacy at all, and I wondered how one person could work there, let alone two, though I had my suspicion that Harry used his truck more than this space.

I heard the woman inside say, "I know your bill's past due. We're doing what we can to pay it, but we need more time. You need to work with us, if you ever expect to get paid." Finally, she said, "Go ahead, get in line and call a collection agency. Be a real jerk about it, why don't you?" She slammed the phone down, and started wading through a stack of bills on her desk when she noticed that I was standing there.

I spoke up and asked, "Is Harry here? I saw his truck out front."

She looked at me and said in an exasperated voice, "He's around somewhere. Do you want me to call him on the two-way?"

"No, if it's okay, I'll go look around a little myself." I figured there wouldn't be much chance of catching him doing something incriminating, but if my presence was announced, the probability would fall all the way to zero.

"Help yourself. Take a set of yellow tags, a lot sheet, and a black marker with you."

"Why should I do that?" I asked.

"You might find a tree or a bush that you like. If you do, tag it with a yellow marker, and then make a note on the lot sheet so we can save it for you."

"Thanks, I'll do that," I said. I'd been looking for a tree to replace a pin oak in our yard that had been struck by lightning during a violent summer storm. It had blown the bark off both sides of it, scoring it nearly the entire length of the tree. I'd had hopes that it might recover, but small piles of fine sawdust around the base told me that it was most likely a hopeless cause.

As I walked among the trees, I got so caught up in envisioning each one by our cottage that I almost missed Harry down on his knees pruning an evergreen.

"There you are," I said, clearly startling him.

"Savannah, I didn't know you were here," he said as he stood and brushed off his pants legs.

"I didn't realize that you had to prune every tree and bush on the place. How do you ever get anything else done?"

"It's not a chore if you love doing it," he said as he holstered his pruning shears.

"That's a yew, isn't it?"

"Yes, it's an English yew. They're very popular around here."

"They're also really poisonous, aren't they?"

Harry waved his hand all around him. "This whole place is full of poisonous plants. It doesn't mean anything as long as you don't ingest any of them." Harry wiped the sweat off his forehead with a green paisley bandana as he asked, "What can I do for you?"

"I was looking for a tree," I said suddenly, realizing

that I might have more luck questioning him if I was a little more subtle about it.

"Then you came to the right place," he said with a smile. "What kind of tree are you looking for?"

I recounted our lightning-struck pin oak, and he started showing me a host of replacements.

"Have you heard what's going to happen with the land deal you had going with Joanne yet?" I asked idly as he showed me yet another oak tree.

"No, it appears that the lawyers are going to end up sorting it all out. If Laura Moon gets Joanne's share, like everybody in town thinks, I might be able to work something out with her. I understand she's in some pretty serious need of money herself."

"Where did you hear that?"

"Word gets around. Now, we have some nice ornamental plums over here. They have some pretty spectacular foliage through three seasons."

"I'll have to check with Zach," I said absently. "Would it be a bad thing if Laura inherits Joanne's share?"

"I don't know," he said. "She would have to be easier to deal with than her cousin. I'll tell you what. That was my last deal with Joanne, no matter how much money we stood to make."

"You didn't like doing business with her?"

He shook his head. "She was always looking over my shoulder, giving me opinions and advice that I didn't need. I like my partners a little more on the silent side, if you know what I mean."

"I can understand that," I said. Trying to be as casual as I could, I asked, "Did you ever get any letters from Joanne?"

He nodded. "Yeah, the crazy old bird sent me one once a few years ago. She said I'd better keep my nose clean, or she'd tell the world what I was up to."

"What did she mean by that?"

"She accused me of cheating a client of mine; it was some friend of hers who accidentally got billed twice for some work I did for her."

"But you didn't mean to cheat her."

He laughed. "Not on purpose. My accountant made a mistake and double-billed the woman. I paid the money back and gave her an extra maple tree to make up for it."

"Did that fix the problem?" I asked.

"I have to believe that it did. She was happy the last time I saw her. Is there anything else? I've got a ton of work to do."

I was about to ask him another question when my telephone started quacking like a duck.

When I tried to ignore it, Harry asked, "Aren't you going to get that? I can't stand a ringing telephone, even if it is quacking."

"It's just Zach," I said. "It can wait."

"Not on my account. Like I said, I'm jammed for time. You should talk to him." He paused, and then smiled. "While you've got him on the telephone, ask him about that plum tree. You won't be sorry, I can promise you that."

"Okay, I'll do that," I said reluctantly as I answered. "Hello?"

"Hey, you're the one who called me first, remember? How did your little chat with Sandra go?"

"It was illuminating," I said.

"You're going to have to give me more than that."

I didn't want to admit that I'd called him earlier more

as a safety issue than actually wanting to speak to him. "Okay, but this isn't a great time for me. Can I call you right back?"

"Why? Where are you now?"

"I'm at Harry Pike's nursery. I've been looking at trees," I said loud enough for Harry to hear, though he'd started to walk away to work on another subject when I'd answered the telephone.

"Don't buy anything without me. We agreed, Savannah."

I lowered my voice. "Take it easy, Zach. It was just an excuse to talk to Harry," I admitted.

"That's not bad," he answered, lowering his voice as well, though I couldn't imagine why. "Did you have any luck?"

I looked around, but Harry was already out of sight. I might as well tell Zach what I'd uncovered so far. "He believes that Laura will be easier to deal with than Joanne was," I reported. "Is that motive enough for murder?"

Zach laughed at that. "It might be. You can't blame him for feeling that way. I can't imagine why he ever went into business with her in the first place, can you?"

"From everything I've seen, he needed her money to make the deal happen," I said. "But I'll be honest with you. He didn't seem all that excited about the prospect of working with her ever again."

"I'm not sure I could ever need somebody else's money that badly. Did you find out anything else?"

I lowered my voice, though Harry was now completely out of sight. "He admitted that Joanne sent him a letter threatening to expose him as a crook a few years ago, so that fits in with those letters I found at her place."

"Why would he ever admit that to you, Savannah?"

I laughed. "Maybe I've got a trusting face."

"There's got to be more to it than that. He had a reason to tell you. You just don't know what it is, yet."

"I don't think there's anything sinister about it, Zach. Harry explained that it was all just one misunderstanding. His accountant double-billed a friend of hers, but he made it right with a full refund and a free tree thrown in, to boot."

"What else have you been up to?"

"You already know that I spoke with Sandra."

"Sure I do, but you never told me what she said."

That was true enough. "She claims that Joanne did her a favor breaking up her relationship with a married man, and Laura confirms that Sandra even thanked Joanne for it after the fact."

"So that's good news. We can strike her name off the list."

It was true, as far as it went. "It still leaves quite a few names under consideration, doesn't it?"

"Don't get discouraged," Zach said, clearly trying to buoy my spirits. "Nobody ever said this process was quick. Hang on." He covered his mouthpiece with one hand, so all I could hear was some mumbling. "Sorry, Savannah, but I've got to go," he said.

Before I could say good-bye, the line was already dead.

Worse yet, Harry was gone, and I doubted that I'd ever be able to find him on his home field, especially if he was through with me.

It seemed that no one wanted to talk to me.

I wasn't about to let that stop me, though.

I had a mission, and I was going to see it through, no matter what.

Chapter 16

. . .

"**I** USUALLY DON'T CUT WOMEN'S HAIR," GREG SAID WHEN I walked into his barbershop twenty minutes later. There wasn't an ounce of humor in his voice, and I knew that I was going to be fighting an uphill battle getting him to talk to me. There was a man in his sixties in the chair getting the finishing touches on a flattop, and the crown of his head was so smooth you could land a toy airplane on it.

"That's good, because that's not why I'm here," I said with a smile.

Greg nodded, and the electric clippers in his hand bobbed with him. If the man in the chair noticed it, he didn't say anything, and if he did, I had to admire him for not even flinching.

"Talking is extra," he said as he pointed to a sign

mounted on the brick wall behind me. It had been clearly hand-lettered, and after listing the price of a haircut, it said, "If you take a cell phone call in the chair, it's going to cost you a dollar a minute. If you complain about it, get your hair cut somewhere else." Below that, he had added, "If you want to talk to me and not get your hair cut, that's a dollar a minute, too."

After the man in the chair examined his cut in the mirror, he nodded and stood as Greg removed the apron around him. Silently, he handed Greg a twenty dollar bill, got his change, and walked out the door with a wave, but not a word.

"He's a real talker, isn't he?" I said.

I handed the barber a ten dollar bill, and he stared at it a second before looking back at me. "What's this for?"

I pointed to his sign. "I figure that should buy me ten minutes. I want to talk to you more about Joanne Clayton."

He shook his head and handed the bill back to me. "No thanks. I don't want to talk about her. Keep your money, Savannah."

"What's it going to take to get your cooperation? Do I have to come back here with Rob Hastings?"

Greg smiled at me. "That would be a cute trick, since I heard that he threw you out of his hardware store. You just lost your biggest ally, Savannah."

"Not even close. How about my husband, Zach? I can have him over here in ten minutes if I have to. I know you don't like talking to me, but what if he brings the state trooper investigating the murder with him? Will that make it easier on you? We can close the barbershop and have ourselves a little party."

Greg thought about fighting it—I could see it in his

eyes—but he finally just slumped down in his chair. "Okay, you win. I'll give you one question, and it's on the house. After that, call your husband. I'm not afraid of him, or the cop tagging along behind him."

"You probably should be," I said.

"Of which one?" It was clear that he didn't think of either one of them as a threat. Wow, was he ever wrong.

"As far as I'm concerned, you should be worried about both of them."

Greg sighed audibly. "Savannah, do you want to keep dancing around this, or do you want to get to the point?"

I nodded. "That's fair enough. You say you had nothing to do with Joanne's murder."

"That's not a question, it's a statement."

"So it is. How about this, then? What would you say if I told you I have reliable witnesses who tried to get haircuts ninety-five minutes apart on the day that Joanne was killed, and they were turned away by your 'closed' sign?"

"I'd say they were either lying, or badly mistaken," Greg said, though it was clear that he was shaken by my statement.

"Fine. If you want to play it that way, you win. I'll call Zach, and he and Captain North can ask you the same thing. They might have to use their flashing lights and siren when they come, though, what with traffic being so heavy and all." We both looked out the broad window and could see an empty road. "What's that kind of show going on out front going to do for your business? You might be the only barber in town, but Asheville's not that far away."

Greg looked at me in disgust before he finally said, "Fine, I admit it. I was gone for more than an hour that day."

"Were you in Asheville?"

"Sorry, I was at home on my couch," he said. "Before I had lunch, I stretched out for a few minutes. I fell asleep, Savannah, and I never left Parson's Valley. I didn't kill Joanne."

"I don't suppose anyone saw you at home."

"I'd love to be able to tell you that my girlfriend was with me, but she was being murdered in Asheville at the time."

"But you can't prove that you didn't do it yourself," I said.

"You're right, I can't. I thought only guilty people needed alibis."

"Why on earth would you think that?" I asked. "An alibi is what keeps you from being arrested for murder."

That got his attention. Greg sat up in his barber chair. "Are you saying they're going to arrest me?"

"I don't know what the police have planned," I said, which was about as true a statement as I'd ever made in my life. "All I know is that you're on their list of suspects."

"So are you," he said.

I nodded. "That's why I'm trying to find Joanne's killer. Why aren't you looking, too?"

"I'm just a barber," he said as he waved his hand around the shop. "I cut hair. It might not be all that exciting, but it's what I know how to do."

"I'm a puzzlemaker," I said, "but that's not keeping me from digging into Joanne's murder."

"Well, maybe we all don't have cops around town backing us up. All I know is that no one saw me while I was at home taking a nap. I dropped my car off at Carl's service station for an oil change that morning before work, and then I picked it up on my lunch hour and drove straight home. My car sat in my garage until I woke up, but I can't prove that, either." He stood up as he added, "Now if you don't mind, I'd like you to leave. Either call your husband, or clear out."

"Wait a second," I said.

"I'm not kidding, Savannah. I'm done with being grilled by you," he warned, and I could tell by his voice that he was dead serious.

I couldn't let him brush me off now, though. "Do you want me to go, even if I can find a way to clear your name?"

Greg had every right to look confused at me as he asked, "How could you possibly do that?"

"The last time I had Carl change my oil, he took down the odometer reading of my car. I remember it, because he made a fuss about forgetting it at first, and he wouldn't let me leave until he had written it down on my receipt. Did he get your mileage as well?"

"I have no idea," he said. "The receipt's in the glove box. Go ahead and see for yourself."

"You're coming with me," I said. "Grab your keys and let's go look."

After Greg unlocked his vehicle, I reached in and opened the glove box. The receipt was exactly where he'd said it would be. I checked the mileage myself, not even letting Greg touch the receipt he'd gotten from Carl, so there could be no question that he hadn't tampered with it. After that, I looked at his odometer and saw that he couldn't have driven to Asheville and back, not if that mileage was correct. There was less than four-tenths of a mile added to the odometer since the oil had been changed last.

"I don't know what to say," Greg said after I called my

husband and told him what I'd found. He was on his way to confirm what I'd discovered, and Greg and I were both waiting in his car. "Thanks, Savannah. I'm sorry I was so rude to you." He grinned at me and added, "I'd offer you a free haircut, but like I said, I don't cut women's hair."

"How about giving Zach one, instead?" I asked. "He's been looking a little shaggy lately."

"It would be my pleasure," he said.

My husband showed up, but he was without Captain North.

As I greeted him, I asked, "Where's your partner in crime?"

"She's on a conference call with Raleigh," he said. "They're asking her for a progress report, and I don't think her supervisors are all that happy about what she's got to tell them. We'll be doing her a favor if what you told me was accurate."

"You don't doubt me, do you?" I asked as I handed him the receipt.

"Of course not," he replied as he checked the odometer reading himself. I would have expected nothing less from him. "Okay, we're good here."

Greg clearly couldn't believe that it was going to be that easy. "Is that it? Am I off your suspect list?"

"I'm going to show this to the investigating officer, but if everything checks out, you should be off the hook."

"It's not for nothing, either. You get a free haircut for my hard work, Zach," I said.

"Thanks," he said as he ran his hand through his hair, "but I'm not allowed to accept it."

"You're not on anyone's payroll," I said.

"No, but I'm volunteering my time with the police force, and that amounts to the same thing in my eyes." He looked at Greg and asked, "Is it okay if I borrow your car for a few minutes?"

Greg tossed him the keys. "Be my guest."

He went back inside the barbershop, and I asked Zach, "Why did you do that?"

"I need to run over to Carl's. Care to tag along?"

"You bet," I said.

I slid into the passenger seat, and my husband started the car and headed for the garage. I said, "We're going to check the garage's paperwork and make sure Greg's receipt is valid."

My husband was holding back on me; I could tell it by the way he spoke. "That's right."

"And then what?"

"What do you mean?" He was smiling at me, always a good thing as far as I was concerned.

"You didn't need his car to check his paperwork. All you had to have was his receipt."

Zach smiled. "You're right about that."

I thought about that for a second, and then I said, "But you do need his car if you're going to see if anyone fiddled with the odometer."

"That's good work, Savannah. I'll make a detective out of you yet."

I grinned at him. "Funny, I thought I already was one."

"You are, and don't let anyone tell you any different."

We got to Carl's, and after a quick check of the records and a look under the hood, he made his pronouncement. "The paperwork's accurate, and the cable hasn't been messed with."

"Are you certain?"

"I sure am. Do you mind telling me what this is all about? What's Greg been up to?"

"Just cutting hair, as far as I know," Zach said.

We headed back to the barbershop, and I said, "So, we can officially cross another suspect's name off our list."

My husband wasn't about to give in that easily. "He could have borrowed someone else's car, or for all we know, he might have another vehicle stashed somewhere else."

"So, go ahead and check out all of the other angles, but as far as I'm concerned, he's not guilty."

Zach shrugged. "That works for me. You're making a real dent in this case, aren't you?"

"I'm doing my best."

We pulled up to a stoplight, and Zach asked, "Who do you think might have done it now? Are there any particularly good candidates?"

I thought about it as the light turned green and he started driving again. I said, "As far as I know, it could be Harry, Laura, Hannah, Barbara, or Rob."

"Or someone we don't even know about yet," he said as he pulled into the empty parking lot.

"That kind of thinking doesn't do me any good," I said. "I have to assume that we wouldn't have gotten that note if we hadn't talked to the murderer at least once during our interviews."

Zach nodded as we got out and he locked the car. "That's the rational way to think about it. Any ideas on where you're going next?"

"I don't have a clue," I said with a grin.

"That's my girl," he said. "I'll drop the car keys back off with Greg, and then I need to get to the police station. I have a report to make."

"See you at home," I said as I got into my own car.

Zach didn't need me for the rest of the day, but that didn't mean I was finished. It had been a productive time, and I hated to stop when there was a single chance that I might be able to wipe someone else's name off my list before the sun set again. As things stood now, I still had a substantial list of suspects. There was an outside chance that one of the names I'd struck from my group might be guilty, but if that turned out to be the case, it was going to be up to Zach and Captain North to uncover it.

I WAS DRIVING TO BARBARA'S FOR A CUP OF COFFEE WHEN I noticed Hannah's craft store on the right. On impulse, I pulled in and decided to pay her a visit. It had started to rain, more of a drizzle than a downpour, but from one look at the sky, it was a harbinger of things to come. This wasn't a warm, bath-temperature rain like we sometimes got in summer; it was a cold-shower storm that left everyone in its wake shivering.

I grabbed my umbrella from the backseat and walked into Hannah's shop. She had a stand near the door, and I slid my umbrella into the rack and fought an involuntary shiver.

If Hannah was displeased about seeing me, she didn't show it. "Have you decided to get a little crafty today, Savannah?"

"I'm thinking about it," I said. "What do you suggest?"

She looked around her shop, and then said, "We've got a new line of card supplies you might like. I especially like the new kits that come with lots of options in stationery."

"That sounds good. Let's see what you've got."

As she showed me the cardstock, I asked, "Could I ask you something, Hannah?"

"Certainly," she said.

"It's about Joanne Clayton."

I could see her tense up at the mention of Joanne's name. "I'm not sure what I can say that I haven't already covered with you before."

"I'm sorry. I don't mean to keep harping on it, but the police are stepping up their investigation, and it's hard to tell what's going to happen. I'm just trying to eliminate as many suspects as I can."

She sighed deeply, and then said, "Go on, then, if you must."

"You told Rob and me when we were here together that you were running errands on the morning that Joanne was poisoned. Did those errands happen to be in Asheville, by any chance? If they weren't, I can tell Zach, and he can take you off the police's list of suspects."

"I would if I could, but unfortunately, I cannot."

I felt a twinge of excitement by the news that she'd been in town the day of the murder. "Did you see Joanne that day when you were there?" I asked. It was important to get my most essential questions out while I had the chance. Knowing Hannah, anything I asked could set her off, and I didn't want to get thrown out of her shop until I'd covered the most necessary questions.

"No," she said with a shake of her head, "but I have no idea how I might go about proving it. I never realized what a precarious position I was putting myself in when I went there." Hannah put down the card packet she'd been showing me, and then stared out the window at the ever-increasing rain. "It's going to flood if this keeps up. I can't believe how much moisture we've had lately."

"It's been wet," I agreed, but I couldn't let myself get distracted. "Were you anywhere near Pack Square that day?"

"I drove past it, of course. It's difficult to go anywhere in downtown Asheville without passing that obelisk."

"That's true enough. It's really too bad we can't pin your timeline down better than that."

Hannah frowned. "I'm sorry I can't offer you anything more specific, and I'm even more saddened that I decided to go into Asheville that day, leaving me without a better alibi than what I have. All I can say is that I was back here in Parson's Valley in time to open at nine A.M."

"It was really that early? Can you prove it?"

Hannah nodded. "I can. Edith Andrews was waiting for her new Christmas tree candle mold, and I had special-ordered it for her. She can vouch for me." Hannah said it with a hint of triumph in her voice.

"I'll tell Zach," I said. He'd told me that the poison had been administered between eleven and two, so if Hannah was telling the truth, she was in the clear.

When I told her the news, she nodded happily. "I'm glad we cleared that up." Almost as an afterthought, she added, "Savannah, if you're looking for suspects, I hope Barbara Brewster has made your list."

"Barbara? Why would she kill Joanne?"

Hannah stared out the window again a few seconds before speaking. "There's something buried deep between them, a bone of contention that's been there for years, though I don't know exactly what it might be."

"How do you know there's a secret, then?"

Hannah looked at me. "Let me ask you something. Do you consider Barbara Brewster a charitable woman?"

"I'm sorry?"

"I said, do you think of Barbara as someone who gives her coffee and scones away for the sheer joy of it?"

"She treated me to breakfast," I said.

That got Hannah's attention. "Without an agenda of her own?"

As I looked out the window, I remembered Barbara's eagerness to share with me all of the dirt she'd managed to dig up. "No, I have to admit that it wasn't given to me without strings," I acknowledged.

"Then why would Barbara give Joanne Clayton free coffee and scones every day since two years ago?"

I turned to stare at her. "How could you possibly know that?"

"I have my sources around town as well," she said. "There's something there, but I haven't been able to excavate it. So you see, there are more fingers ready to be pointed toward people with reason to see Joanne dead."

"I'll talk to her about it when I get a chance," I said. "Thanks for your time, Hannah."

"What about the card pack?"

I shrugged. "I'll have to think about it."

"It will be here whenever you're ready for it," she said.

I grabbed my umbrella and opened it as I stepped out into the rain. By the time I got to my car, my jeans were wet despite the umbrella. I was tempted to drive home, take a hot shower, and start a fire, but Hannah's news about Barbara was too good to ignore. Maybe a good cup of coffee would help take the chill off as well. At least I'd have that, even if Barbara decided to stonewall me.

But first I had to call Zach and tell him what I'd found.

HE DIDN'T HAVE TIME TO TALK, WHICH MADE ME WONDER why he'd answered his telephone in the first place, but as soon as I told him about Hannah's alibi, he seemed happy to hear from me. After we hung up, I drove downtown to take care of the next person on my list.

The coffee shop was nearly deserted when I walked in, shaking my umbrella to dislodge some of the water still clinging to it. Barbara was wiping down the counter in front, and she nodded toward me as I approached. There was just one other customer in the place, a man huddled over a cup of coffee by the front window.

"What can I get you?" Barbara asked.

"I'd love a cup of black coffee, and the chance to chat, if you have a second," I said.

She looked around the coffee shop. "It looks like you're in luck."

She got my coffee, and then asked for payment. I slid the money across the counter to her, and after she took it, Barbara drew a cup for herself. At least she hadn't asked me to pay for hers, though it looked like my free breakfast was a one-time offer. In a way, I was happy about that. I might have felt a little guilty interrogating her while I drank free coffee.

We found a table as far away from her lone customer as we could.

"What can I do for you?" she asked as she took a sip of her coffee. "Do you have any follow-up questions?"

"In a way," I said as I took a healthy swallow myself before diving into the fray. "I just learned that you gave Joanne Clayton free coffee and scones for the past two years. I'd say that was out of character, wouldn't you?"

She looked at me as though I'd slapped her. "Savannah, what are you talking about?"

"I heard it from a reliable source," I said, hedging my bets. I had no interest in giving Hannah up unless I absolutely had to.

"Was it one of my baristas?" she asked with a wicked look in her eyes. "Give me a name and I'll fire them before it stops raining."

"It wasn't anyone who works for you," I said. "I give you my word on that. From your reaction, I take it that it's true."

"First things first. Let's agree that I never admitted anything to you about the validity of the claim you just made," Barbara said as she stared at me. "False rumors can be just as damaging as true ones, and I mean to step on this with both feet."

"Why fight it, Barbara? It's easy enough to prove, don't you think? I'm sure you had your reasons."

Barbara stared at me, and after a few seconds, she smiled gently. "Maybe I'm just being paranoid, but it sounds like you're coming after me personally now. I'm surprised by it, to be honest with you. I was under the impression that we were on the same side."

"I want to find Joanne's killer," I said.

"I understand that."

"Then help me. If it doesn't pertain to the murder, I won't tell a soul, and that includes my husband."

She clearly thought about it, and then finally nodded. "I know what that bond means to you, so I'm going to trust you. Regardless of what your source told you, it wasn't every day. I gave Joanne coffee occasionally, and a scone here and there. It wasn't that big a deal."

"Then it shouldn't be a problem telling me why," I said.

Barbara nodded. "That's true enough. I owed her a favor. She helped me out once, and I was grateful for it, so I showed her my appreciation with a freebie every now and then."

"How did she help you?"

"I'm not about to go into that with you," she said. "It had nothing to do with her murder."

She started to get up when I asked, "Where were you the morning she was murdered?"

"I was here, where I am every day," she said dismissively.

"Don't you take a morning off now and then?"

"I do," she said.

"Then it shouldn't be hard to learn if you were here then or not."

She frowned at me, and then finally said, "Fine. I took some time off that day. I had a headache, so I decided to sleep in."

"When did you come in?"

"I was here in time for lunch," she said.

"So, you had the opportunity to get to Asheville and back, and no one would have been the wiser."

"That might be true, but as I said, I had no reason to wish Joanne harm. If anything, I owed her for past kindnesses."

"So you say," I said.

"Savannah, I'm finished with this conversation."

She walked into the back before I had a chance to say anything. A young employee came out to watch the front the second she disappeared, and I knew our interview was over.

I had no idea what favor Joanne had done for Barbara, or if any of what she'd just told me was indeed true. Returning a favor could be her motivation, but so could a low level of blackmail. I couldn't imagine what that might be, but I was determined to find out. We had a new player in our list of suspects, and I was going to go after her, regardless of the consequences.

Chapter 17

∎ ∎ ∎

WHEN I GOT HOME, I FOLLOWED THROUGH ON MY promise to myself to grab a hot shower, and after I toweled off my hair, I lit a fire in the fireplace. Zach wasn't home yet, but there was a message from him on the machine.

"Hey, your telephone is turned off. Did you know that? Call me when you get this. I'm worried about you, Savannah."

I checked my phone and saw that my cell battery was dead. It had been having trouble holding a charge lately. I had to get a replacement battery, and soon, since I lived and died by my phone.

I plugged it into the charger, and then dialed Zach's number. "Sorry about that; my battery died again."

He sounded relieved as he asked, "Is everything okay?"

"I'm fine," I said. "I found out a few new things that are interesting."

"I'm listening."

I brought him up to date on my conversations with Hannah and Barbara—leaving out the reason why, as I'd promised her—and he whistled when he heard about Barbara's generosity. Zach said, "I never heard a whisper about that, did you?"

"No, but for a place that can spread rumors at the speed of light, some information is pretty tightly held around here."

"Tell me about it," he said. "Why was she doing it, anyway?"

"I promised I wouldn't say," I replied.

He seemed to mull that over, and then finally said, "That's good enough for me, then."

I loved how my husband could switch gears so quickly. "Zach, is there any chance you'll be home in time for dinner tonight?"

"I'm nearly finished here," he said. "What did you have in mind? I could pick up a pizza on the way home if you'd like."

Pizza was part of our fallback diet, but I was frankly getting a little tired of it. "How about some potato soup, instead?" I suggested. "It might be good on a night like tonight."

"That sounds great," he said. "I'll be home in an hour."

"It'll be ready when you get here," I said as I hung up. I started boiling the potatoes and carrots as I thought about what I'd learned. Someone had killed Joanne Clayton, but it seemed like every time I thought I was making progress in my investigation, someone new popped up. I'd eliminated three suspects, and added a new one along the way. Barbara Brewster was a curious case. She could have had a reason to kill Joanne that she hadn't told me, and the fact that poison was used gave me a vague sense of unease. Why did I think she even had the means to kill Joanne? It wasn't as though she had anything poisonous around her coffee shop. Something kept nagging at the back of my mind, but the more I focused on it, the farther it distanced itself from my grasp.

THE SOUP WAS SIMMERING AWAY ON THE BACK BURNER when my husband finally made it home. "The rain's really picking up out there," he said as he ran a hand through his wet hair. "I left my coat on the porch." He sniffed the air. "That smells wonderful. Is it ready?"

"You have time to grab a quick shower if you'd like to," I said. "The soup can wait."

"Ordinarily I'd choose food over cleanliness, but right now I'm soaking wet. That sounds great," he said.

As Zach went upstairs, I turned the heat off the soup and set the table for our meal. While I had the chance, I got out the Parmesan cheese and the Microplane grater. I'd discovered the cheesy addition by accident once, using some leftover Parmesan from another meal. We'd found that the added touch raised the level of flavor in the soup tremendously.

Ten minutes later, Zach bounded downstairs wrapped up in a soft robe I'd bought him for Christmas the year before. It was covered with cartoon bears, moose, and pine trees, and he loved it.

"I'm starving," he said as he rubbed his hands together. "Is there any sourdough bread?"

"I've got it warming in the oven," I said.

"Do we have any real butter on hand?"

"It's already on the table."

He wrapped me in a bear hug. "Have I told you lately how special you are to me?"

"I bet you tell that to all the girls who feed you," I said with a smile.

"Just you," he said as he released me. "Why don't you sit down and I'll serve us both."

"I'd like that," I said. Zach dished out the soup, and then took the toasted bread out of the oven.

I grated the cheese over both our bowls, and we had a lovely meal that was uninterrupted, for a nice change of pace.

After we were finished eating, he asked, "Is there any chance we have dessert?"

"There might be some ice cream left in the freezer," I said.

"Sold. You want some, too?"

"Why not? Let's eat it by the fire."

"Sounds great."

As we settled in, I said, "I had a pair of interesting conversations with my uncles today."

"Listen, before you get upset, let me explain."

I shushed him. "There's nothing to apologize for. I know you're just looking out for me. Did Uncle Barton tell you about his Alaska property?"

"Are you kidding? He had me drooling within the first thirty seconds with his description. I can't wait to see it."

"We could just drop this and leave tonight," I said.

"What about Joanne Clayton? You can't just let this case go any more than I can."

"I know, but I can dream, can't I?"

He smiled at me. "The second we have this wrapped up, we'll be on a plane for Anchorage, and that's a promise."

I shivered. "Now? It's going to be freezing up there this time of year."

"Then we'll have another excuse to snuggle up to the fire."

I laughed at him. "I don't know about you, but I don't need any excuses." I moved over beside him just as my telephone rang. "Somebody has wretched timing."

"You could just let it go to voice mail," he said.

"We both know better than that," I said as I grabbed my telephone.

"Hello?"

"Savannah, we need to talk."

I hadn't been expecting to hear from Barbara on the phone, certainly not at this time of night.

"I'm sorry, but I'm in for the night," I said.

"This is important, and it won't keep until morning."

I'd had about enough of her hot and cold attitude toward me lately. We hadn't exactly left things on the best of terms earlier, and I was in no mood to trudge through the rain to meet her anywhere. If she was angling for an invitation to my house, she was even more delusional than I could have imagined.

"Sorry, I can't do anything about that."

Zach tapped my knee, and I heard him ask softly, "Who is it?"

I shook my head and held my hand up toward him as I waited for Barbara's response.

"Fine. Can you at least come by the coffee shop first thing tomorrow?"

It was a reasonable request for her to make, but I wasn't feeling very reasonable at the moment. "I don't know about getting there that early, but I can probably make it by eight," I said.

Barbara paused, and then finally said, "If that's the best you can do, I guess I'll have to live with it."

"See you tomorrow."

I hung up, and Zach could barely contain himself. "Who was that, Savannah? If you need to go somewhere tonight, I can drive you. It doesn't have to be a big problem."

"It's not. I just hate being treated badly."

"Who's messing with you?"

"Barbara Brewster has something to tell me, but it's going to have to wait until morning. I gave her plenty of chances to talk to me today, but she stonewalled me every time I turned around. It's not going to hurt her to stew over it a little, at least until it's more convenient for me."

He shrugged. "It's your call."

"You aren't seriously going to try to convince me to go see her right now, are you? I have a tough time believing you'd ever do that."

"It's your investigation," he said as he collected our ice cream bowls and rinsed them in the sink. "I know how much I hate being second-guessed, and I'm trying my best not to look over your shoulder all of the time."

"I appreciate that," I said as I kissed his cheek.

"I'm glad, because it's tough holding my tongue sometimes."

I laughed at him as I offered my hand. "I know it's not all that late, but I'm exhausted. Let's worry about the case tomorrow, okay?"

"That sounds like a plan to me," he said.

* * *

I FOUND ZACH DOWNSTAIRS MAKING BREAKFAST WHEN I got up the next morning. "Wow, this is a real treat," I said as I kissed him good morning. "You're usually gone by the time I get up."

"I figure that since you're doing all of the heavy lifting on this case right now, it wouldn't kill me to lend a hand around here now and then. After all, you cooked last night."

"You won't get any arguments from me," I said as I took a sip of orange juice and sat at the table. I wasn't there thirty seconds before he put a piece of French toast on my plate.

"Eat fast," he said with a grin. "You've got a meeting in twenty minutes."

I took a bite, and found it delightful. "I can be a little late. It can't really matter that much."

"That's where you're wrong," he said. "You made an appointment with one of your suspects. You can't afford to just blow it off, no matter how you might feel about her."

I took another big bite, and then smiled at him. "You can be a real slave driver; you know that, don't you?"

"If I ever forget, I'm sure you'll be there to remind me."

I took another big bite, and then asked, "Do you want to tag along with me and see what Barbara has to say?"

"I'd love to," he said as he served himself, "but I've got a pretty full agenda myself. I'm going to Asheville with North. She wants to do a little more digging there, so I'll be out of touch for a while."

"When are you leaving?"

"Right now," he said after he finished another bite.

"Did you get enough to eat?"

He smiled at me. "That was my third piece. I think I'm set." He turned off the griddle, and then added, "Just leave this mess. I'll take care of it tonight."

After he was gone, I decided to ignore my husband's instructions. I didn't have time to wash them in the sink, but at least I could rinse the dirty dishes enough so the syrup wouldn't harden by the time Zach got to them.

I got dressed in a hurry and still made it to Barbara's just a few minutes after eight.

What I didn't expect when I arrived was that she wouldn't be there.

"**W**HAT DO YOU MEAN SHE'S NOT HERE?" I ASKED ONE of the baristas.

"What can I tell you? She called this morning and said that she was going to be running late. I expect her to show up any minute."

"Then I'll take a cup of coffee while I wait," I said.

I found a spot near the window, and I had barely taken my first sip when someone tapped my shoulder. It was the barista who'd served me a few minutes before.

"Savannah, Barbara wants to see you."

"I want to see her, too. Did something happen to her?"

"No. She asked me to bring you back to her office so you can wait for her there."

I looked around at the other customers. "Thanks, but I think I'll wait right here."

It was clear that the poor woman didn't quite know

what to think of my refusal. The barista started stammering about Barbara's request, and I finally couldn't take it anymore. I picked up my coffee cup and said, "You win. I'll wait for her in the back."

She started to lead me to Barbara's office when I shook my head. "Don't bother. I know the way. Thanks anyway."

I took the same seat I'd been in a few days earlier and once again looked around for something to read while I waited. The stack of library books hadn't been touched, and I studied the titles again.

That's when it jumped out at me.

I suddenly realized what had been nagging at me since the last time I'd been there. With my hands shaking, I reached into the pile and pulled out the book on plants indigenous to North Carolina.

There was a torn piece of newspaper she was using as a bookmark in the pages, and I opened the book right to it.

The chapter was headed, "Deadly poisonous plants in the region, and the toxins they create."

It appeared that Barbara had been doing some homework on deadly poisons.

"WHAT ARE YOU READING, SAVANNAH?" BARBARA glanced at the book in my hands with a frown on her face. "That's mine."

"Actually, it belongs to the library," I said. "Is this what you wanted to tell me, Barbara? Have you been studying up on poisonous plants?"

She shrugged. "Among other things. What can I say? I have eclectic tastes."

"Are you trying to tell me this has nothing to do with

Joanne's death? I don't believe in those kinds of coincidences."

She shrugged. "Believe what you will. I had the book all along, and when I heard about what happened to Joanne, I started looking for some information on plant poisons so I could figure out why she died."

"It's tough to prove which came first, isn't it?"

She didn't like that comment one bit. "I don't have to prove anything to you, Savannah."

I looked back at the bookmark and saw that the piece she'd torn off had a date on it. It was from yesterday's paper.

"Sorry, I shouldn't have jumped to conclusions like that," I said.

She took the book from me, but I held on to the marker. "No, you shouldn't have. What changed your mind so suddenly?"

I held up the newspaper fragment. "It's dated yesterday. That backs up your story."

"You don't miss much, do you?"

I shrugged. "Once I get into something, it's impossible to get me to let up on it until it's finished."

"You don't have to tell me that. It's the reason you're here."

"Why is that, exactly? You were kind of evasive on the telephone last night, Barbara."

"I'm sorry about that," she said as she put the book back on the stack. "I want to come clean with you about Joanne."

"I'd like that," I said, being sure to keep my position closer to the door if I could manage it. Just because she'd satisfied my curiosity about the plant book didn't mean that I'd absolved her of the murder.

"The truth is that Joanne was blackmailing me," she said, her voice breaking a little as she admitted it.

"Were you having an affair?"

"What?" Barbara asked, genuinely shocked by my suggestion. "It was nothing like that."

"Then what was it?"

She frowned, and then admitted, "A few years ago, Joanne caught me in a rather embarrassing position. She sent me a note telling me what she'd discovered, and then made it known that free coffee and scones every now and then would be enough to buy her silence."

"So, she was blackmailing you with her knowledge, but asked for just coffee and a snack now and then. How can I know that it didn't escalate? If her demands started increasing, it could be a reason to get rid of her."

"No, the stakes were never that high. She had something that would embarrass me, but it wasn't illegal."

I shook my head. "It would help a great deal if you told me exactly what she knew about you."

Barbara found that amusing. "If I tell you, then you'll have something on me, too, won't you?"

The idea of it mortified me. "I'm not about to blackmail you, Barbara. You have my word."

"And that's supposed to be enough?"

I didn't know what to say to that. "You can tell me, or tell my husband, but one of us is going to know."

"Then I choose you," she said a little reluctantly. "If you must know, I used to have a thing with Harry Pike."

"Harry? What's so bad about that? He isn't married, and neither are you. There isn't anything embarrassing about that."

"Perhaps not, but we thought the door was locked when she came in after hours. You knew Joanne. She could spin things so far out of control their resemblance to the truth was sometimes hard to imagine. I didn't need the aggravation, so I gave her the coffee she asked for just to keep her quiet."

"Is there any way to confirm this?"

She rubbed her forehead, and then said, "You can ask Harry. I'll call him and tell him you're coming."

"I've got a better idea," I said. "Why don't we go there together?"

Barbara laughed. "So I won't tip him off, is that it?"

"Something like that. Do you mind?"

"I don't have much choice, do I? Let's go, Savannah."

We went out the back and got into my car.

I placed a call to warn him that we were coming, only to be told by his receptionist that Harry was working in the nursery, trimming some maple trees that were getting a little unruly.

Sure enough, that's where we found him when we got there. He didn't look all that surprised to see us, so I had to assume that his receptionist had told him that I had called. "Harry? Can we talk?"

"I heard you two were coming. What exactly are you up to?"

"I need to confirm something," I said. "Do you have a minute?"

"For you? Sure." He turned and looked at the coffee shop owner. "Hey, Barbara."

"Harry," she said curtly.

I couldn't imagine the two of them together under any circumstances, but then again, sometimes love made the strangest matches. There was no way to dance around the question, so I dove right in. "Harry, did you and Barbara ever have a fling?"

He looked startled by the question, and then started to look at Barbara. I couldn't have that. I said, "Keep your eyes on me, if you don't mind."

He did as I asked, but that didn't keep him from talking. "Barbara? Should I answer her?"

"Go ahead," she said. "I trust her. Tell her what happened."

"Yes, it's true," Harry told me. "I didn't find out about Joanne blackmailing her for coffee and scones until after we bought that land together, or I never would have made the deal. It was cruel the way she treated Barbara, and I let her know exactly how I felt more than once."

"It was fine, Harry. I told you that."

Harry shrugged, and then turned to her. "Barbara, would you like to have lunch sometime?"

"I don't think so," she said.

Harry just nodded, accepting it as though he was unsurprised by her answer. "If that's it, I've got work to do, ladies."

"That's all I needed," I said.

Once we were back in the car, I asked Barbara, "If you don't mind me asking, why won't you date him? Is it because of his reputation as a ladies' man?"

"Please, I've been over worrying about that for too many years, and I know Harry likes women. What's wrong with that?"

"Nothing. As a matter of fact, it's a trait I cherish in my husband. So, if that's not it, what is?"

She let out a short breath of air and said, "Honestly, it wasn't the fact that we were seen dallying by someone else," Barbara told me. "It was the way that we were caught like a couple of teenagers. I'm not sure I'll ever be able to get that moment out of my mind."

I'd seen something in her eyes that belied her negative response to him. "You must still like him."

"Must I? You aren't matchmaking, are you, Savannah?"

I laughed. "No, I wouldn't dream of it. Thank you for sharing that with me. You can trust me. I won't tell anyone about it."

"I've changed my mind. You can let your husband know," she said. "I trust him as well."

"Thanks, I appreciate that."

When we got back to the coffee shop, I stopped in front to drop her off. "Thanks for sharing that information with me."

"It was either that, or have you digging around until you found out the truth on your own."

I nodded, and then drove away. It was amazing to me that this strong woman would let herself be embarrassed by being caught with a man. Then again, knowing how proud Barbara was, it was probably worth a cup of coffee and a scone now and then to keep her reputation intact.

At the very least, I felt comfortable scratching Barbara's name off my list, and that made up for learning an embarrassing secret about someone I saw just about every day of my life.

It was progress, but I wished that I could strike Harry's name as well. That would require another form of proof, though.

I would just have to keep digging until I found it, or something that pointed out the real killer.

Chapter 18

■ ■ ■

NOW THAT I KNEW AT LEAST A PART OF HARRY'S SECRET, I decided to speak with him again. With any luck, I could catch him with his guard down.

He was exactly where I'd left him, pruning the lower limbs off a few trees in his nursery.

"Do you have another second for me?" I asked. "I don't mind if you keep working while we talk."

He looked up, clearly startled to see me again. "I thought you left." Harry looked past me. "Is Barbara still with you?"

"No, I took her back to the coffee shop."

He nodded. "Then I'll do as you suggest and work while you talk, if you honestly don't mind. I've got a lot going on right now."

"That's fine with me. Harry, what are the exact terms of your deal with Joanne?"

"What? Why are you asking me that?"

"I need to know if you had motive enough to kill her," I said bluntly.

"Of course I didn't," he said, with the outrage clear in his voice.

"That's why I'm asking you to your face instead of going behind your back. Harry, I wish I could believe you," I said.

"Savannah, frankly, I don't care what you believe." He stopped pruning and took a step toward me with his shears. I noticed for the first time just how sharp they were. What had I gotten myself into?

I took a step backward. "Zach knows I'm here," I said. It was the first thing that came into my mind.

"Good for him," Harry said as he took another step toward me. I was about to scream when he kept walking and brushed past me, heading directly toward his office.

"I'm not finished here," I said.

"Stay as long as you'd like," he replied, "but I've got an appointment I can't afford to miss."

I'd just seen an angry side to Harry that I had never seen in him before. When he'd moved toward me with those shears, I swear that I could see the hint of a killer in his eyes.

It wasn't proof good enough for Zach and his fellow officers, but it certainly made me realize that Harry was right where he belonged, near the top of my list of suspects.

THERE WAS SOMETHING I HAD TO DO, BUT I'D BEEN DREAD-ing it too much to act on it. I suddenly realized that I couldn't put it off any longer. I knew in my heart that it was time to try to talk to Rob again. I couldn't afford to be accusatory with him anymore, but that didn't mean I was ready to strike him off my list. The only way I could do that was to talk with him again and see if he could convince me that he didn't belong anywhere on it.

MY NERVES WERE JANGLING WHEN I WALKED INTO THE hardware store. Generally, I hated confrontations, and having one with someone I considered a friend was the worst kind of battle there was in my book.

I scanned the sales floor, but Lee was working by himself.

"Is your boss around?" I asked as I walked to him.

"Yeah, but I'm not sure he's going to be all that excited about you being here, Savannah. You're not exactly his favorite person in Parson's Valley right now, if you know what I mean."

"I'm willing to take my chances."

He shrugged. "Go ahead, then. It's your funeral." After a moment's pause, he added, "Hang on. That was a bad choice of words. If I can't talk you out of it, go on. He's back in his office."

I found Rob going through a stack of invoices on his desk when I walked back through the narrow hallway that separated his office from the retail floor space.

He looked up when I walked in, but the second he saw it was me, the smile that had been forming quickly vanished. "Savannah, I'm not entirely certain that you're welcome here anymore."

"Rob, we've been friends too long for this to end it."

"Then maybe you should have thought about that before you accused me of murder."

"I never accused you of anything," I said. "Rob, I was just confused when I found out that you didn't tell me your wife was poisoned the same way Joanne was killed."

"I didn't kill Joanne," he said. "How many times do I have to say that before you believe me?"

"So then it's just a coincidence? Is that what you're saying?"

Rob leaned back in his chair. "Savannah, I know it's not something we talk about all the time around here, but what happened to Becky was no great secret. What would be the best way to frame me? I'll tell you, because I've had a lot of time to think about it. If anyone in town wanted to point a finger at me as a murder suspect, what better way would there be than to duplicate my wife's death on the anniversary of the very day she died?"

"Becky's death wasn't a homicide, though, was it?"

He frowned. "No, everyone involved said it was accidental, and there was no reason to dispute it, then or now."

"This has to be incredibly difficult for you," I said, trying to put a little sympathy in my voice.

"More than I can say," he said.

"Then let's try to clear your name and make it go away." It was risky trying to enlist Rob's help after what had happened between us, but I couldn't question him if he continued to hold me at arm's length.

"Thanks, but no."

"You don't want to be absolved?"

"Absolution is for priests," he said. "I expect my friends to believe in me. Good-bye, Savannah."

"What makes you think I don't believe in you?"

He shook his head as he stared at me. "Because you have to force yourself to look me in the eye."

I hadn't realized that I'd been doing it, but I wasn't all that shocked to hear it. I was going to have to get better at this if I hoped to keep investigating crime. Even though making puzzles was my first love, that didn't mean that I was ready to turn my back on a murder if it touched my life in some way.

"Now if you'll excuse me, I've got work to do," he said as he stood up and brushed past me.

I was ready to follow him out of his office when I noticed a framed photo on his desk.

He was in winter-weather clothing, and his cheeks were red from the cold. The background was familiar, and it only took a second to realize that it was the same scenery from the photograph I'd taken from Joanne's house.

The question was, had it been taken before Becky Hastings's death, or sometime later? On impulse, I picked up the frame and tucked it into my bag.

"Savannah, are you coming?"

I looked up to see that Rob had come back to his office. Evidently, I'd taken too long to follow him.

"May I use the restroom?" I asked, hoping he wouldn't notice the photograph's absence until I could take a closer look at it.

"Go on," he said. "You know where it is."

I walked into the ladies' room and quickly locked the door behind me. My hands shook a little as I removed the photo from its frame.

The picture had been folded back, and I saw that there had been three people in the original version.

Looking happy and joyous, Rob and Becky Hastings were standing there with Joanne Clayton between them, their arms all locked together. If he was fine with Joanne, why had he effectively taken her out of the shot? Another question I had was why he hadn't put his late wife's picture forward instead of his own. The photo posed as many questions as it had answered. I couldn't wait to see if Joanne's photograph was a duplicate of the one I was holding, or if it hid something different from plain view.

I WAS COUNTING ON ROB TO BE GONE WHEN I SLIPPED OUT of the restroom. I'd replaced the photo as it had been when I'd first found it, and now I was hoping I could return it to his desk without his being aware that it had ever been gone.

I looked down the hallway and couldn't see anyone in the retail space, which meant that no one there could see me.

I hurried into Rob's office, only to find him sitting at his desk.

"I thought we were finished here," he said. "I'm not going to budge, Savannah, so don't waste your breath."

"I'm not going to try to change your mind." I tried to think of something I could say to distract him, but I couldn't come up with anything. Then it hit me. "My cell phone battery is dead. May I use your phone?"

"No, I don't think so," he said.

"Rob, I'm still a customer here, no matter how you feel about me at the moment. I deserve at least that basic courtesy."

"Fine," he said angrily as he shoved his desk telephone toward me. "Make it quick."

I picked up his phone, waiting for him to look away. When he didn't, I knocked the cup full of pencils on his desk onto the floor.

"I'm so sorry," I said as I made an attempt to lean down, the telephone still in my hand.

"I'll take care of it. Just use the phone and leave me alone, Savannah."

I dialed my home number as I slid the photo out of my bag and back onto his desk.

"What are you doing with that?" he asked.

Here I thought I'd been so clever, and now it appeared that I hadn't gotten away with it after all.

"I KNOCKED IT OVER WITH THE CORD WHEN I REACHED down to help with the pencils," I said.

He shook his head. "I'm not buying it. I've never seen you this clumsy in all of the time I've known you."

"What can I say? Maybe my nerves are a little on edge."

No one answered my phone at home, which was exactly what I'd been expecting. I hung up, and Rob asked, "What's the matter? Can't find your husband?"

"No worries there. If I ever lose him, I know that he'll find me. Thanks again, Rob."

"You're welcome," he said, without the slightest hint of sincerity in his voice.

I didn't care how sarcastic he was being. I was getting out of there in one piece, and that was all that mattered to me.

OUT IN THE CAR, I COULDN'T WAIT TO DIG OUT THE PHOtograph Laura had given me at Joanne's house. I'd been expecting a duplicate of the photo I'd just seen, and that was what I found. It was interesting that both people who had the same photograph had chosen to show only themselves, and not the late Becky Hastings. Was it too painful to look at that sunny smile of hers, a reminder of unhappier times, or was there a deeper reason?

IHAD A FEW VIABLE SUSPECTS LEFT WHO WERE STILL TALK-ing to me, so I decided to see if Laura had any interest in getting lunch with me somewhere. Maybe if I could get her to relax, she might tell me more than she meant to. It wasn't exactly a master plan, but it was the best thing I had in my dwindling arsenal.

I checked at Joanne's first, and I was relieved to see Laura's car sitting in the driveway. The stack of Goodwill donations on the porch was quite a bit larger than it had been before, and the trash she'd taken to the back now lined the curb in front of the house.

As I walked up the steps of the porch, Laura came out of the house with two more garbage bags, barely able to contain what was inside.

"Hey there," I said.

She was so startled by my presence that she dropped both bags in her hands. "Savannah, you surprised me."

"Sorry, I didn't mean to creep up on you like that," I said. "How's it going?"

"Believe it or not, this is the last load," she said. "I'm ready to turn it over to the real estate agent this evening, and then I'm out of here."

"Where are you going?" I asked.

"I can't stay in town, not with all of the tongues wagging about me. Does anyone think I don't hear their snickers when I walk past them in the grocery store? Everyone's talking about how I got a little too lucky with Joanne's death, and isn't that a little odd."

"It's understandable, but you can't let them drive you away."

She frowned at me. "Savannah, don't you know they're talking about you at least as much as they discuss me? Joanne might have been murdered, but we're both victims here, too."

"Then we need to stay here and fight for our reputations," I said.

"You fight. I don't have the energy anymore."

I picked up one of the bags and put it with the other pile. "Would you like to go have lunch before you go? My treat."

"Thanks, but no. I've got a long list of things to do before I leave town. If I were you, I'd take off, too. Think about it, Savannah. You're not like most of us in Parson's Valley. You don't have any family here or any ties at all."

I wasn't about to concede her point. "It's my home, Laura, and no one's going to make me leave it."

"Suit yourself," she said. Laura threw the last bag onto the pile, and then locked the front door of the house. "That's it. I'd say I'll see you around, but I doubt it. At seven tonight, I'm meeting my agent here, and then I'm getting out of North Carolina just as far and as fast as my car will take me."

As Laura drove off, I kept waiting for her to look back at me, but she never even glanced my way once.

It was clear that as far as she was concerned, we were finished.

But was she leaving because she had grown tired of being a murder suspect, or was she a killer leaving while she still had her freedom?

I just wish I knew which it was so I could act accordingly.

* * *

ZACH WASN'T HOME WHEN I GOT THERE, WHICH WAS NO great surprise. Though he wasn't officially on the case, he was as obsessed as he ever was when he was on the clock. Murders were mysteries for him, much like my puzzles, and he wouldn't be able to rest until he uncovered the truth and came up with a solution that suited him. Maybe we had the same personality type; I could be just as obsessed when I was working on a puzzle.

It was time to take a hard look at the three suspects I had left, and search for a solution by treating their actions as one giant puzzle.

Harry Pike had admitted openly that he wanted control of the land deal he had made with Joanne. He was in trouble financially; I knew that from the conversation I'd overheard his assistant have on the telephone with a bill collector when I'd been at the nursery. What if he'd wanted to sell their property to generate enough cash to save his business, and Joanne had refused to take the deal? If Harry was desperate enough, it could certainly be a motive for murder. It didn't help his case that he'd been in Asheville that day, according to the murder victim herself. The fact that he knew plants so well wasn't in his favor, either. If any one of my suspects knew how deadly chokecherry could be, it had to be Harry.

Next on my list, whether I liked it or not, was Rob Hastings. It was hard to imagine him waiting so many years to avenge his wife's death, but the poisoning and its timing were both too much of a coincidence to pass up. The problem was that I knew Rob, and while I had a difficult time seeing him as a murderer, if he had decided to kill her, the ironic justice of using the same date and method of execution would be right up his alley. Rob had been in Asheville picking up supplies at the Asheville Hardware Store that morning, so he was in proximity to where the murder occurred. I knew from personal experience about his broad knowledge of everything he sold, and that included plants in his gardening section. There were books there on native flora as well, so he had a readily accessible source of information. I hated the thought that my friend might be a murderer, but Zach had told me time and time again that murder was often an aberration in someone's personality, and that there was no way to tell exactly what a killer might look like.

That left Laura. She had motive enough, if what I'd heard was true. She needed money, and not just a little of it, and killing Joanne would get her out of the debt she was drowning in. If she'd asked Joanne for a loan, I was pretty certain the woman would have laughed in Laura's face. Even if she'd come through, Joanne would have held it over her head for the rest of her life, and I couldn't imagine how humiliating that might be. It could have been a desperate act by a woman at the end of her rope. As for being in Asheville, I'd seen her there myself. In fact, she could have just as easily made a mistake and poisoned me instead.

That was it. I had three suspects left from the long list I'd started with, each with viable motives, ample opportunity, and the means to acquire enough poison to kill.

I had the facts down, but where did my gut lead me? Zach had often told me that the facts, not his instincts, were what made him so good at his job, but I didn't work that way. I had to feel it in my heart to believe that it was true.

I was still mulling over what I knew when the landline

rang. I'd forgotten to get a new cell phone battery, making that phone pretty much a paperweight.

"Hello?"

"It's your husband again. Savannah, is your phone off?"

"No, I think my battery's shot. It won't hold a charge at all. I'll get a new one tomorrow. What's going on?"

"We're close to making an arrest, and I thought you had a right to know before we made our move."

Chapter 19

∎∎∎

I NEARLY DROPPED THE PHONE WHEN HE SAID THAT. I HAD MY list down to three people, but evidently Captain North and Zach had already eliminated two of the names still in contention for me.

I just had to know who had done it. "Who are you arresting?"

"I'm sorry to have to tell you this, Savannah, but it looks like Rob is the one who did it."

I couldn't believe it. Not Rob. Somewhere in my heart, I'd been holding out hope that he was innocent. "What exactly are you basing that on?"

"North got a tip to check out his garden area in back. She found some evidence that he should have gotten rid of the day he killed Joanne. There was a sample of poisonous plants in one corner in a solar dryer. You could kill half of Parson's Valley with what was in there."

"I'm guessing there were chokecherry leaves there."

"That's just the beginning. According to the plant expert North brought in from UNC Asheville, we found jimsonweed, larkspur, foxglove, hemlock, yew, pokeberry, nightshade, and monkshood, too. It was a regular assassin's selection of poisonous plants. Rob had his pick, and if he'd been a little more careful, he just might have gotten away with it."

"I still can't believe it, Zach."

I could hear the heaviness in my husband's voice as he said, "You know what I always say, Savannah. You can't tell a killer by looking at him. Anyway, I thought you should know. I'm turning my cell phone off; it drives North crazy when I get a call, but I'll be in touch later."

"Thanks for calling," I said. I was still numb from the news as I hung up. My friend Rob, the man who'd helped me countless times since we moved to Parson's Valley, was a murderer. I just couldn't believe it.

I started pacing the cottage floor, flashing back to all of the projects he'd helped me complete, all of the laughs we'd shared over my rookie remodeling mistakes. Suddenly, everywhere I looked, I saw his face staring back at me.

I had to get out of there before I went crazy.

Grabbing my car keys, my bag, and a jacket, I locked the cottage up and got into my car with no real destination in mind, just a desire to get away. I started driving toward town, but then I realized that I didn't want to be around people at all. I'd accused too many of my fellow townsfolk to be welcome anywhere. The more I thought about it, it might be the perfect time to take Zach and go to Uncle

Barton's Alaskan refuge, regardless of the chilly weather there. Giving people in town a chance to forget how I'd interrogated them so relentlessly might be the smartest next move, and if we were secluded in the wilderness, I could catch up on my puzzles and actually buy myself some breathing room for the future. My syndicate had been running a few puzzles from my backlog, but I knew better than my syndicator how shallow that pool was becoming. As I drove aimlessly around, letting my thoughts skip from subject to subject, I found myself at Harry's nursery. An apology was in order after the way I'd browbeaten him, but I wasn't sure I was up to delivering it, until I saw Laura's car already parked in his lot.

It was long past his closing time. What was she doing there? I pulled up beside her car and started to wonder what was really going on.

And then it hit me. Could my husband be wrong about Rob's guilt? A new way of organizing the facts started to form in my mind, dancing like the numbers from a puzzle as I worked the solution from a different angle. What if Harry was the real murderer? I knew he needed money, probably more desperately than Laura did. Could it be that he'd murdered Joanne for control of their jointly held property, only to find that Laura was stalling to sell, too? If that was the case, he wouldn't have any choice, at least in his murderous frame of mind, but to kill another obstacle in his way. Harry could have lured her to his nursery on some pretense, just to eliminate her.

I reached into my bag for my cell phone to call Zach, and then I remembered that my battery was dead, and his phone was turned off. I'd have to drive to Rob's hardware store to get him there.

I was about to put my car into gear when I caught a

glimpse of Laura beckoning me from inside the tree lot. From the way she was moving, it appeared that she'd been hurt.

I knew I was taking a chance, but I couldn't just pretend that I hadn't seen her. She was in trouble, and I could very well be her only hope. I got out of my car and rushed to help her. As I neared her, I saw that there was blood on her blouse, and I was afraid that I was already too late.

"Laura, did Harry do this to you?"

"He stabbed me with a pruning knife," she gasped.

I put my arm around her to help her back to my car. "Come on. I'll take you to the hospital."

"We have to go back," she said. Her voice was calm and her breathing was tight, but she was still managing to fight me at every step.

"No, the hospital's not far. I'll drive you there, and then we can tell Zach what happened."

Only then did I see the blade in her hand as she righted herself. "Why would we do that, Savannah? After all, it's not like I want to get caught."

"**Y**OU KILLED JOANNE," I SAID, STARING UNBELIEVING AT the blade. It was sharp steel, finely honed to a cutting edge, and now it was pointed straight at me.

"You had to keep jamming your nose into this, even after I warned you to stop," she said. "Move." The command was followed by a jab in my direction, and I didn't need any more incentive than that.

I started to piece the puzzle together yet another way, and in a split second, the new scenario began to play itself out in my mind. It had been Laura who had been greedy and driven to murder. First she had murdered Joanne, her closest living relative, and then she must have gone after Harry for his share of the property. I wasn't sure how she was planning to work it, but I had a suspicion that the deed Harry and Joanne shared was worded in such a way that if there was no direct beneficiary to either party, the surviving one got all of the land. It was the only way the facts all made sense.

"You killed Joanne for the money, and then half of the land deal with Harry wasn't enough for you when you read the actual deed," I said as we walked deeper into the nursery, past the office and toward the gardening shed. "There is a clause that allows you to inherit it all, isn't there?"

Laura laughed, and there was more than a tinge of madness in it. "Very good. Poor Harry. He had no one in the world to leave his dying business to, so as his land partner, I get his half, too. It's a tough break, wouldn't you say?"

"Then he's already dead?" I asked.

"Not yet, unless he's already managed to bleed out. I was just getting ready to finish him off when I decided to look around for witnesses. You can't be too careful, you know."

I stopped walking. There was no sense making this any easier for her. "You planted those poisonous leaves in Rob's solar dryer, didn't you?"

"Very good, Savannah. You're becoming quite the detective. I bought a book in Asheville on poisonous plants, and then it was just a matter of collecting them and planting them near Rob." She frowned as she added, "The only problem was that I was beginning to believe that no one was going to be clever enough to find them. I had to call in the tip myself before the police made their move."

"They're going to know it was you," I said.

"Keep moving," she said. As she jabbed the knife at me, I felt it bite into my arm. A sharp, burning pain took over as warm blood started to seep out, and I decided the only chance I had was to do as she asked.

"You're the killer, and my husband will figure it out and hunt you down."

"How could he possibly know I was even involved? Granted, he may be surprised by what he finds here tomorrow, but no one will be able to link it back to me, and I'll have it all." She seemed to think about that for a second, and then frowned before she spoke again. "You've ruined my suicide angle for Harry, though. I knew what kind of desperate shape he was in to sell. His business was dying, so why shouldn't he kill himself? Hmmm. How about a murder-suicide? That could work, if I stage it just right."

"You've got a problem," I said. "Why would Harry want to kill me?"

She shrugged. "Who knows? Maybe you two were having a torrid affair."

"My husband would never believe it," I said.

"I bet I could make him have doubts, especially if I strip you both and make it look like a love affair gone bad. Yes, that's what I'll do."

I knew my husband would never believe it, no matter how incriminating Laura might make it look, but knowing it and proving it would be two different things. The police might not back him, but that wouldn't stop Zach. "You don't want to kill me. Believe me on this, Laura. My husband will figure it out, and he'll make you pay."

"You have too much faith in him, Savannah."

"No, you don't have enough."

We were nearly to the shed, and my arm was really

starting to hurt. That pain suddenly became secondary when I walked inside and saw Harry. He was on the floor of the dirt shed, trussed up and completely helpless. His hands and legs were bound together with silver duct tape, and there was a piece over his mouth as well. No big surprise, there was a great deal of blood welling up on his forehead, and it looked as though he'd suffered a massive wound.

But then I looked into his eyes and suddenly felt a little better.

He wasn't frightened, though he had every reason to be terrified.

Instead, he caught my attention, and then looked sharply to my right. The second time he did it, I saw what he was motioning to.

The sharp shears I'd seen him pruning tree branches with were on the ground three feet from where he lay. They might as well have been across the country for all the good they did him, but I had one chance, if I just dared to be bold enough.

Laura had her back turned to us, securing the door. I only had a few seconds, so I had to act. I dove toward the shears, grabbing them despite the pain in my arm. As I turned, Laura was on top of me, and I saw the blade stabbing down at my heart.

I jerked my body sideways, but not quickly enough. The blade missed my heart, but still managed to graze my side. The sensation was intensely sharp, a blinding white pain that took my breath away. Driving the pain back, I swung the shears at her, and managed to get her arm as she tried to block my strike.

The sharp tip of the shears bit into her flesh, and she cried out in pain.

The problem was that she didn't drop the knife.

It was time for a new plan, and I had to come up with one quickly. The only thing within my reach was a pole saw. I couldn't use the blade in close quarters, but I could use the pole itself as a weapon. I grabbed it and struggled to pull myself up to my knees. As I swung it toward Laura's head, she ducked just in time, and it bounced out of my hands as it hit the wall. The impact of the strike drove me to the floor, and I was vulnerable again.

I was out of weapons, and she started to come at me for what was going to be the final blow. As Laura got closer and closer, I felt the weight of regret that I wouldn't be spending the rest of a long and full life with Zach, and it not only saddened me, it made me mad.

I couldn't let it end like this.

I WASN'T ABOUT TO GIVE UP, NO MATTER HOW BAD IT looked. As I scrambled away from her on my hands and knees, Harry startled us both and found a way to free his legs enough to lash out and kick Laura in the thigh. The impact of it knocked her back, and I had a free second to try to save us one last time.

I scooped up a handful of dirt from the floor of the shed and threw it into her face. It blinded her for a second, but thankfully, that was all I needed. There was a square-edged shovel hanging from its peg nearby, and I grabbed it. I swung it at the back of Laura's head, and this time I didn't miss.

It made a satisfying thud as it struck home. Laura went down in a heap, and I grabbed Harry's shears and started to cut him loose.

"This is going to hurt," I said as I pulled the tape from his mouth in one swift motion.

He jerked as I did it. "Thanks. I could barely breathe." He looked over at Laura. "Is she dead?"

"I don't think so. I hope not." I didn't want her death on my hands, but if that's what it took to save our lives, I would find a way to live with it. It was a price I would willingly pay to go on living.

"Cut me loose, then. We can't trust her, Savannah."

I used the shears and broke him free of the tape. He rubbed his hands together as he said, "I thought I was going to lose the feeling in them. She's absolutely insane, isn't she?"

"I hope not," I said.

"Why is that?" he asked as I started to help him up.

"Because then she's not going to be able to stand trial."

"Savannah, look out," Harry shouted as he shoved me to the ground. I'd made a mistake taking my eyes off Laura, even for a second. She had apparently only been stunned by the blow to her head, no doubt cushioned by her thick hair, and while we'd been distracted, she'd retrieved her knife and had lunged toward me with it.

Harry saved me, but he took the blade straight into his chest.

I swear I could see a smile on Laura's face as the knife point found its mark. I didn't even hesitate as I picked the shovel up and hit her again with it while she was struggling for the knife with Harry, who was mortally wounded but unwilling to give up.

This time when she went down, I had a feeling she wouldn't be getting back up anytime soon, if she ever managed to do so again.

* * *

I STILL DIDN'T HAVE MY PHONE, AND WE WERE FIFTY YARDS from the office. It might as well have been fifty miles. I knelt down beside Harry. He was still breathing, but it was causing him pain. I could see him wince with every breath he took.

"Hang on, Harry. Do you have a cell phone?"

"Pocket," he said, his voice barely over a whisper.

"Hang on. I'm getting help."

As I grabbed the phone, he asked, "She dead?"

"I don't know, but she's not getting up anytime soon. Harry, I'm sorry I didn't hit her hard enough the first time."

"It's not how you start that counts; it's how you finish," he said, his breathing more labored with every moment.

"Stay still, Harry," I said as I dialed 911.

After telling them we needed two ambulances and the police, I hung up and turned to Harry.

His eyes were shut, and if he was still breathing, I couldn't tell.

It appeared that Harry had fought his final battle when I passed out from my own loss of blood.

Chapter 20

■ ■ ■

I WOKE UP IN A HOSPITAL BED, FEELING WOOZY FROM SOME-thing. "Did they drug me?" I asked when I saw Zach looming over me.

"You were in pain," he said. "Of course they did. How are you doing, sweetheart?"

"Harry's dead."

I started crying for the man who had died fighting to save my life, but when I looked at my husband, Zach smiled at me. "It was close, but they managed to patch him back up. He's going to be okay."

The relief flooded through me in wave after wave. Harry had taken the blade that had been meant for me, a sacrifice as noble as anyone can make for another human being, and I knew that I owed him my life.

And I was thrilled that I'd have the chance to thank him for it.

"Don't you want to know about Laura?" Zach asked me.

"I suppose so. I hope I didn't kill her, but if I did, I won't lose any sleep over it. She's the most wicked person I've ever met in my life."

Zach stroked my cheek lightly. "You won't have her blood on your hands. She's got a pretty sizable concussion, but she'll be fine."

"That's good. That means that she can stand trial for murder."

He brushed some of the hair out of my face, and saw that I was crying again. "Hey, are you okay?"

I tried to move my left arm, but it was still too sore, and every motion brought a new wave of pain. "I'm not, but I will be."

He looked into my eyes. "Savannah, I'm sorry I wasn't there to help you. I will never forgive myself for not being there when you needed me. We finally figured that someone planted those leaves at the hardware store, and the tip was too good to be true. Anyone could have had access to the back where the dryer was, and Rob never wavered on claiming that he was innocent. North and I had just started to realize that we'd been wrong when your call came in." He touched my face again lightly with his hand, as if he wanted to make sure that I was really there. "I can't believe I almost lost you."

"We both have Harry to thank for that."

"We will."

"Rob came by," Zach said. "He left you this."

It was a small piece of chestnut, sanded and waxed, buffed to a perfect sheen. I took it and smiled as my fingers lightly touched the wood.

"What does it mean?" Zach asked.

"That things are going to be all right between us," I said. I shifted a little in my bed and felt a twinge of pain in my side. "How bad is my wound? Did the blade do any permanent damage?"

"There's going to be some rehab when you're feeling better, but all in all, you got lucky," he said.

"Funny, I don't feel lucky," I said.

"It could have been a great deal worse than it was. You should be out of here in three or four days, and after that, you can recover at home."

"As soon as I'm able to travel, I want to go to Alaska," I said.

He kissed my forehead. "There will be plenty of time to do that later," he said. "Right now, you need to rest."

"I made myself a promise back there, Zach, and I mean to honor it. With or without you, I'm going."

"We'll go as soon as the doctor clears you for travel, then," he said.

"Good. I need one more thing, and then I think I'll pass out again, if you don't mind."

He nodded. "I know what you're asking for. Tom and Barton are on their way. They were both pretty shook up about what happened, but I think I finally convinced them that you were going to be okay."

"That's good, but that wasn't what I wanted."

"Anything," he said as he stared into my eyes. The poor man seemed as though he wanted to burst out crying when he looked at me, but he was holding it together as long as he had to, and that was what made him strong in my eyes.

"I need a couple of pads and some pencils."

"Savannah, you can barely keep your eyes open," Zach said, "and one arm is useless at the moment. How on earth are you going to make a puzzle?"

"You're right; I can't work. At least not yet. I just want them around me. Having something familiar and safe right now means more to me than being able to make a puzzle."

"I'll have them here for you when you wake up again."

"Thank you," I said, immediately feeling better.

As I drifted off, I thought about how close I'd come to dying on that shed floor. If it hadn't been for Harry's act of bravery, I knew in my heart that I would be gone. I never took advantage of Uncle Barton's great wealth, but I was about to call in a pretty big favor. Harry needed a silent partner, someone who knew business and had a deep bank account to keep them going through hard times, and I knew my uncle was just the one to do it.

It was the least I could do for the man who had saved my life.

And I planned to hold Zach to his promise to take me to Alaska. From hearing my uncles talk about their trip there together, I knew that it would be the perfect place to start my recovery, surrounded by the men I loved.

I might even get a puzzle or two finished while I was there.

Stranger things had happened.

I wasn't exactly sure what the first puzzle would be, but I already had the snippet to accompany it written in my head.

Salvation sometimes comes from the strangest places. A friend can look like a foe, but in the end, the people we surround ourselves with are all that really matter in this life.

This puzzle is dedicated to Harry Pike, the man who saved my life, and to the memory of Joanne Clayton, who always wanted a puzzle of her very own.

Word and Math Puzzles

■ ■ ■

NAME THAT COZY WRITER

Example:	AC	Agatha Christie
	Initials:	**Hints:**
	1. LJB	Cats
	2. CH	Bookstore
	3. CM	Ag school
	4. TM	Penn Dutch
	5. MJ	More cats
	6. EDS	I forget
	7. LC	Tea for 2
	8. JC	Chocoholic
	9. EF	Patterns
	10. EP	Egypt

Answers:

1. Lilian Jackson Braun
2. Carolyn Hart
3. Charlotte MacLeod
4. Tamar Myers
5. Miranda James
6. Elizabeth Daniels Squire
7. Laura Childs
8. JoAnna Carl
9. Earlene Fowler
10. Elizabeth Peters

MYSTERY MOVIE TITLES

Example: NBN   North by Northwest

         Initials: Hints:

         1. TMF   Golden bird
         2. TUS   Round them up
         3. C   Where? With what?
         4. TDVC   Symbols
         5. KTG   Alex angry?
         6. TSOTL   Shhhh!!
         7. MOTOE   Trains
         8. RW   Watching
         9. P   Mommy issues
        10. DMFM   Don't answer

Answers:

1. The Maltese Falcon
2. The Usual Suspects
3. Clue
4. The Da Vinci Code
5. Kiss the Girls
6. The Silence of the Lambs
7. Murder on the Orient Express
8. Rear Window
9. Psycho
10. Dial M for Murder

WHAT'S YOUR SIGN?

(Fill in the missing mathematical signs. As an added bonus, try doing these in your head first.)

Example: 2__3=6 is 2x3=6

PUZZLE 1

1q. 8__5__8__6__3=5

PUZZLE 2

2q. 7__4__6__3__16__2__3=12

PUZZLE 3

3q. 11__22__3__3__5__4=10

SOLUTION 1

1a. 8+5 (13) + 8 (21) − 6 (15) ÷ 3=5

SOLUTION 2

2a. 7 − 4 (3) X 6 (18) X 3 (54) − 16 (38) − 2 (36) ÷ 3=12

SOLUTION 3

3a. 11+22 (33) ÷ 3 (11) − 3 (8) X 5 (40) ÷ 4=10